GEOFFREY WOLFF'S

PROVIDENCE

"*Providence* is a comedy in the classical sense, a tale about reintegration into moral society.... As narrative, an essay in novelistic effect, a meditation on degeneration, or a stylistic tour-de-force, there is little in recent fiction that can equal it. It is simply the pleasurable/morally terrifying novel one always hopes to find and seldom does."
— *Village Voice*

"Wolff shifts smoothly from... cultured prose style to hoodlums' post-literary speech as easily as a performance car moves into top gear. With barely any sensation of transition, you're out of... tasteful houses and orderly lives and into [an] amoral, stoned world.... Ingenious structure, flawless rhythms of speech, elegantly restrained imagery."
— *Los Angeles Times*

"Death is lurking and disaster hangs over every page—a nerve-racking suspense takes over early on. The crisp, abrupt style in *Providence* suits the story perfectly. It will give any reader a stepped up pulse."
— *People*

"*Providence* is a history, a veiled commentary on how America as we know it came to be.... Like any novelist who makes a tale ring true, he presents a world balanced between images of hope—whales cavorting with each other off the New England coast—and hopelessness: Lisa, aspiring torch singer and utter druggie, crooning in a hotel lounge to a roomful of deaf-mutes."
— *New Republic*

"Wolff has accomplished the impossible: a masterpiece of braided lives. What makes this book knock-your-socks off great is the language. If Wolff were a musician, he'd have perfect pitch." — *Hartford Courant*

PROVIDENCE

PROVIDENCE

A NOVEL BY

GEOFFREY WOLFF

▲ ▲ ▲ ▲ ▲ ▲ ▲ ▲ ▲ ▲ ▲ ▲ ▲ ▲

VINTAGE CONTEMPORARIES

VINTAGE BOOKS

A DIVISION OF RANDOM HOUSE, INC.

NEW YORK

First Vintage Contemporaries Edition, November 1991

Library of Congress Cataloging-in-Publication Data
Wolff, Geoffrey, 1937–
Providence: a novel / by Geoffrey Wolff. —1st Vintage contemporaries ed.
p.   cm. —(Vintage contemporaries)
Originally published: New York : Viking, 1986.
ISBN 0-679-73277-2 (pbk.)
I. Title.
[PS3573.O53P76   1991]
813'.54—dc20   91-50017
CIP

Manufactured in the United States of America
10 9 8 7 6 5 4 3 2 1

For Justin and Nick:
wanted men

AUTHOR'S NOTE

W H I L E the geography, neighborhoods, streets, and ancient history of my *Providence* are generally those of that New England city, this is a place of the imagination. I have, for example, re-routed a river to suit my purpose, and every contemporary character who dwells within these pages is an invention; they who live and die here are not intended, should not be misunderstood, to be "real."

PROVIDENCE

1

▲ ▲ ▲ ▲ ▲

THE MORON

S H E was a reporter, had been around the block a time or two, thought she'd seen it all, but she was wrong. Her back to Superior Court, knees jammed against the police barricade, looking across the narrow Providence River toward the Federal Courthouse, looking up, the reporter perceived the cargo net's freight to be a humanish dead something-or-other, dripping mud and seaweed. The wire net hung slowly spinning from a tow truck's crane while now, early morning of this fine March Saturday, her colleague snapped pictures.

The *Providence Journal*, like the city it serves, has a connoisseur's interest in hugger-mugger, and today—as happens so often in so small a city—coincidence had smiled on the city desk. A *Journal* delivery driver, drinking coffee and eating a doughnut, sitting on a stone wall to enjoy the break of day, had found the body. He knew enough to phone Action News' Tipline ($25!) before he called the newsroom, which he called before he called the police. He had sniffed out the guy lying on the river's muddy riprap, sucked by the falling tide, bloated, cripes! Even from up there he could see the holes in those weird clothes; the truck driver knew this was A Story.

The homicide detective beckoned the reporter across the barricade. The reporter felt one way, and she felt another way. It was nice to have the attention and envy of the gawkers, to be "Miss Hutchins" this and "Miss Hutchins" that (even if it was *Hutchinson*) to Lieutenant Cocoran, but she wasn't sure she wouldn't prefer watching from back there with the civilians while the crane lowered its weight.

She crossed the barricade, and watched her photographer try to make sense of the bad-looking mess leaking stuff on the sidewalk. She had been around long enough to know the newspaper always wanted such pictures, and never printed them. Most people live and die without seeing anything as ugly as that sight there, and almost everyone can get through breakfast, thanks anyway, without having to look at what she was now discerning, and let's not even mention the smell.

The lieutenant invited her close for a look before they zipped the body bag, as though this would please, or instruct. She had seen dead people, and photographs of many more, as recently as yesterday, in Judge Kiely's courtroom, State's Exhibits six through nine. If her curiosity was satisfied about the physiognomy of deceased males, it was also true that Lieutenant Cocoran was offering a gift or a challenge, and either way it seemed to the reporter obligatory to observe up close and personal that thing now untangled from wire mesh, soon (but none too soon for her) to be snugged in a black plastic mummy bag.

"He was somebody's precious baby," the lieutenant told her. "Once upon a time some mommy and daddy dandled him on their knees, and had his booties bronzed." The reporter suspected this was not the first time Lieutenant Cocoran had made such an observation, and that he would probably make such an observation soon again, probably to the WJAR reporter lurking yonder, beside his cameraman.

No getting around it, she had never smelled anything like that smell. In movies, to suggest such a smell, they show some hardened cop or medical examiner or reporter puking, but she was too interested to feel sick.

The dead man had been whacked twice in the head, probably with a .22 or .25, close range, the usual. It looked like someone had clubbed his face, ho-hum; this made him look routinely dead. But not so usual, he had been stabbed again and again in the belly and side, so he looked deader than dead. He was also the worst-dressed corpse fished that day or any from the Providence or any river. See those high-top black sneaks—Keds, according to Lieutenant Cocoran—and Ban-Lon bell-bottoms cinched by a white patent-leather belt, and a black blouse affected by karate enthusiasts, according to Lieutenant Cocoran. The martial arts angle could also be inferred by the dead man's bracelets, "karate stars," steel bands studded by sharpened spikes such as pit bulls wear as collars and punk musicians as ornaments. His neck was deeply cut. The gold chains must have been roughly snatched to be sold cheap for melt-down, too garish for his killer to wear. But the finishing touch (this was the Eighties!): the stiff was wearing a Nehru jacket!

"Jesus," the lieutenant said, "who's his tailor?" The lieutenant was dressed for success: creased flannels, gleaming loafers, black blazer, sharp, on the case.

"Who is he?" the reporter asked.

"Anthony Mirabella." He waited while she figured the spelling, raised his brows when she got it right without asking for help, smart lady. "The Moron."

"Who?" she asked, her pencil ready.

The lieutenant shrugged. Next time she'd listen. "Just a dumbbell, a coulda-shoulda specialist."

Now WJAR horned in: "Who did he say?"

The ProJo reporter shrugged at the television reporter, whose videoman was taping the Investigation Unit's German shepherd.

The newspaper reporter got her story, and left to write it. Walking past the Action News reporter she heard the lieutenant reflect, with feeling, on camera:

"Once upon a time his mom and dad dandled that boy on their knees. They had his booties bronzed. Now look at him, all tucked away nice in his plastic Doctor Dentons. . . ."

That night the Action News team featured the dog, "Mandy, with three years on the K-9 force, skillfully searching for clues along the bank of the Providence River in the mysterious gangland slaying of Anthony Mirabella. . . ." Lieutenant Cocoran didn't make the final cut.

Providence.

2

. . . . .

ADAM

FROM his office in the Turk's Head Building, Adam regarded the scene below. Now that the body had been fished out and salted down, the spectators were losing interest, wondering whether Providence held a livelier attraction that Saturday morning, deciding it probably didn't. Adam wondered if they knew they were gathered at an historic site, the Crawford Street Bridge, held by the *Guinness Book of World Records* to be the widest bridge in the world. Whoever had dumped whomever they croaked middle of downtown was either too dumb to know the tide would uncover him, or wanted him found pronto. One or the other. Most circumstances, Adam reckoned, were one or the other.

He'd never quit hoping for good tidings in the mail, though what gratuitous benison could befall him at forty-six he couldn't conceive. In the weekend quiet of his small office, his father's before his, he leafed through bills, opened a mannerly solicitation for affection and money from Exeter, ignored the importunings of magazines for renewal, read a letter of thanks from the mother of a car thief he'd last week plea-bargained down to six months, suspended. She'd enclosed a check—less than his fee, more than he'd expected. Maybe she calculated her family would need Adam again; maybe she wanted to do the right thing. If he knew anything, Adam knew not to judge motive; he liked to believe actions speak for themselves, *res ipsa loquitur*.

Still. He held a square envelope, that heavy gray linen you see now enclosing invitations to weddings and bar mitzvahs, in the old days coming-out parties. Engraved paper from the Racquet

Club in New York. Adam's father had played there in a squash tournament when the boy was twelve or thirteen, and now he remembered that match, how proud he'd felt. Amos Dwyer had been a ruddy-faced, open-faced, soft-spoken man, willing to let people think he didn't catch their drift as quickly as his legal colleagues in the big cities north and south of Providence. But the old man was plenty quick, and when Adam was old enough to recognize this, by the time of that trip to New York, it was a good secret between them. His father, down two games to one in the quarter-finals, down 5-12 in the fourth game, had favored his elder son that afternoon with a wink just before he began to play way over his head, finishing off that cocky smart-aleck with drop shots before the smoothie discovered he'd been roughed up. Adam's father had been a man to rise to occasions, on the rare occasions when they mattered to him.

That night they'd eaten alone together at Luchow's, and listened to Edmund Hall and Wild Bill Davison at Condon's, and spent the night at the Yale Club. That night Amos had confided in his son what he called "hard-won wisdom": *Fool me once, shame on you; fool me twice, shame on me.* And when his father got whipped three-zip next morning in the semis, he took it well, probably too well, Adam thought then.

He looked now at the postmark; it took a long time to get a letter to Providence from New York. Sometimes the greater world seemed so much farther away than two hundred miles he wondered if he'd ever have a reason good enough to see it again.

He opened the envelope. Paper-clipped to the sheet was a crisp twenty:

> Here's the money I lifted from your overcoat pocket junior year at Fence Club, I think the weekend of The Game, though maybe the weekend of merely A Game.
>
> From what I hear you need it worse than I need it. Fact is, you needed it worse then. Fact is, I wanted it, and now I don't. So you can have it back. Anyway, here you go, Boola-Boola.

No salutation; neither, of course, was the fastidiously lettered note signed. Adam thought of Davis Somebody, the thief at

Pierson College. People knew he stole, and people pretended not to know. It was difficult to talk about that kind of thing, and besides, Davis was a bruiser with an ugly temper. Sophomore year, the Monday before Thanksgiving vacation, Adam had been paid for eight weeks' work in the student laundromat, fifteen hours a week, a dollar seventy-five an hour. He remembered the amount now, almost exactly, two hundred and change; he remembered because the laundromat was hot and humid, and he'd given up intramural football to work there, and because dirty clothes are dirty clothes. He remembered because he'd planned a jamboree with Clara, drinks at the Biltmore, dinner listening to Red Norvo at the Embers, dancing on the St. Regis Roof. He'd cashed the check at the Yale Co-op, and the money was in his wallet, and when he came back from his shower the money and the wallet were gone. One of his roomies had been robbed, too, just a few dollars. Everyone seemed embarrassed. There was an odd want of anger, and compassion, as though Adam and his roommate, like those other victims, had somehow, by being robbed, violated probity and scruple. Maybe his friends felt that excluding Davis from Fence and Deke, then Wolf's Head and Bones, would be punishment enough.

Adam wanted his money back. He didn't really know Davis, had said maybe two sentences to him in the dining hall, had seen him shout and break glasses one night at the Old Heidelberg, had wanted to say something about the words and the glasses, and had not. But now he went to Davis's room, and found him there, sorting his record collection.

"I'd like to borrow some money from you."

Davis Whosis didn't even counterfeit surprise: "How much?"

"Some shitweasel stole two hundred and fifty dollars from me just now while I was in the shower. I'd like to borrow two hundred and fifty."

Davis Whatsis showed surprise. "I could maybe let you have two hundred and ten, about."

"I'd prefer two-fifty."

Adam might have shared the profit with his roommate, but he didn't. This didn't surprise his roommate, but it surprised Adam.

Now, holding paper from the Racquet Club, he recollected Davis the Thief. But Davis was ten years dead. Plane crash, something, train maybe, public carrier, litigation, gorgeous tort. So now Adam could spend the rest of his life wondering which of his Yale friends had wanted twenty dollars badly enough to steal from him, or had disliked him enough to steal twenty dollars from him. One or the other.

Adam drove an inconvenient detour to avoid the mop-up of The Moron's terminal particulars. On his son's sunny birthday, he had no appetite for a crime scene. Crime scenes he'd seen.

On his way home to Benevolent Street he picked up Ike at the Brown rink. The boy tossed his skates and pads in the battered car's trunk, and began babbling wonderfully about his final practice, how he'd slapshot this one in, put that guy on his ass. He was excited, and then he remembered himself and clammed up. He liked to think of himself as a cool customer, but at school he still hugged his mother in the corridors between classes, or blew kisses to her in the lunchroom. He still said "boy oh boy," and his chums teased him for "jeepers!"

Ike was fourteen today. Before the car had rolled to a stop behind his uncle's Porsche, parked at a hydrant in front of the house, Ike was out the door and up the steps, where Adam's brother sat, smirking: Asa.

(How could the old man have done it? Amos, Adam, Asa. It was the only unambiguously stupid impulse to be laid at Amos Dwyer's door, the cute symmetry of those names. Adam once asked his dad, with no little irritation, why he had named them that way.

"I can't really explain it. Adam didn't mean a thing to me, nothing symbolic about it, just a name I'd always liked to hear. If I'd bought a dog before we had you, would have called him Adam. Then when Asa was ready, we looked through a dictionary of names, skipping ancestors. Give me credit for that—neither of you is named for ship captains or slavers. Asa was the first one I marked, liked something about it, and by the time I got to Zachary, hadn't found anything I liked better. There's the beginning and the end of it."

"People think Adam stands for something."

Amos shrugged. Other people's opinions of him and his usually made Amos shrug.)

Ike tried to keep his eyes off the gift-wrapped package and black leather bag in his uncle's free hand, while he hugged that man and traded high-fives with him. Asa had standing with the boy, and little wonder. Young, single, disreputable (he called referees "assholes" at Bruins games), reputable (he was a doctor), irreverent, extravagant (Beacon Hill apartment, ski vacations, toys), generous, incapable of exhorting his nephew to Be Good or Work Hard, he seemed to Ike, and indeed to almost everyone, like the genuine article.

If Adam was nagged by doubts about his only brother, doubts beneath the level of articulation, this was probably because Clara, now opening the door for them all, did not like Asa, and—perhaps unpardonably—would not tell why.

The cake had been eaten, and while Clara brewed coffee and Ike unwrapped his gifts, there was a look on Asa's face, Adam thought, that an uncharitable witness might interpret as condescension, a kind of benign wonder that someone of energy and wit would content himself with such snug familiarity. Adam watched his little brother examine the house where they had grown up.

"They gave us a good life here," Asa said. "I miss them."

Adam knew his brother meant what he said, and Adam felt shame to have doubted his brother's goodwill. Adam thought he should know better than to trespass on another's mind. He felt uncomfortable, the sour residue of the morning's mail.

Ike was exclaiming, as well he might. "Outstanding! Outstanding! Oh, Asa!" That kind of thing.

"I used it in medical school, and during my residency. Take care of it."

Ike said he'd use it at medical school. Clara told her only child he might not want to go to medical school. Ike said he knew what he wanted, he wanted to be a doctor, like Asa. Adam smiled. Clara said maybe he'd want to be a lawyer like his father, like his grandfather, or maybe even, *mirabile dictu*, a teacher, like his mother. Ike said he knew what he wanted. This didn't hurt Adam. Really, it didn't hurt. What did hurt, just sometimes, and not as much as Clara assumed, was Asa's assumption that it hurt, and the solicitous way he'd manage to change the subject whenever Ike's ambitions were expressed.

"When I was your age, I wanted to be a ski bum," Adam said.

"Maybe he can be both," Clara said, glancing toward her brother-in-law. "A doctor and a ski bum. Nothing's impossible."

Adam cocked his head at her. She seemed jittery. He wondered if a storm was making up.

Asa showed Ike how to focus the knurled knobs of the microscope. He taught him to switch magnification levels, and adjust the slides. Ike was content at first to investigate the strangeness of ordinary matter, of water, dirt, his own hair. Then he asked to look at blood.

It surprised Adam, and pleased him (forgive him), to see that Dr. Asa Dwyer was not eager to give his nephew a drop of blood. He remembered Asa's squeamishness, some unexpected lapses of courage during visits when they were kids to the doctor's office for inoculations.

"I'll give you blood," Adam told his son.

Adam welcomed quiet tests of courage, which he willingly confused with grace. When he was eight or nine and the neighborhood gang mingled bloody hands in a compact of eternal loyalty and community, he hadn't flinched when the Buck knife cut the soft flesh of his palm. Adam's knife, in fact. In fact, he had proposed the test. He wondered where his boyhood friends had gone, what they'd say if he tracked them down, asked some simple favor of them. Now he used a needle from the black bag Asa brought to the house to impress Ike. Adam wanted to hold a match to its tip, but his brother assured him it was sterile. He drew a bead of blood while he talked, taking care not to break the serene cadence of his speech. He watched his son watch him.

He smeared the blood from his finger on the slide, and Asa took the slide to the microscope, set up on a card table across the room.

It was a large room, cluttered with ship models. Many of these rested on the surfaces of fine examples of early American furniture, the kind antique dealers call "important." There were prints of sailing ships on the walls, and export China displayed in a corner cupboard. The ceilings of this house were high, and late afternoon light worked through the high windows and struck a bull's-eye mirror.

Ike had been looking through the eyepiece while his uncle, seeing the blood in his mind's eye, had told the boy what was what.

"Look, it moves," the boy said.

Asa told him to notice the distinction between cells, red and white mixed in a happy community of interests.

"They all look the same to me."

It was perhaps the sun striking the bull's-eye mirror that caused Adam's brother to blink hard as he bent to the eyepiece. Explaining the principle of cell locomotion to his nephew as he adjusted the focusing knob, without breaking his teacherly rhetoric, his eye lost its casual droop. Asa bore down hard against the eyepiece, and when Ike asked a question, he got no reply. When Ike shoved close to see what was so interesting, he was gently waved away. So it came about that Adam, slouched in the deep cushions of a chair his father had also favored, watched himself sentenced to death.

He glanced at Clara, and was glad she had not noticed. She was reading *The New York Times*. Asa finally, with transparent reluctance, lifted his eye from the birthday gift. They say we'll die sooner or later; *sure*, we say, *sure*. They tell everyone. Adam had believed them. But Jesus, now? So soon? Why him? It didn't make a lick of sense. What was his capital offense? Forget he asked, he knew it was a dumb question. Life had been good to him; he knew that. He only wanted it to be good a little longer.

———

Imagine Adam's Sunday. Asa had asked to talk with him right away, Providence or Boston, his brother's choice. But Adam had chosen to wait another day, not to defer the miserable lesson he knew he'd learn, but to hide it from Clara and Ike. So he faked his way through Sunday, and busied himself with household chores, trading storm windows for screens, repairing a rotten sill, maintenance.

Sitting in his little brother's Boston office two days after his son's birthday, Adam wished three things. He wished Asa didn't feel it necessary to wear a white gown over his street clothes during this particular meeting. He wished his brother had better sense than to clasp his hands behind his head while he talked. And he wished he didn't believe what Asa was telling him.

Asa recited the obligatory hedges: "they" wouldn't know for sure till "they" did a marrow biopsy, and even then there was much "they" didn't know. But he was a good doctor, and he didn't horse around with I-pray-to-God-I'm-wrongs. Building engineers called such a glitch a *structural surprise*, and weren't much surprised. He told Adam his blood was awash with white cells, blast cells, and the fatigue and joint pain and swollen spleen were just details piled on other details in a rotten narrative.

"I'm sorry. It's upside down. You're too young for this. Not medically, you're just the perfect age for leukemia medically, right on the money, mid-forties, the actuaries wouldn't bat an eye."

Like everyone, Adam thought he had prepared himself for this day. He wanted to be brave. He had dreamed awake (and maybe not utterly with dread) of the moment the Bad News would come. He had pictured himself, after a persistent sore throat, or the surprising feel of a lump growing big under his arm, sitting like this, scared like this. . . . He had wondered how it would come to him, a hunch in the bones, a declarative sentence? He had wondered how he'd take it.

He had hoped he'd take it well, of course. No gagging on someone else's words. No pounding his fist against the doctor's desk, or face. He had been sure he wouldn't head for the nearest saloon, or blurt out his sorry story to the first stranger he met. But then he had also been pretty sure he wouldn't ask that dumb question:

"How much time do I have?"

This was the occasion for Asa to unclasp his hands from behind his head, and mime a traffic cop's halt signal: "Whoa! We haven't even had a second opinion. It's not unknown to confuse acute leukemia with . . . say . . . infectious mono."

"Have you ever confused them?"

"No."

After appropriate silence, Asa suggested what might be in store: five, six, maybe nine months. (Adam believed he was brave. Sailing through a bad storm with friends, he knew he'd behaved well, like them. They were still friends. When the storm had hit, they'd talked just loud enough to be heard. Mostly they had done what was to be done, and had not pretended they were unafraid. No drama, just remedy. The storm had lasted a long time, seventy-two hours in the Gulf of Maine, bad, bad storm. Nine months: Adam wasn't sure he'd stay brave. Adam had been a civil rights lawyer in Mississippi, early Sixties. He hadn't buckled, but he had carried an open airplane ticket to Boston, always. No ticket home from this. He wasn't at all sure he wouldn't buckle.) Chemotherapy, evident remission, anemia, not unbearable pain. No immediate need for hospitalization unless, of course, Adam wanted to go the distance, take radiation.

"Would you?"

"No."

Adam was grateful for those blunt monosyllabic replies. Now he trusted his brother, and wanted to ease his brother's pain, even as he appreciated the impropriety of this misfit ambition. He had binocular vision now, watching his brother watch him, feeling Asa feel respect for his sensible bearing, his sympathetic thrust past the decorums. Adam was sensible that he was playing a zero sum game, that whatever he did now, or said, or felt would seem merely passionate (and cowardly) or calculated (and false). Nothing's what you expect. What the hell? Adam had just learned he was about to check out, and still he was angling for his brother's respect.

"Tell me all about leukemia."

And, Jesus, did he ever! Asa knew his stuff, and now he got into it, pacing his office, summoning a nurse to fetch schematics of the spleen and a cutaway model of bone and marrow, bringing Adam to the microscope to examine his own languidly swimming flaws, those miniscule, tragic clumps, about the wrong business entirely. Oh, Asa was deep in it now; Adam, to his surprise, found it difficult to listen. He was—could this be?—bored by his brother's analogies and sketches. He didn't want to gaze at the slide in his brother's microscope, a death sentence simply enough parsed. He realized that what Asa was doing Adam did when a defendant sat across from him, inquiring into some consequential point of law, how it might work for him, work against him. Asa was explaining the machine (*the body's a delicate mechanism, ta-rum, ta-rum*), plumbing its mysteries and ugly surprises with real interest, fully engaged now with its quiddities, here was the thing itself, first cause and end. . . .

"I want you to do me a favor," Adam said.

"Anything," Asa said.

"I want you to give me a clean bill of health—"

(Adam watched his little brother try to conceal surprise, a flicker of contempt. He realized Asa thought his big brother had refused to hear what had been said to him. He imagined him thinking this was going to be harder than he had expected. Was it ever! Asa, he thought, hadn't the faintest notion how hard it was going to be. . . .)

"Let me explain again—" Asa began.

"I want you to sign over a clean bill of health so I can buy more insurance. I haven't got much to leave."

Adam thought he saw Asa's relief. *Oh, that's all you want . . .* Asa blinked.

"Jesus, Adam, don't ask me to do that; I can't do that. You know I can't do that. What you're asking, it's not right to ask me to do that. Come on, you're a lawyer! It's not even right to want it."

"You're right," Adam said to his little brother, wanting it. "Right you are."

Asa said: "Let's go to lunch."

Adam said: "No. No, thanks." Then Adam said: "I want to go home now."

The vinyl pew of his bent-fendered X-Car felt slippery and cold; the car and its setting in the hospital parking lot were second-rate. Adam turned the key and heard a sullen whir, then a few sad clicks. Then nothing. *Dead* came to mind, and he thought how from now on—whatever seasons, season, months or weeks, *from now on* might describe—words would mean things to him they did not mean to other people. He had built his life on the precision of small print; you might say he had pitched a lifelong battle against metaphor.

Now his car had died, and he figured he might as well weep for that fact, and be done with weeping. If Numero Uno of Fortune's Five Hundred couldn't make a car that would run, what chance had God, let alone a Providence lawyer, against a fucked-up white blood cell count? So he tried to weep, and failed at that.

The man from AAA looked under the hood, and shook his head. "You've got starter problems." Hours later, gridlocked with commuters on the Southeast Expressway, driving home with a rebuilt starter, Adam regretted he hadn't thought to say he was really having finishing problems. But when the man from AAA, staring dolefully at Adam's grease-caked works, told him gravely, "You're in deep shit, friend," Adam had laughed, at least.

3

▲ ▲ ▲ ▲ ▲

CLARA

HER senior year at Barnard, his last at Columbia Law School, Adam asked Clara to marry him. He proposed in a conventional, sweet way, downtown at the White Horse, a tavern she liked. Adam wore his heart in plain sight. She drank her ale, and at the bottom of the mug was this sudsy emerald ring, his mother's, her mother's, her mother's, Clara lost track of the regressions. She admired Adam's gentleness, and he had a quick, loud laugh that she also liked, and shared. He had courted her by a relentless display of warmth, zest, boyish decency. If she sometimes felt his values subtly self-congratulating, cocksure, Clara relished Adam's patience, and she couldn't think of a single reason not to marry him, except that she suspected she might be too smart for him, except also that she didn't want to, and back then, 1962, these weren't reasons enough.

Even so, she didn't say yes at the White Horse; Adam wore her down that spring, waves of warm water gently eroding soft stone. At that far-off time, Asa was a bodacious sophomore Yalie, all teeth and trimmed hair, fine-tuned, slang up to the jiffy. Bright as brass, Ace to his classmates, of course. Clara, despite herself, backed the kid into an admission that his older brother was stolid, a fellow you'd sooner have execute your estate than share your ski lodge. A month before the August wedding, Clara got cold feet, and borrowed Adam's car to drive from New York to Providence to explain to his mother why she couldn't, it wasn't enough, she wouldn't do it. Clara suspected that Adam's mother would tell her she was right not to do what worked against her hunch, but she never found out. Four blocks from the house on Benevolent Street Clara ran a stop sign on Hope, got whacked by a tow truck, and woke up in Rhode Island Hospital.

That's where they were married, with Clara still in traction. The truck driver had towed Adam's MG-TC; Adam had loved that car; his father had left it to him. It was a goner. The driver sued Adam, who was so good about it all, so attentive, so genuine in his indifference to the mess Clara had made for him that she never screwed up the nerve to tell him she didn't want to be his wife.

In fact, she suspected he knew this, that he knew he had boxed her into a cul-de-sac. She wished he hadn't known it, because it wasn't what she felt now. To tell the truth, she sometimes wondered what cards might have been dealt her in a game played away from Providence, back in New York, where she had been born and raised. Like Adam, she despised deceit, but she hid from him her resentment that they never had quite enough money. Truth to tell, she was seldom irritable, except with herself, and of course with Asa. Her students told her the most awful dirty jokes, and she couldn't help herself, she laughed at them. Laughter was her hobby, she might have said, might have been proud to say, because hard work as a high school history teacher sapped her pep. She tried not to complain, but it sometimes galled her that her husband was famous for not complaining. On the other hand, he deplored injustice (suffered by third parties, of course) more bitterly and publicly than she, and in his deploring mode he was also famously tedious. On the other hand, unlike Adam, she could not teach herself not to believe a ringing telephone brings bad news.

But to tell the truth again, she didn't wish now she hadn't run that stop sign then. That was a fact, even though she had been drawn to other men, even though time was when she acted on a couple of those attractions, long ago. No, she was glad she ran that stop sign. Otherwise, for one thing, there'd be no Ike. Another boy, perhaps, or girls, or boys, but not *this* boy.

———

When he returned from the hospital that Monday, he asked Ike how was school today. Then he poured himself a beer. Then he loosened his tie, and didn't lose himself in the front-page story about some erstwhile mobster called The Moron. Then he sent Ike out to shoot baskets, and told her he was going to die, soon, and Clara listened. Her attention surprised her. She would have guessed her response would be operatic, that she'd indulge rage and doubt, that she'd feel terror. Instead, she strained to follow every throughway and back road in his account, let him back over thoughts he'd already expressed, nodded when she believed she understood. She didn't weep, didn't ask if there could be some mistake, didn't object when Adam said they had to think hard about after, about money, Ike's future, what he could do now to ease things for them later. She thought she didn't want to say anything she didn't mean exactly, and that she'd better understand every word he said. Clara thought she had waited a long time for something consequential to happen to her, and now it had, and it was the wrong thing. She thought she didn't know what to think, and she was listening for a single false note, some sign that he wasn't truly as brave as he seemed, because if she heard that from him, she thought she might break in two.

The shit that's written about dying. Nobody knows anything about it. For a while, learning it was coming, that was all there was, all they could think about. Walking on eggs, threading through the minefield, Clara would squint trying to figure him out. When Adam's father had fallen like a tree, dead, playing squash at the Agawam Hunt Club, after his second heart attack, Adam had said he was glad it had happened that way, what a great way to go. And Adam had played the next year, fiercely, in the New England league, and then desultorily, till one day he put away his racket for the last time, and then quit the club. He wore his father's suits, too short in the sleeves and legs, and wouldn't have them fitted to him, and when Amos's old friends remarked a likeness between father and son (*Your Dad! To the letter!*), Adam sometimes beamed and sometimes frowned. Clara had begun to understand even then that death had aspects the living weren't destined to comprehend.

She sort of understood why Adam seemed to lose his affection for Bozo, their Golden Retriever. The dog exuded dumb health, with his healthy, shining coat and wet, healthy nose. She understood why Adam managed to hide his pain and fear from Ike, at least for the time being, and why he'd call her at school and hang on the phone like a teenager, making her tell how the morning had gone, what she was doing now ("talking to you from the history department office"). She understood why he was preoccupied with sums, and had abandoned work as a Public Defender to squirrel away money in private practice. Sensible. But why the three-year subscription to *Cruising World*, a pair of last-a-lifetime custom-fitted shoes, a Defiant woodburning stove? Why now, for God's sake, a video tape recorder, with a two-year membership in a discount tape club?

Clara paid attention. She tried to imagine how he must feel, about to die, soon. What if she were Adam? Well, she was Adam, and he was Clara. She knew this, but she couldn't feel it. She knew how synergy worked, but who could feel it working? She tried. She didn't want to say the wrong thing. She didn't know what to say. She suggested he quit law, he must be bored by now, they could travel on their savings. He just stared at her. He took offense.

"Remember the Lawsons?" he asked.

She remembered. A couple they'd known in Boston, good people, smart and generous, good marriage, kids, solid. He'd come home late from his purse-proud law office, and before he was into his slippers and a see-through he'd bitch about the firm: Yeah, he was a partner, but he shouldn't have joined, he'd missed his calling, should have practiced pro bono publico, environmental, civil rights, consumer advocacy. She'd tell him he didn't really mean it, and he'd argue, turning the dials, muttering, "Wish I could quit spinning the wheel like a goddammed hamster." No sooner did she believe him than he ran out on her, whining that she'd never respected his work, never asked how it was going at the office.

"I remember the Lawsons. Thinking of running off with a bimbo? The car wouldn't make it to Mexico."

"To New London. I've made a couple of wrong turns. I know that. But I'm pretty much what I am now. No surprises, Clara."

She said she knew this. She said this was fine by her. Look, she said, he'd always wanted to take *Warlock* on a voyage? She'd take a leave from school, never mind dough, they'd find a way. By God they'd do it, cross the ocean, never mind what she'd said before about sailing across the ocean, think what it would mean to Ike. Well, at least to the Islands, or down the Inland Waterway? Well, should they sail to Maine again?

Adam said, "We'll stay home. I want to do this carefully, no grandstanding."

Adam said he wanted the time left to count. He wanted to open himself to chance, answer yes to questions, but here (touching his heart), and *here* pointing to the center of his father's house, their house, the kind of substantial (and draining) place realtors call a terminal home, what Clara called a grownup house and didn't yet feel connected to, hadn't learned to inhabit.

Thus it was, two weeks after he got his bad news and gave it to her, that they ate dinner in Bristol with a couple whose invitations Adam used to dread. The couple had "redone" a clipper captain's house, right on the harbor. The view was great. Guests in that house learned a lot about the floors, how that glistening wide pine had been, "incredibly," covered by layers of tacky linoleum. Guests got to look at before-and-after photographs, and hear from the horse-face's mouth that dust gets everywhere, "and I mean everywhere," when floors are sanded. (Behave yourself, Clara, Clara told herself.)

He was an Exeter classmate, she played serious golf at the Agawam. That's not fair, she did other things too, Clara supposed. She was really a dedicated golfer, for example, and her golf game was really very good, and the sun, when it shone on the fairways, had etched handsome lines in the corners of her eyes, which were said to be steady as she addressed the ball. Her husband was in a respectable business that required a decision every four or five months, and he gave generously of his time to the school where Clara taught, and he played golf.

During dinner, Adam and his old friend Tubby reviewed Exeter anecdotes. The golf woman urged the golf man ahead, "Oh, Edward, tell about . . ." and "Oh, Edward, don't forget to tell about . . ." and "Oh, Edward, don't forget to remember . . ." She adored her husband, who wasn't tubby any more, who thought she was a great little gal, and eating dinner with them was like listening to *The Love Boat* seep in from the house next door.

Adam seemed to love it. He was expansive, as serene as a man who has just got a promotion and raise. What was he thinking? What were they doing in that place? What was wrong with her husband? This was *it*, for Christ's sake! This night was a night gone forever, a measurable fraction of every night they had left. Adam was laughing, as though from the heart, at another unlaughable run of words. Clara wondered if she was nuts. Clara knew she wasn't nuts.

"Edward," the golf wife was saying, "didn't you tell me some story about Adam and the admissions office?"

So Tubby told, and Clara listened. Tubby remembered that Adam's father had brought him for an interview, and advised Adam that what he said in that office couldn't wreck his life, but could make it probable that his son would have a happy life, and to make a mistake in there would be to make a mistake that would count.

"Wanted to put Junior at ease, right? What were you, thirteen?"

"About," Adam said, with a loan officer's smile. Now Clara was interested; her husband did not retail anecdotes about himself, finding himself uninteresting in a way she had never trusted.

"So Amos, class of 'twenty-eight . . ."

"Nineteen-thirty . . ."

"Whatever . . ."

"It was the Depression."

"Hey," the golf man said, "I've heard of the Depression; you're screwing up my story. Let me fill your hand?"

Adam covered his wine glass with his hand. He looked at Clara, who was watching the golf man get watched by his adoring golf wife. The air was buzz and static; Clara's skirt clung like a wet sheet to her legs, and her hair bristled. She heard thunder boom down south, a storm rolling across the mouth of Narragansett Bay. The sullen thump alerted Adam's face. He was sure a sailor.

"So old Amos launches the squirt here on the admissions office; the quality of his whole cee-vee's on the line, *Who's Who in the East* is waiting to hear how this half hour turns out, and coming out of the office, preceded by those famous bushy eyebrows and that hawky honker, Himself Himself, the Headmaster, Patrick Patrician. Well, we get the dutiful, bored pleasantries, and the look down the slope of that nez from an altitude that would make a mortal nose bleed, down Salty stares at this mite, and then he asks it: 'What did you do with your summer, young man?' So he gets his answer: 'I mixed drinks for my mother.' "

"I didn't know your mother's an alky," the golf woman said. "Or at least till Edward told me that story."

"She isn't," Adam said. "She's dead."

"Sorry, I meant was."

"Is that story true?" Clara asked. "I've never heard it before."

"Tubby tells a good story," Adam said.

Tubby crossed his heart. "Gospel. True fact. They let him in because he was interesting, I think. Let's drink to Exeter, by God. They were interested in what was interesting."

"That's an interesting story," Clara said.

"Hell, I've got a dozen about this guy."

"Let's talk about someone else," Adam said, gently.

"Well," Tubby said, "you mentioned death a minute ago. I heard one this week at the club . . ."

Clara rose, on the pretext of using the bathroom, admiring the golfers' house, any pretext at all.

Adam said, "Sit down, Tubby tells a good story."

Clara cocked her head at her husband, and he winked, nodded, sit down, for me, a favor.

". . . so this guy goes to his sawbones, says, 'Doc, it's probably nothing, but I've got a sore throat that won't quit.' The medico says, 'Let's have a look. Oh-oh, I want to run you right over to Rhode Island Hospital and biopsy that lump under your jaw. . . .'"

Clara stared at Adam. He smiled at Tubby, encouragingly. She wondered if Adam would share her pleasure in a lightning bolt, right now, let it hit the TV antenna mounted on the golfers' widow's walk and run right down the wires and blast out of that chandelier right there above this idiot's head, and fry him. Adam's encouraging smile never flickered.

". . . so the guy protests, 'Jeez, Doc, it's Friday, can't we wait till Monday?' The doctor says no, 'not on your life.' " (The golf lady got it; Adam's grin came in a little late, but it came.) " 'As soon as I've cut into that lump, I'll give you an answer. We might have to operate.' Well, the poor chump wakes up, and the doctor's nowhere to be found. The nurse sends him home; he sweats out the weekend, trying to get the doctor on the phone, but the medic's at the Homestead." (Tubby stood up, did a nice golf swing, a doctor pantomime; he was an accurate mimic.) "Monday, the patient gets through to him. Over the horn, he hears the doc slap his forehead: 'Jesus, how *could* I forget, your biop! Christ, forgive me—slipped my mind! Well, I've got great news, and a little bad news.' The guy says he'll take the bad news first. 'It's malignant,' the doctor says, 'and within three months you'll be dead.' The guy wonders, what could be the great news? 'Great news is I finally corked my receptionist Saturday night.' "

Clara looked past him, beyond the bow window, into the dark. Tubby said there was an alternate version, " 'Great news is I birdied the fifth hole at the Homestead.' "

Adam was laughing. Adam was laughing at the first version. Clara said none of it was funny. The golfers shut up, stared into their wine glasses, spun those wine glasses in their hands.

Tubby cleared his throat. "I didn't know you were a libber, Clara. Sorry to tee you off. But it's a funny joke." Tubby looked at his old Exeter classmate for confirmation, and his old Exeter classmate gave it.

"That's a good joke, Tubby. You tell a good joke. To tell a good joke's a gift. Hang on to it. When they hook up the colostomy bag, hang on to that gift."

"Yuck," said the lady golfer, fingering her drop-pearl earring. "Bad taste."

"Now that's gross," Tubby said. "I don't think that's very funny."

Clara laughed, and then everyone felt better. Except Adam, and of course Clara. And Tubby, who seemed almost to be thinking about something.

After, they lay on their backs laughing. She rested her head against the crook of his arm; twenty years had taught Clara just where to put her weight so they could lie that way time out of mind. The storm was receding, and she strained to hear its display, listening like a sailor lost in fog for a mournful horn. Adam had become quite the black humorist lately, quite the collector of the macabre. He'd read somewhere that leukemia can be caused by lightning, so lightning had caught his interest. He'd read her the passage in Melville's "Bartleby" in the voice of that Wall Street lawyer "thunderstruck" by the abrupt sea-change imposed on him by a nay-saying clerk:

> For an instant I stood like the man who, pipe in mouth, was killed one cloudless afternoon long ago in Virginia, by summer lightning; at his own warm open window he was killed, and remained leaning out there upon the dreamy afternoon, till some one touched him, and he fell.

He told her about Roy Sullivan, in the 1983 *Guinness Book of World Records* with the widest bridge in the world. Sullivan had been struck seven times by lightning, pulled through every time. Shot himself after the seventh hit. Suspense milled him down. They lay there laughing. Or a couple of old scudders past eighty, quarrel over who discovered America, gunplay, one dead, the other arraigned, indicted, convicted, jailed. Adam laughed and laughed. Or the woman *way* past eighty, crippled, hauling herself out of her wheelchair to beat her husband to death with her cane and his towel rack.

"His what?"

"You know, walker."

"What the hell are we going to do?" Clara said.

"Classmate of mine at Yale, his father built a bomb-shelter. Used to check on it every weekend, the integrity of the locks, the canned goods, the cooling and heating systems. Flicked the switch after church one Sunday, nothing. Lit a match to see what was what, kaboom! Hell of a shelter, my friend never even heard the propane go, just a kind of thud. He told me, my pal was drunk, it sounded like a fart in a bathtub. When he told me, he laughed, couldn't help himself, poor bastard. Never had much to say to me after he told that story."

"You've told that story before. I've never thought it was funny."

Adam laughed now till the tears flowed. "Jesus, you're wrong there. Stay. Don't move. Please."

So she made herself listen, bowing to the fact that she hadn't the slightest notion what he felt, what she could do. He talked on; she let him. She willed her body not to tense; she tried to blank him out when he told about the bathers sunning on the rocks near Marseilles while the French Mediterranean fleet, cruising at flank speed, edging close to eyeball topless beauties, spread huge waves against the rocks, dashing dozens to their death that placid Sunday. He wouldn't quit. He'd heard a weird one at the courthouse. A sophisticated gentleman, a Hartford lawyer, had been scared to death by a Halloween mask. Just a kid, trick-or-treating, wearing some rubber get-up with black wiry hairs sticking from moles. Croaked. That would cost some kid's dad a pretty penny, Adam said.

Clara wondered if her husband was not just a little drunk, and she asked him. He said he didn't think so, but he looked as though he were studying the question.

"Maybe it's the chemo," he said.

Clara asked him please, no abbreviations, no familiarities, no fraternizing with the enemy. Adam squeezed her hand, nodded.

"You know," he said, "there are worse hands dealt every day. Client of mine, little crime wave all to himself, asked me to plead extenuating circumstances, post-adolescent trauma. Of course it's a crock, but turns out his story's kosher. He and his brother were fishing the Georges Bank on different boats out of Point Jude. His brother fell overboard, drunk they think, night, boots must have filled with water. Calm, clear night. My client didn't get the word aboard; everyone thought it best to break it to him on shore. Two days later my client's vessel was dragging, and they pulled his brother up in the net. There's your older brother, Catch of the Day, tangled in the monkfish, pollock, cod."

Adam said that was a worse sight than a 400X magnification peek at a bunch of pale plastic beach balls bouncing around your blood. Of course, Adam said, he didn't know how he'd feel "down the road." Maybe the deep six, drunk, on a warm night, maybe that wasn't so bad for the swimmer. Sure bad, though, for the fisherman.

Had she read about . . .

Clara laid her finger across Adam's lips, and he kissed her finger . . .

Had she ever read about the guy ("cross my heart") carrying a case of champagne to his wedding reception ("right here in Providence"), who slipped on ("I swear") a banana peel. Dropped the case; it exploded; "good night, nurse."

"Shut up," she said. "Hush, baby."

"I'm a little scared," Adam said.

"What's that?" she asked.

"What's what?" he asked.

"Downstairs. Something. Listen."

"It's nothing," he said. "Just the dog. He's scared of the thunder. Shush. Don't be scared. Everything's okay. I'm here."

4

▲ ▲ ▲ ▲ ▲

SKIPPY AND BABY

BABY had duked out a backyard cellar window, but they hadn't gone in, yet. Downside was the beast. That leash tied to the back porch was sturdy, for a big mammal. Meat-eater. Happy-side, look at the carton jammed in the trash, Sony Beta-Max, a better machine altogether than the RCA Selecta-Vision, according to *Consumer Reports*, but worth less on the street, maybe a dime on the dollar. Still. Sony family's a family worth getting to know.

You could work around the dog, of course. Baby scared them quiet. Skippy had heard that a few years ago, during a daytime home invasion, Baby was attacked by a Pekinese, yappy little assailant wrapped around his ankle like a muckluck, biting or boning, who knows a dog's mind? Story was, Baby bit it, tore out its throat, cashed its check. Skippy would ask Baby about those stories, and Baby would shrug. Skippy thought they were bullshit, but you couldn't tell. Baby could weird you out. One story Skippy knew was true, from years back, when they were kids, and it might explain why Baby got so sore at the Peke (if he did). They were checking out this convenience store, 7-Eleven, Dutchland Farms . . . it was Cumberland Farms, over near Rehoboth? No big deal, beer and smokes was all they were after, they knew the register was empty, about five in the morning. So Baby got bit by this guard dog, came from nowhere, tearing out of the stock room, Jesus, a shepherd. Well, that dog got a piece of Baby, and they lit out, better believe it. So next day in the *Journal* there's this story, the pooch had rabies, the thief's life was in danger. Oh, boy. Skippy figured the story for bullshit, it had to be a scam. But maybe not. So Baby went for the shots, we're talking *many* needles, in the belly. Skippy thought it was pretty funny, but he didn't laugh about it much when he was around Baby.

For sure Baby would poison a dog, put the pipe to its head, but not on the job with Skippy. Poison was for creeps. Skippy liked to feed a dog chunks of raw rump, show some class, be friends. Skippy liked dogs.

Couple of weeks ago he'd had to put Scout down; the old hound went back to his dad's time. His dad had told people who shopped at the bakery there was wolf in that dog, and it might have been true. Before Skippy's big brother had run off to Atlantic City, him and Scout were tight as ticks, so to speak. That big fellow would ride around in Mike's convertible, along Blackstone Boulevard, say, or better yet along Thayer Street, where all the rich-bitch Brownies hung out. Red light? Great: Scout would jump from the front seat, kill some pedestrian's animal, and be up front again, sitting pretty next to Mike before the light changed. A quick dog. Got a lot of respect. (They kept him off Federal Hill, of course. You didn't want your dog cutting a new asshole in the pet of some connected guy's niece.) That was before; then Scout lost his hips, and after Skippy's dad passed on, after Mike took off for the big bucks in Atlantic City, the pooch just moped around Skippy's pad, raising hell with Skippy's allergies, whimpering at wild dreams, like some burned-out speed freak. Finally he couldn't even eat without Skippy holding his head to the bowl. Sunset City. The vet said Skippy could go two routes: a shot, or decompression. With decompression they just cut back the oxygen, and then there was this snooze, about eleventy zillion winks. It cost a bundle, but decompression was the only way to go. Class was Scout's middle name. Skippy had his friend's tags on his key-chain, and he figured if there was a dog heaven, Scout was looking down at him right now. Scout had gone to that vet trusting him. He'd let Skippy take off his flea collar—"You won't be needing this, old pal." If Scout was Up There, Skippy figured he'd be saying, "You son of a bitch, you ratted me out."

They were in the cellar. Leadpipe cinch. Baby was holding a piece, wimpy chromed .25.

"What's that for, asswipe?" asked Skippy.

Baby said he'd grease the fucking mutt if it hassled him. "I'm not checking out with a dog necktie," Baby said.

Skippy hated artillery. "Put the fucking weapon in your pocket," he whispered, taking a hit off his inhaler. Baby muttered, and put the automatic in his pocket.

"What's that noise?" Baby asked. They were at the top of the cellar stairs, in like kind of a hallway.

"Thunder," Skippy whispered.

"Bullshit. Did you fart, man?"

Now Skippy could see him, a big guy, rattling his chain, Golden Retriever, wagging his tail. Now he laid another one.

"The dog cut the cheese," Baby said.

"No clue, Dick Tracy. Jesus," Skippy said to the dog, "cut it out." The big dog was nuzzling Skippy's nuts, licking his hand. Holy smoke, it had a ball in its mouth!

Baby looked nervous. "Put your hand in your pocket," Skippy told his old friend, "and I'll set your hair on fire. Let's get to work."

Even before they found the BetaMax, the Orientals, the TV, the candlesticks, the old-timey boats, the Ted Williams autographed ball, the pictures, the video and audio cassettes, the Cap'n Crunch, even before they knew by evolved sense there was no alarm system, Skippy spotted the keys and purse on the hall table, where the chumps always tossed them if they were first-timers, or if the last time was just an irritating memory. This was good. Either way, there'd be fresh pickin's. It was a pain in the ass to go to the trouble of breaking in some fancy house like this and find sloppy seconds or thirds, sometimes fifths or sixths, sometimes elevenths, fifteenths.

GM keys. Shit. Skippy hoped at least it wasn't an X-Car. He crossed the living room carefully (no wall-to-wall to muffle the noise, what they call "area rugs," sometimes they were worth a nickel or two) to check out the wheels in the driveway. Oh, no, 1980 Citation! The pits! Skippy was surprised the guy upstairs hadn't left the motor running. People wore out their knees praying their Citations would be heisted. One thing, you'd never find a Chapman Lok on an X-Car; another thing, they could drive around all night without worrying about a report; they could drive a hundred thousand before the guy would report it. That is, if it could rack up a hundred thousand. That is, if the brakes didn't lock up on the way to the fence, or the transmission didn't drop on Benefit Street, or the power steering decide to kill them on Wickenden. Whatever, it was better to limp along in that cheerless Detroit wreck than to jakeleg along the sidewalk with a clock radio cord tangled around Skippy's knees.

Baby was trying to shoo away the mutt, who wanted to play. Baby was pushing at his muzzle, and the beast was making fake growling noises, pretending to protect his tennis ball. This was getting noisy. Baby was pissed, checking out the pocketbook for cash and cards.

Skippy whistled the mutt to him. Patted his head till the animal got this blissed-out look and tried some more to lick him. Skippy whispered to the dog to lie down, and the sweet thing lay right down. He wondered if he could get him to roll over, like Scout, but when he asked, the dog just vegged, head between its paws, and sighed, like he'd heard it all before.

"Tell the fucker to play dead," Baby said.

They were working hard now, moving stuff to the kitchen door, near the car. There was always a chance the doors were wired, so it was prudent to move everything out in a rush. Speed was wise: wham, bam, thank you, ma'am, you're down the road.

Good eye! Sony Trinitron, 23-inch with digital tuning and remote, the mighty Tron! A yard at retail, three centuries from a private buyer. This was fun.

There was a shitty stereo. Well, low-end, good enough sound, but minimum resale. Good tape deck, six years ago, when they first came out. Skippy unplugged it all. The system was always worth more than the sum of its parts. That was a law he'd learned in high school, and on the streets. A guy might buy a set-up like this for his kid, say, to take to college or use in his bedroom. Skippy was filling a laundry bag with tapes. The homeowners had recorded on them, but what were bulk erasers for? These were reserved for Skippy's personal use; the fence wouldn't take them for free. Most of the video tapes were new, cellophane hadn't even been torn. These had value. He rolled up some rugs. They'd been in there ten minutes, max, about three times longer than they usually stayed.

Skippy found the old Rawlings baseball on a stand. A bruise from a bat, and an autograph. The handmade stand was worth liberating, too. "Line drive foul to deep left, hit by the signatory and caught by Adam Dwyer, Fenway Park, August 28, 1949."

"Hey," Skippy said. "Ted Williams signed this."

While they worked, they talked about the Red Sox. Whispered, really. Well, a little louder, no strain to hear each other. Lamented the stupid loss of Fisk to Chicago, the pitching problem.

"Eck's got good smoke," Skippy said.

"Bullshit," said Baby. "No control."

"Bullshit," said Skippy, "he can put the ball in a bottle, when he fucking wants."

Baby had found some silver. Now he was taking these old-fashioned boat models off their wood stands and dumping them in his sack. What's the point, Skippy asked him, they're just getting smashed. Won't be worth shit. Baby kept at it, skipping some he didn't like, the half-models of hulls, a couple of others. Skippy was flipping through the record collection, old stuff, scratched, ancient history, some ten-inchers, he didn't even know they made teensy LPs. Jazz, jazz, jazz. Classical, what Baby called "opera" when he switched it off the radio. Quick hands when the opera started fiddling and tooting and wailing and whining. Some of the disks were in a fancy wood box, hand-made. What the fuck, there was room in the hatchback, he'd steal them. He also grabbed, for Lisa, albums by these singers she liked, Bobbie Holiday, Bessie Holiday, whatever.

A bed creaked upstairs. They flashed their lights at each other, not at their eyes. They froze. The bed creaked again. They heard a headboard slapping against a wall. They smirked; they knew what was up; that would keep mine hosts busy. But then Skippy saw it wasn't a headboard; the dog had climbed to the stair landing, and he was lying there whacking his tail against the floor.

"Jesus, not bad!" Baby was at the piano in the living room, stuffing silver picture frames in his sack. They framed family photographs. There was an old fart with white hair standing next to a guy about twenty. He had his arm around the younger guy. The two gents were dressed in white shirts and shorts, holding these little rackets, smaller than racquetball rackets, with long skinny handles. They were sweaty, looking at each other, grinning like a couple of homos. There was a picture of the young guy older, middle-aged, standing with *his* arm around a kid, maybe nine or ten. They were holding these dumb-looking fishing poles, useless, skinny fucking things, with the reels attached to the bottom of the pole. Vests with bugs stuck to them. The kid was holding a string of bitty little fish. Waste of fucking time, Skippy thought. He'd read in *True* about fly-fishing, when he was a kid. Himself, he'd used worms. And if they didn't work, blasting caps.

But Baby's exclamation had been provoked by another photograph, and he was holding it. It too was of the young fisherman, in this scene even younger, no more than three. Wearing a bathing suit. Sprinkling someone with a hose. But fuck the kid. He was sprinkling this fox, probably his mommy, and she was wearing a bikini, and sticking out her tongue at the kid.

"Now there," Baby observed, "is a stand-up piece of ass. Inspect the tits." Baby stuck his tongue against the lady's tongue, and licked the glass, and moved his hips against the edge of the piano.

"Give me that," Skippy said.

"Ooo, he's in love," Baby said, dropping the frame in Skippy's sack. "Wait till I tell my cousin Lisa you're in love."

It was silent in the house. There was nothing on the ground-floor small enough to take worth taking, and Skippy never worked upstairs. If there was one thing he knew, Skippy knew he wasn't ready for, wasn't interested in, *upstairs*.

"Let's go," Skippy said.

"I've got the munchies," Baby said. "Let's check out the ice-box."

Skippy said to hurry, he'd load the car. When Baby was cranked like this on reefer and coke, there was no point arguing with his appetite.

In fact, when Skippy had finished humping the goodies into the Citation, he decided he could use a bite himself. They had a long night ahead of them. They fought over the Cap'n Crunch, to get at the plastic treasure chest buried at its bottom. There was supposed to be a coupon in one of those treasure chests worth a thousand. Skippy figured this for another con, but he always checked it out, digging through the cereal at Star Market and Almacs whenever he went "shopping." Inside the plastic chest were three worthless disks, like always. Skippy finished up in the kitchen while Baby took a last look around the house. Skippy thought he heard Baby on the stairs, and called softly to him ("No way!"), and heard his accomplice leave the house. Okay, done.

Baby found a ten-speed outside the kitchen, and just for drill went through its chain one-handed with his bolt-cutters. The weird fuck took off on it, making motorcycle noises; Skippy took charge of the wheels. The car flooded when Skippy tried to start it, and some loud dumb jazz blasted out of the speakers before he hit the eject button on the deck. Skippy got the junker going, and backed out quietly, and drove sweet and easy down Benevolent, without a care in the world. At the corner of Transit he passed his partner, and picked him up after Baby dumped the bike behind a hedge. They'd get it by and by, when they had more room in the car, if they had nothing better to do, if someone else didn't steal it first. Later, they forgot about the bike, because they got lucky. They invaded three more houses in the neighborhood, and hauled a shitload. By the time they dropped it with the fence and went off the nightshift, they couldn't remember, because they didn't care, what stuff came from what sucker's house. Except Skippy remembered, more or less, where he'd copped the picture of the stacked mumsy, whose finger bore the freight of a green rock the size of her baby's fist.

Sometime during the night Adam was stirred by music. Adam's ears ached, early symptom, and sometimes filled with the roar of breaking surf. He thought pain had waked him, but it was music. Wild Bill, "Time After Time," he recognized Cutty Cutshall. Maybe Adam smiled before sleep abruptly shut off the sweet, unsentimental ballad.

Next morning, descending the stairs to the kitchen while his mom showered, Ike shuffled, just like every morning. Heaped at the landing lay Bozo, like always, positioned to catch them coming or going. What? Bright red beads splashed on his neck; he was bleeding! Dead! But when Ike bent to him, he saw it was his own foot bleeding; he had cut his heel on the blade of the boning knife put there on the stairs.

Adam uncoiled from bed fast at the sound of his son's confusion. Adam's joints ached more every morning, but he was quick enough to get there, to wrap Ike in his arms, and quiet the excited dog. Now Clara saw it, her son bleeding. Her hair was wet, dripping like sheets of tears against the side of her face, staining her silk robe. She mopped at Ike's bleeding foot with the silk Bangkok robe, green and white, with bamboo blown by a breeze, placid hills, smutched now bright red. Adam had bandages. The cut was superficial.

"Don't come downstairs."

Adam knew what to do, they thought. So he was first to creep through the downstairs of his suddenly unfamiliar house, moving as fastidiously as a thief, wondering if "they" were gone. The knife, their signature, implied that they were gone. If he had had the serenity to review what he knew about these things, he would have known the house was empty. The knife was a warning, a gesture of contempt. Mature invaders. Teens left their own mark, scat on the living room rug.

They were gone. The back door was open to the cold dawn. The car was gone. Adam shut the door. Now Clara and Ike were beside him. The three stood at the center of the living room, wheeling like clockwork dancers to take in what was gone, what had happened. The dog stood with them, stretching, wagging its tail. Adam took the dog outside, and tied him to his leash. The gentle man considered, just a moment, popping the pet one on the snout. Adam stood in his bare feet on the cold dirt, staring at the broken cellar window. He wondered which ones did this. He knew the pros, had seen them all in court, had defended most of them.

Clara, the bloodstain on her robe already going rust to brown, leaned over the sink, cleaning blood off the boning knife, throwing cereal bowls in the trash.

"What are you doing?" Adam asked.

"They ate our food. They put our dishes in our sink."

Ike was at the icebox, reading a note attached to the door with a magnetic mouse:

"We won a grand in the Cap'n Crunch. Thanks, everybody!"

"They won a prize," Ike said.

"I don't think so," Adam said.

"My bike's gone," Ike said.

"Our pictures are gone," Clara said.

Adam saw that his baseball was gone, with the Ted Williams autograph; he saw that the ship models were gone, most of them. He bent to the bare floors to collect broken bits of rigging. The room he had known since he first knew anything was terra incognita.

"At least they didn't steal the model you built of *Warlock*," Adam told his son.

"They didn't like it," Ike said.

Then, Adam didn't know what to say. Clara couldn't think what to say. Ike climbed the stairs to his room, and shut the door, and locked it, and tested the lock. Outside, the dog barked to come in, louder now, disturbing the peace.

5

▲ ▲ ▲ ▲ ▲

TOM

H E was middleman in a lineup with four other clowns. Three pals from the Shriners ("Uncle Sham," "Bunky," "Crybaby"), Tom ("Yo-Yo"), and an out-of-town freelance, hiring out for chump change at the malls, called himself "Howdy." PPD called him "A Suspect." Lineups spooked Tom. It was bad enough witnessing in court, strangers listening for you to stumble over your grammar, or lick your lips when you got nervous, or blink when you had to fib a little. At least you could stare them down in court. But now, it was dark out there; you couldn't even see them. They always picked the one in the middle. And it didn't make it better fun to know that "they" were several grade-school girls with a felony morals beef against a clown. In fact, a terror of clowns. Tom Cocoran slipped a few places to his left.

The kids had told their parents that some creep with a red ball nose (just like Tom's now!), bald wig with frizzy red fringe (Tom's on the money, ditto "Uncle Sham's"), white eye-sockets and black shoe-polish brows (ever see a clown without them?), polka-dot pants with red suspenders and a droopy butt, tiny hat on the bald wig, thick scarlet lipstick (gets a mite creepy, no?), and a handy way with balloons, twisting them into the likeness of poodles and bunny rabbits—such a one had been stopping kids homeward bound (or hanging out?) after school, inviting them into a van with an elephant painted on its side, kissing their little cotton panties, or whatever else he could frighten them into letting him kiss.

This was not what had brought Lieutenant Cocoran to

clowning. His daughter, Maisie, when she was younger than those kids out there in the dark, horsing around with matches and a can of gas for the lawn mower . . . They patched her chest, and shoulders, and scalp, they fashioned her a face, they kept her going at the Shriners' burn hospital, near Boston. Grafts, plastic surgery, tough pep talks, gentle pep talks. She was okay now, a junior at St. Agnes', good student, cheerful, considering. She wouldn't be Miss Rhode Island or even Miss Cranston, but plenty of teenaged girls didn't win beauty contests. She had plenty of sand, and smiled as often as most teens, Tom hoped. But nine years ago, her history measured by square inches per month, wrapped like a mummy in gauze, hurting, hurting, hurting, she'd brood; Deirdre's faked grins and remorseless sunniness made it worse. But one Saturday, rock bottom, Tom didn't want to remember the night before, a couple of Shriner clowns ("Bunky," first in the lineup to Tom's right, was one) came to Maisie's ward. They made her laugh with their dizzy stunts. It hurt her to laugh, and they made her laugh anyway, knowing this, and the nurses pretended to try to shoo them away, and pretty soon they had Tom, for Christ's sake, laughing. So nutty. Pretending to be milkshake blenders, alarm clocks, popcorn! Name it: they told knock-knock jokes. Pretended to eat an apple, and found a worm. That's the one Maisie remembered, and liked to see her dad act out.

Anyway, Tom wanted to give something back when they finished with his little girl, and he offered to be a clown. Sure, Shriners were Freemasons, but plenty of Catholics were members. George Washington had been a Freemason, so Tom figured it was okay for him. With the Shriners, people thought there was a catch. But there wasn't, just helping kids was all, and maybe a little fun with the Motor Corps, and maybe a highball after the parade. Tom knew the world wasn't in danger of running out of Shriner jokes. Most people say "Shriner" and think "asshole," loudmouths wearing tassled fezzes. At first he thought of his clowning as charity, and it felt goofy. He was particular about his appearance, a conservative dresser, had his hair razor-cut every three weeks, never mind the cost. Tom was a little vain (maybe more than a little); he liked to be taken seriously. But he also got to like the clowning, its anonymity, what he could get away with, the way he could go up to anyone with a kind face, anyone, and give that person a hug, or maybe tease that person, pull his necktie out of his vest, or squeeze her nose and honk.

It wasn't easy to make people laugh. You had to learn how to make up your face, how to fall on your ass. Tom went to a Shrine clown school. "Show me happy; give me some happy," the instructor said. He was a pro from Ringling's, a friend of the late and great Emmett Kelly (1898-1979: Tom never missed a Kelly performance hereabouts; he'd bawl at the end, when that sad-face swept up the last of the spotlights when the circus shut down). "Show me sad; your pup just died!" He learned how to work balloons into shapes; the tight, squeaking rubber made the children squeal when he twisted it into a poodle, or a rabbit. They didn't teach Tom to kiss cotton undies.

When the lineup broke, the investigating detective sent the freelance away. The kids had fingered Tom, and Tom's friends, but not the out-of-towner, the one now in the middle. That guy was scared, but clean. Number one, no van. Number two, checkable alibis. Three, nobody was stupid enough to pull shit like that and hang around town, in his costume. The perpetrator would be in Boston next, or Worcester, or Hartford, or Springfield. Or he'd wait eight months. Or he'd never do it again.

"Hey, Yo-Yo, can I have your autograph?" the duty sergeant asked, in what he must have thought was an accurate simulation of a kid's voice.

Lieutenant Cocoran wasn't in a humor to be ribbed: "I'll be the clown, okay? You be serious." He peeled off his wig.

"Officer?" (The civilian was in the waiting room, hanging over the duty sergeant's desk.) "Could I steal a couple of minutes?"

Tom recognized him. A local mouthpiece. Adam Dwyer. This wasn't court business; his family was with him, hanging back a little. They all had that dazed look, that "why me?" look. There was that tremor along Counselor Dwyer's cheeks, fury. The victim (mugging? car? no sex—he wouldn't have brought the kid) was too smart to ask, *How can this happen?*, longed to ask, was too smart to ask, *What are you people going to do about this?* There was also a small wrinkle here, as both men appreciated: Providence was a peewee metropolis, and the probability was high that whoever had wronged the attorney and sometime Public Defender was an ex-client.

"Let me get out of my gear," Tom said. "How did you make me?" Tom figured Dwyer would say something light; he had an easy way in court, good-natured, smart on cross but never a bully. Tom figured he'd say something like *Your fame precedes you*, some lawyer remark.

Dwyer said: "The sergeant pointed you out."

Tom tried to comfort the girls, put his red ball nose on one, some greasepaint on another. They didn't laugh. Their parents didn't laugh. Tom figured they'd had their ration of clowns. He thanked them for coming to Fountain Street, suffering the aggravation. To tell the truth, Tom wasn't sure he hadn't had about enough of clowns. His friends seemed to feel the same. They agreed to meet later at the 19th Hole in Quonset for solace, a couple of shooters.

"I don't know," Bunky said.

"Mondo weirdo," Uncle Sham said.

"Mondo bizarro," Tom said. "What can I say?"

Counselor Dwyer and his family sat in Tom's office and told what had happened. Tom liked them. Mrs. Dwyer was easy on the eye, smart, feisty. Very pissed off. The kid was sweet, open smile, scared, pretended not to stare at the remnants of Tom's grease-paint, polite for a kid his age. Adam Dwyer was just the slightest bit paunchy; most people wouldn't even notice, but Tom was in great physical shape, and prided himself on noticing things. His street instincts were known to be impeccable: "I know how to go where the music takes me," he liked to say.

He had trouble reading the lawyer. Dwyer was in charge, but he also seemed to tune out now and then. Also, he spoke softly. So did Tom; people had to lean into Tom's words to catch his drift, sometimes even cock an ear. Tom liked this in himself, but when he'd been cross-examined recently by the defense counsel, the judge had admonished them. ("Don't whisper, gentlemen, please; share your disagreements with us.") Tom had winked then at his adversary, and maybe this had caused Dwyer to unload his troubles on him now.

Because a pissant B & E, even with Grand Theft Auto, was not the territory of a Gold Shield. Never mind, it was a quiet morning. Tom took the inventory of stuff, touch-typing the report. He had learned to type even before he finished at the Police Academy; it pleased him to run against the stereotype of the hunt-and-peck bumbling cop, awake till dawn banging typos on coffee-stained reports.

No, he told Mrs. Dwyer, he wouldn't dust for prints. No one had been hurt. Yes, they'd use the credit cards, some right away, more later, after everyone had quit paying attention. The cards had been reported stolen? Great, wouldn't cost the Dwyers anything, just the hassle was all, life in the Twentieth Century. The car? Tom shrugged: not much of an automobile, it would probably turn up, if the Dwyers were unlucky, probably stripped, if they were really unlucky. Had they read about the Chief's car? Yesterday afternoon's *Bulletin*? Well: '74 Olds Cutlass, piece of junk nobody would want to take around the block, left at a retread shop for some new shoes. The repairman raised it on the lift, did his stuff, lowered it, backed out of the bay, left the engine running while he wrote up the bill. The Chief sat in a waiting room, in his uniform. Paid the bill, found air where his Olds had been. He was sick about it, "just like you people."

Mrs. Dwyer didn't seem to feel better when Tom told this story. She said they took her appointment book. Mr. Dwyer tried to comfort her, said his plans had changed, he'd be home more than he'd expected.

"I feel like we're under siege," Mrs. Dwyer said.

"You are," Tom said. She didn't seem to feel better when he told them not to feel singled out, or take it personally. They had been chosen because they had what someone else wanted, and didn't even want that badly.

"The ship models matter a lot to us," Adam said. "They've been in the family a long time. My son liked them. He makes models himself; they overlooked his models."

Tom liked that. "I know how you feel," he said, looking at Ike, "but at least nobody got hurt." He explained that what thieves couldn't sell, they'd keep, or junk. It wasn't likely they could fence the models. It wasn't likely they'd be recovered. To explain this, he'd stopped typing. Counselor Dwyer was staring at Tom's quiet fingers. The nails were manicured. Tom wondered if the lawyer misread the meaning of such an extravagance.

"Officer, we'd be grateful if you could help us find those models. I'd be really grateful."

Tom wondered if the honorable member of the Rhode Island Bar was offering a *quid pro quo* across his desk, a little something for a little something. Tom hated envelopes. He'd sooner give his palm than his fist, if only no one offered an envelope. Not that he was a prig. Tom understood bending, and not just once, every day. He understood how it worked. A break on a clean used car, tickets to the Celts even, more likely a turkey and a jug at Christmas, a free cup of coffee, what friends do for one another, forget power. But envelopes were different: "Officer, let me put some worldly goods in your rec room, what do you say?" That was different, and for that Tom would cuff your hands behind your back, and maybe fuck up your Rolex.

"What do you want me to do?" Tom asked.

"Ask around about the models."

"And what will you do?"

"I'll describe them to you. Show you pictures of them. What else can I do? There's nothing else I can do."

Tom said: "Sure. We'll ride around together." Tom smiled at Ike: "Maybe we can find the bike, if we look quick."

Clara said she didn't want Ike riding around in a police car. Before Ike could plead with her, Tom said of course not, he wouldn't let his daughter ride with him, why would he let Clara's son?

"We won't get the boat models back," Tom said. "But we'll

look for the bike. But we probably won't find it. But if I don't waste time looking for your stuff, I'll waste time looking for something else."

Ford Fairmont, shocks like a New York taxi's, no doorknobs or window cranks back there behind the cage. Dynamite communications, first-class radio, the dispatcher came in static-free to Adam, Tom, Tom's brother and sister cops, hobbyists, villains, anyone willing to spend $300 for an FM scanner, or boost one from Radio Shack. Tom said it was a problem. No broadcast was secure. Setting up a major drug bust last week, the TV van beat them to the drop, had laced their fucking cables all over the importers' front lawn before Tom even arrived. Adam wondered why none of the arrested dealers had sought his services.

They stopped at Saturn's Rings, a video arcade at ground-zero downtown, couple of blocks from the Biltmore. This was a naughty place, and the dangerous young layabouts feeding the machines with quarters stolen from parking meters knew Tom. The few who didn't sometimes got in his way, and then they got out of his way. Not that he hissed at them, or swung a stick on its thong, or showed his weapon, or tapped a flashlight against his palm, or grabbed kids by the collar. He spoke with cultivated courtesy, just as Adam had heard him speak in court. The policeman was seamless, Adam suspected. But he had a reputation for rage; for this Adam had chosen him.

Adam had once defended a wise-guy, a petty hood who liked to give cops his lip, and the finger. Tom had been a uniform then, on his way up. The charge was small-change, loitering, public nuisance, maybe gambling. But Tom had busted Adam's client in a third-floor apartment on Federal Hill, had come through that window wearing a motorcycle helmet to protect his head, a towel over his face, ski mitten on one hand, weapon in the other. That was *through* the window, *through* the glass; he'd been lifted up there by a cherry-picker. "Crap-out!" he'd said, busting through the glass with his revolver. He was evidently cross with Adam's client, and that was how Tom had expressed displeasure. Tom had left an impression on the sportsmen, and now people pretty much got the hell out of his way, and told their little brothers and nephews and young friends to get out of Tom's way.

Tom didn't trouble to ask questions at the arcade. He just checked out the bikes, and went about his business. Heading toward Fox Point, he got a call. This was a domestic dispute, serious, one of Tom's specialties. They peeled out toward North Main Street. Adam wondered if this weren't central to the officer's image of himself, scaring the lawyer. The siren screamed; the car was unmarked, and Tom hadn't bothered with a light. He seemed to enjoy it, and Adam, with time later to reflect, might understand why. Braced so hard against the firewall he was afraid he'd punch right through, Adam felt the adrenalin kick in, and terrified as he was, he was thinking *we* got a call.

This was to "quell a domestic disturbance."

"There's nothing worse," Tom said.

Terrifying the citizenry (what red light?), Tom reminisced, granddad rocking on his porch. Adam knew this was an affectation, but he was impressed anyway. Tom whipsawed the Ford around a delivery van and ran the inventory of weapons turned against him in domestic incidents: screwdrivers, hammers, lumber (popular weapon), forks, a six-pack. . . . Tom said the only time he'd been hurt badly enough to do hospital time was trying to break up a lovers' quarrel between a couple of fairies. They'd seen him coming; one of them dumped the other's stereo out the window, and busted Tom's shoulder. Well, that was his only overnight hospital time. He'd also been treated at St. Joseph's five years ago.

"I was patting down this Negro near Daddy's House of Ribs, on Broadway? No big deal, looking for ganj. So I got bit by an alligator. No shit. Eighteen inches of cayman in that man's pocket, and whatever else he had in there, I didn't care any more."

This was something. Screaming rubber, screaming siren ("a practiced bad guy can distinguish between sirens: fire, ambulance, us . . .), and all those complete sentences . . .

Here they were. Adam was shaking, of course. Tom was pre-
dictably expository:

"What do you want? That wasn't bad. The chases are bad,
one death per hundred chases. You can get into it, though, especially when some teen is looking to make you look like a donkey.
What do you want? Fifty-five? Stop on red?"

"I didn't say anything," Adam said.

"But I know what you're thinking."

"Nobody knows, Officer, what anybody thinks."

This was the usual, and Tom handled it well. He beckoned
Adam to follow him up the stairs of the clean two-family Victo-
rian frame house near Olney Street. A man and a woman
screaming at each other, awful threats, primitive curses, from
the heart. People once in love wished their nearest and dearest
dead, "burning in hell," and Tom knocked, and announced himself, and they cursed him. So he kicked through a chained door,
cheap as paperboard. It made satisfying splinters, and now Tom
had their attention. She had (shades of Jiggs & Maggie!) hit him
with a fry-pan, and blood was congealing above his eye. It was
the head of household's ambition to scrimshaw his initials in her
face with a broken Orange Crush bottle. They weren't the least
bit drunk.

Adam eavesdropped. They didn't ask who he was. They must
have figured they had no standing to ask questions. Tom heard
their stories. "His Nibs here" had complained about the food.
"Her Majesty" had thrown out an album of snapshots ("he spent
all his time looking at pictures of his dead fucking wife"). He always chose the television programs. She made her side of the
bed. He couldn't stoop to make the bed. He had arthritis. Adam
lost interest pretty soon, but Tom was in it deep, working to
cross-index their torts. Adam had heard enough torts. He figured
the couple at seventy, maybe older. Their apartment was spot-
less, hospital standards. Adam wanted to go home, take care of
his wife and son, be cared for, lock their goddammed doors. He
sat in the police car, waiting. Chills were taking charge, what

Asa called the shakes and bakes. Tom was still upstairs. Adam honked the horn, lightly. He felt ashamed to honk the horn, but he honked it again, urgently. He waited. About ten minutes later, Tom came down. He said nothing about the horn. He didn't apologize, either.

"They're okay now. Things just piled up, the way they do."

Adam said he'd like to go home, back to the station, he could catch a cab, to his office, wherever.

Tom wanted to look one place for the bike. He drove there slowly, a park near Fox Point, just off Gano Street, the Portuguese section, an uncertain neighborhood of derelict apartments and houses spruced up by junior faculty at Brown and Rhode Island School of Design. They drove to a monument to Vasco de Gama, and saw a gang of kids circling the statue, a dozen and more kids hunched over the bars, clicking their ten-speeds in circles. Pretty soon they'd do this in hot Firebirds and Fieros, down at Kennedy Plaza, cruising anti-clockwise past the Post Office, railroad station, Biltmore, Fleet National Bank, Ming Garden, Federal Courthouse, Post Office, round and round, fish in a bowl, throaty gurgles from the exhaust, dumb music distoring stolen speakers, amplified by stolen tape decks, powered by stolen batteries. . . . Tom parked. They stared.

"Hey," Adam shouted. "That's Ike's! There's his bike!"

Every kid dumped his bike, and booked. They split in all directions, showing the flash of their sneakers, Puma Intimidators, perpetrator boots, seventy bucks at Stride-Rite, free of charge at Midnight Haberdashery.

Tom helped Adam load the Peugeot into his trunk. It did not escape his notice that this bicycle was not precisely as described on the stolen articles inventory.

"It's okay," Tom said. "It evens out. Tell your kid this is a gift from the Providence Police Department."

"What a world," Adam said.

"Tell him we're sorry about the boat models. Tell him we'll look around."

Adam stared out the side window of the car. Dusk was coming down. He thought about things. He didn't think about ship models, or bicycles, or domestic strife, or criminals, or police officers.

Tom knew what the lawyer was thinking. "What a world," he said. Tom didn't know a thing about the lawyer, or the lawyer's thoughts.

This runt town of 156,000, declining population, could serve your security needs. The *Yellow Pages* list more than eighty alarm companies, five pages dense with display ads for closed circuit television, ultrasonic, stress, infrared. The *FeelSafe* system, for example, sold by Ace Alarm: "If you're afraid of robbery, rape, fire, vandalism at home, you have good reason. And we have good news."

Alarms would be installed next week. Tonight, less than twenty-four hours after It happened, the Dwyers' house was like Fort Knox, like a jail. Greased sills. Cellar doors sealed. Quarter-inch plexi on the ground-floor windows. Couldn't shoot through it, sure couldn't punch it out with a brick. In summer, no air would pass through it, either, and the sunlight would be broken by steel bars, due next week with the *FeelSafe*.

Tonight, there were new deadbolts on the new inner doors, which were steel. The deadbolts were tempered steel; the lieutenant had said brass is butter to a hacksaw. Tonight, there were sash bolts. The floodlights were new, and lit. It would take the Dwyers about five minutes to leave their house, the locks were so many and so complicated. Tonight, they had barricaded the back and front doors with heavy furniture, but of course this was a practice they'd soon abandon.

Tonight, they were upstairs, with some things they treasured. Tonight, after Ike had gone early to bed, and shot his new bolt shut, and laid his rigging knife, open, on his bedside table, then Adam and Clara had lugged up to their bedroom, as they would lug in nights to come, some special things: a few rugs, some photograph albums, Ike's ship model and another they had neglected to steal, some paintings. Adam had learned the trick from his mother, years ago in Jamestown, feeding the raccoons.

His mother would put bread and milk beside the garbage cans, in the hope that they wouldn't make a mess when they came. But the coons tipped over the rubbish anyway, and his mother and father would just smile at this. But Adam thought now he would go crazy if it happened to him. He'd scream into the night at them, scream against their fucking greed, as though this had anything to do with anything. Just nature at work, nothing personal.

But they tried this anyway, rearranging the house with an eye to satisfying "them," leaving stocking stuffers downstairs. A camera; skis; $60. They called this "feeding the roaches," putting out leftovers so the roaches wouldn't move on the larder. Or come upstairs.

They talked about guns. In the days and weeks, with luck the months to come, they would talk often about guns. In this, as in so many aspects of the morning and day leading to tonight, they had much company on the East Side, in Providence, America.

Tonight, they tried to sleep. They felt unlocated anger at each other, a component of shame. Adam wondered what it would be like to catch "them," or maybe better one of "them" (if there were more than one; he knew there were two), and tie him to a chair and consider what to do next, fuck with him some, watch him deal with a sucking chest wound. Adam tried not to think these thoughts. He tried to sleep, and wondered how Ike and Clara would do without him. But last night he'd been here, right here, and so what? Adam had heard many a preacher tell many a congregation of mourners, *We won't see his like again.* Adam reckoned they'd probably see Adam's like again. Or they wouldn't. So what? He didn't ask Clara what she was thinking. He knew. She lay beside him tensed with listening. Adam thought about after. It offended his conservative (and sentimental) aspects to learn he couldn't be planted on his land in Jamestown. Something about the integrity of the water table. He wished they'd built on it, after they had to sell the summer house. Maybe Ike? In the boneyard up the street Adam would be one with his Yankee forbears, by God, stiff-lipped and hollow-cheeked, freezing his rocks off. He thought about his funeral, the memorial service. Clara should charge admission, see who really gave enough of a shit to pay a hundred to see him out. He'd mention this to her; it might make her laugh. But not tonight. He couldn't help himself, he wondered who would cry. He'd cried for his dead mother, not for his father. Surprised himself. Again. He figured Ike would try not to cry, and that was all right. He figured Clara wouldn't cry. Sometimes she was strong, boy he admired that strength. But sometimes, when she didn't cry, when she hadn't cried once these past weeks, he wondered what was going on in there.

"Did you hear that?" she whispered beside him. She was rigid.

Adam strained to hear. "What did it sound like?"

"Someone pushing at the window."

"I hear it. Sounds like the front door, someone testing the front door."

"I don't think so," she said. "Maybe it was nothing."

"I'll check it out."

"Don't go. Stay here! Don't go down there!"

They lay silent, straining to hear.

"I don't know," he said.

"Were you dreaming?" she asked.

"Sort of," he said. "Were you?"

"I don't know. Maybe."

"Listen again," he said.

"I don't hear anything now."

"Maybe they heard us."

"Maybe they left," she said.

"Maybe," he said.

"Maybe they're down there," she said.

"Let's try to sleep," he said.

"Yes," she said. "Let's." And then she wept.

Tom knew most of the bars. Before he joined the force he hung out a lot, and then when he married Deirdre, he stayed home, and especially when Maisie was little. It was terrific watching her grow up. Terrific. Deirdre would read Dr. Spock to him, and he'd read Dr. Spock to Deirdre.

"Isn't that incredible," she'd say, when the baby wrapped its fingers around her finger.

"Isn't that great," he'd say, when she tried to crawl.

"Listen, she's singing!"

"Come here, Tom! She talked!"

He'd get a call in the squad car. "Officer Cocoran, your Maisie was spotted an hour ago, walking."

Then, Maisie started school, and he'd go out at night, after work, no worse than anyone, just to unwind. Then she was in the burn ward, and he spent his off-hours there. Now, Tom knew most of the bars.

Off-duty police like to stick with their own. Most civilian hangouts, you'd run into someone mad at you. Say the brother of a fence, or maybe the fence himself, on work release from the ACI. On the other hand, cops off duty in gangs can pull some wiggy shit. There was that recent horror show up in Boston, King Arthur's Lounge and Motel, a strip joint and truck stop in Chelsea. A vice detective, should have seen enough to last his life, but hadn't, touched a stripper in the wrong place, a little urgently, according to witnesses. She put a spiked heel in his eye. He got bounced. Not blind, but blind drunk, he came back at closing with a dozen cops, and they chased the customers and the girls into a motel room, which got quickly, pointlessly, locked. The cops, all dressed in at-home costumes, glancing now and then at their friend's disgusting mess of an eye, went at the door with nightsticks and a fire ax.

"We're going to kill you!" Several of them decided to scream this. It sounded right to them: "We're going to kill you!"

Someone inside yelled for someone to call the police. That's when the passerby got Maced.

"We *are* the fucking police! No one can help you."

And no one could. Hi and bye for three sad customers. Fifteen to twenty-five for two cops, family men. Who wasn't a family man?

At first, Tom didn't hang out where cops mixed with civilians. So he took his custom to the Fraternal Order of Police Lodge No. 3, a roomy joint on Sheridan Street, dull yellow cinderblock set among derelict brick factories. Very Mill Town. No sign in front. Juke, pool, Pong (when they dreamed up Pong), Space Invaders (modern times), horseshoe-shaped, orange Formica bar, honest-to-God dimies, crackers and dip at Happy Hour (which was every hour, and some hours after legal closing). The walls at the FOP were covered with pictures of softball teams, plaques honoring the patrons for their contributions to this and that, Meeting Street School for the Handicapped, Christmas Feast for the Elderly, Little League, of course. There were also photographs of outings, an old-timey print of old-timey police officers, hundred and fifty of them, pissing over the starboard rail, upwind, of the Block Island ferry, homebound on a July Sunday. Must have been a short-lived tradition, because there was only one similar picture, a circle of hundreds pissing into the Lincoln Reservoir (*No Fishing! No Boating! No Swimming!*), with a huge wave moving before the power of their eliminations.

But there had been hullabaloo on Sheridan Street. The confusion about closing hours. The disagreement between fellow officers about the athletic merits of "The Boomer," the Bosox's recently traded first-baseman; this debate ended with a bullet passing through the fleshy part of the neck of "The Boomer's" detractor. This led to some spoil-sport remarks from the Chief, quoted by the *Journal*: "This should be the safest place to drink in the city of Providence. Instead, it's among the most dangerous." Tom felt the Chief overreacted, a little. True, there had been some wild-west stuff when the kilt-clad members of the NYPD's bagpipe band showed up late, after a parade in Newport, maybe uninvited. True, some weapons had been discharged into the ceiling, and also in the parking lot. But the FOP Lodge No. 3 was not such a knock-down, blow-out joint; not like the Pinecone Tap, where people wound up dead like every week or two. Or the King Arthur Lounge and Motel.

Still, Tom had outgrown the crazy stuff. So now he was slugging down rum drinks to bring in the spring in Quonset (where the quonset hut was invented?), at the 19th Hole, a Shriners' roadhouse. The owner was a fan, and Tom's autographed picture was on the wall with other clowns'. He owned a ceramic mug, with his name on it, "Yo-Yo." The owner played the organ at the 19th Hole, and had a quick mouth. If he liked you, he'd rib you from the organ, give you a real roasting, a Don Rickles kind of thing. He liked Tom a lot. It was special to get picked on at the 19th Hole; regulars appreciated the honor. Tom reminded himself: it was an honor, what was happening right now. Some people got a piece of lemon meringue in the face, but this wasn't Tom's style, and he was sure the owner understood this. He hoped the owner understood.

The rum wasn't doing much for Tom tonight. He'd been talking more than an hour about the shitheel putting his clown moves on little girls, and "Uncle Sham" had said what he'd do if they caught the guy ("I've never asked for favors, Tom, but just this once, so help me, I'm asking, just put me in the cell with him, I'm asking for a few minutes max, just turn your back, it's a favor I'm asking, Tommy . . ."), and "Bunky" was looking like he might cry, and Tom was hoping that waitress coming his way, grinning, bearing something on a tray covered with a napkin, Tom was hoping she didn't think he was someone he was not.

"Lieutenant, we want you to have this, and enjoy it." She was smirking. The napkin came off with a flourish. It was a carved balsa clown, painted, "Yo-Yo." She said a burned kid in Boston made it last month, after a show. Now the owner was playing a flourish. People were applauding, most of them strangers, the way people applaud when someone who just happens to be at the next table gets a cake and "Happy Birthday!" from the waiters. Tom smiled.

"I've got to get home to dinner," he said.

"Yeah," said the owner, sounding from the organ approximately appropriate *yah, yah, yah* strains. "I know what's waiting for you. *Some dinner!* Hot tongue and cold shoulder."

(Laughter.) Tom wanted to say it wasn't like that with him

and Deirdre. Tom wanted to explain he was happily married, a family man. To tell how special it was. How happy they were. Well, to tell the truth, not recently, lately they'd had problems, he had.

6

▲ ▲ ▲ ▲ ▲

L I S A

FEEL that spring sun! Top down, catching some rays, Lisa scooted along Farewell Street, past the Jewish cemetery. Skippy was doing business, so she'd spent her off night in Newport, horsing around, letting a guy buy bets for her at the Jai-Lai. She'd met him driving along America's Cup Avenue, waiting out a light in front of Bannister's Wharf. Lisa had this tic, looked like a wink, and it caught the fellow's interest. Just before the light changed, she'd licked her lips, then gunned her VW across his lane. The chase was on! What a hoot! She loved to drive them nuts, especially when she was cranked on X-Roads. Men were such babies! She let him catch her on Ocean Drive, and talk her into dinner at the Candy Store, and Jai-Lai. First he said he was single; then divorced; would you believe separated? Okay, not all that happy at home? They boogied the night away. Come bedtime, Lisa explained she'd made two resolutions on her twenty-third birthday: no more coke in her eyes, and no married men. He took it like a sport, bought her a room at the Treadway, and now she was zooming back to Providence, feeling fine, letting her long blond hair stream out behind her, looking good, as she knew.

The cemetery made her think of bones. It wasn't just those dead people in there, the skeletons. It wasn't just the memory of the time she got stoned with Skippy, when they did it in the Garden of Heavenly Rest.

These days lots made her think of bones. She needed to mellow out; tonight she'd be singing at Goddard's. Shitski, pressure, what a bummer! So before she hit the on-ramp for the bridge to

Jamestown she sparked this monster bone, a Cheech & Chonger of Maui Wowie stuffed in a Tampax wrapper. *Okay!* The sun was *so* warm, and a nor'wester pushed puffy little clouds above her, and below she saw sea horses breaking down the Bay.

Wait a minute! That guy in the suit and tie, in a *hat*, he was crossing the guardrail. He was staring down, seemed as interested in the sight as someone looking for his bus. Holy cow, he was going to jump, maybe. Lisa cupped her smoke, and checked out the scene. There was a car on her tail, maybe he'd stop and square it away. If Lisa pulled over, she'd have to dump the gizzy, and she'd just copped it, a lid. Heat would make the scene, for sure. She'd tell the guy at the tollbooth, and he'd do something.

GOOD WEED! Lisa took a couple more hits, and forgot to look in her rearview. Another, and she wasn't thinking all that much, if you really want to know, about the man in the suit, eyeballing the water, a hundred fifty feet down. The Newport-Jamestown Bridge was long, and Lisa's attention span was short. Now she was a happy camper, giggling about something she maybe said last night, wondering how Skippy made out. The toll was two bucks; exact change a one-dollar token. The toll-taker didn't accept tokens. Lisa fished out a slug, and sailing into the booths she took a last pull on her roach, flipped it and the slug in the cage, and cruised toward Providence, singing along with the Eagles. It wasn't that Lisa was an uncaring person, she just didn't have an awesome memory. The guy in the suit was archives, for her and for real. He had been looking down at Narragansett Bay for reasons that would provoke questions on the six o'clock report, and answers in the morning paper. Lisa would have saved him if she could; she'd save everybody in the world! When she saw sad shows she cried. But hey, nobody's perfect. Still, she felt like a wackadoo sometimes, even if she knew she was too hard on herself; she should cut herself some slack.

During The Wedding, Lisa got a boot out of people telling her she brought to mind Lady Di. She didn't know about that, but she knew she stacked up okay. Skippy said she was Jodie

Foster's exact double, and Lisa guessed that was possible, too, except she knew for sure Lady Di didn't look a bit like Jodie Foster. Okay, it got confusing, but here was a fine-looking woman. Maybe a little on the chubby side (she had a weakness for yummy drinks, mai-tais and sombreros, black Russians and mimosas), and maybe a tad vacant when she was ripped on chiba, but most of the time she looked brighter than the Brownies up the Hill, and God knows she dressed better than RISD's hippy-dippy art students halfway up the Hill. She kept her eyes open, liked a good time, figured she was going places. Eventually. "Full of beans," the nuns told her in school, "full of beans."

For now, waitress. Waiting tables was a lot of dues, answering to "yo, wench!" or getting ranked on by some snotty fancy-pants whose medaillons de boeuf Rossini weren't pink enough, whose tea was made with bags. Bags was right. But there were consolations. And hadn't Jessica Lange been a waitress? *Everyone* had, and Lisa had the class waitressing gig in Providence, L'Apogee, top of the Biltmore, top of the goddammed *city*, you could see the State Capitol yonder, lots of little buildings twinkling in the distance. Don't forget great tips and some interesting out-of-towners. She got hit on a lot, by businessmen, even by daddies visiting their college kids, trying out the bar after mummy went to sleep early in one of the hotel's fancier rooms. Lisa didn't mind; she knew how to flirt, turn it into a joke. She knew what those turkeys wanted her to say: "Are you from out of town?" No way, José. Lisa's chops had been busted, but she'd never thought of hooking, even when she came up short on coke money.

Really, the money was dynamite. But what made waitressing at the Biltmore such a blast was being able to sing every month or so at Goddard's, the well-known bar, the bar downstairs.

Now Lisa was singing, "I Guess I'll Have to Change My Plan" upbeat, piano and drums behind her. She was the Chris Connor, the Anita O'Day of Providence. That's what people told her.

She had their albums cold, could do all the cuts. In fact, she was pretty good, when she didn't forget the words. As though that mattered tonight.

What was with this crowd? It took Tom a few minutes to figure out the conventioneers listening to that pretty singer. He'd seen her around; she kept evil company, but he'd never busted her, thought she had a clean sheet. There was Tom's world: clean sheet or record, the binary range.

He'd left the 19th Hole figuring to go home. Then he figured he might as well stop by the Station on Fountain Street, see what was going down. But first, he decided, a little pop at the Biltmore. He tricked himself into believing he wasn't looking for action, because he really didn't want to find action. He hated to hunt, to fit himself with beer goggles so everyone began to look tasty half an hour before the bar closed. He tried not to want any. The way Tom saw it, when you looked for it, you usually got it, and then you ate a bushel of remorse. Here it was, half an hour before closing, and if he got laid tonight it would be like sinking one from mid-court at the buzzer, and still losing by one point. Because he had to go home, after.

Deirdre told their friends, in front of Tom: "At least we've never been bored. We've had our troubles, but we've never bored each other."

Deirdre lied.

That pretty girl was singing, and smiling, and screwing up the lyrics, and trying for notes she couldn't hit, and still smiling. Tom figured she was either on something, or the happiest singer in Providence. She was not the best singer in Providence, but forget her pipes. She had a batty smile. Despite the crowd. The crowd wasn't listening, because the listeners couldn't hear. The place was wall-to-wall deaf people; they weren't inconsiderate; they weren't yammering above her ballads. These were silent people. Busy with their fingers, also smiling. Drunk conventioneers, handicapped persons putting out-of-town moves on one another. They'd picked Providence.

———

Lisa figured, it's show business. She noticed Tom at the bar. She knew who he was. He'd busted Baby a couple of times. He was giving her The Look, and she lowered her eyes, a shy gesture she'd practiced; boy, did it work! Now she was singing to a cop wearing a piece under his jacket, and a boner in his pocket. A blast. There were Lisa's binaries, blast/bummer, her conceivable spectrum of chance. She liked his clothes. He had cute eyes, but what a Gloomy Gus!

When the set ended, they talked. She didn't seem to realize she'd been singing to deaf mutes. She said she usually waitressed at L'Apogee, and pronounced it just right, without making a big deal out of it. Tom figured she was French-Canadian. Tom said he didn't drink at L'Apogee, "It's an asshole factory."

Then she did the damnedest thing. Said she had something in her eye. The bartender was standing in front of her, and she pointed to her eye, and said:

"Jerry, lick it out, will you?"

Jerry wasn't buying in.

"I'm busy, honey, sorry."

She turned to Tom. "Be a sport; it hurts."

Tom wondered if she had just possibly asked other men to lick motes of dust from her eyeballs, and he decided he didn't much care. He licked the salt smoothness of her eye, and she drew back, and winked.

"Oo-la-la," she said. "You're adorable," she said, "for such an old coot."

Standing in front of the door to the women's washroom, she turned to look at him. He was staring at her, like she suspected. What the hell. She beckoned to him, and at first he didn't understand. He looked over his shoulder, to check if she might mean someone else. Here he came; here he was. She took his hand, led him into the place, past a startled lady, into a toilet stall.

"You're wicked cool," she said.

"I'm a police officer," Tom said.

"It's okay, sweetness."

Some time passed; customers came and went, most in silence. But Tom heard what women say when they're alone together, and it surprised him. A surprising night for Tom.

"I'm married," he said.

"I'll make you forget your wife. Let her rip."

So how about that, she fucked a married guy after all. Great hairy Ned! She didn't mean to; it just happened, the way things did.

7

▲ ▲ ▲ ▲ ▲

PROVIDENCE

"Where your treasure is, there will be your heart also."
                                —*The Good Book* (*Matthew 6:21*)
"I would plow the ocean into pea-porridge to make money."
                                —*A Bristol privateer, 1750*

I T did not escape Clara's notice that most of the stolen ship models were likenesses of fine sailing vessels with dark histories. Like Rhode Island, the Dwyers had prospered, from Colonial times, as "Guinney traders," in the Triangle Trade. It must have seemed, while it lasted, like a perpetual motion machine, an alchemist's stone, divine providence, the everlastingly free lunch. Let's say in 1750 a Dwyer vessel—the *Planter* or *Prudent Hannah, Warlock*, perhaps, or *Four Bachelors* or *Nimrod*—embarked from the foot of Transit Street, bound for Jamaica, Cuba, or Hispaniola laden with horses, red onions, cheese, corn, and tar. Let's say these were traded, prudently, for sugar or molasses. Back to Providence, where any of twenty and more distilleries (by the end of the decade the Dwyers had their own) translated it into rum. Now for some triangulating!

On the west coast of Africa the rum was traded for men and women, two hundred gallons for a man, hundred eighty for a woman. To make this rum had cost eighteen cents to a quarter the gallon. Leg one. Second leg back to the West Indies, where most of the slaves were sold to cut cane, a disagreeable chore, but necessary to the gathering of sugar, which was necessary to the manufacture of molasses, which was necessary to the production of rum. Sweet sugar. Sweet molasses. Sweet deal. Final leg: at the scalene's apex a slave at market fetched $400 for a man, less for a woman. A dollar won for a dime ventured.

Not that "catching blackbirds," as the project was styled, was a day at the beach, or at any beach you'd enjoy. The sultry heat was a bitch on the Slave Coast, notable for its deficiency of harbors. Coming ashore from offshore anchorages through the treacherous surge was bad enough, but trading with local chiefs, who kept their medium of currency in stockades, called "barracoons," was tedious, and prolonged, especially if the Rhode Island rum had been sampled. Then, if a deal got struck, back through the surf with terrified, moaning natives. Once the morose cargo had been secured aboard, some of the black folk would die (109 out of 167 on a single voyage: bye-bye blackbirds, bye-bye profits). Sometimes the slaves, wishing to escape, essayed mutiny. No one liked the ankle cuffs and iron collars; this was dark work, but someone had to do it.

As in later commercial undertakings, the Dwyers flourished for a time in the human trade, but their stomachs were never as strong as those of their principal competitors. If Simeon Potter, of Bristol, commanded the captains of his slavers to "water down your rum as much as possible and sell as much by the short measure as you can," the Dwyers (bless 'em) left strong rum on the African coast, and healthy slaves in Barbados, Charleston, Savannah, and Rhode Island. No colony had a higher proportion of slaves to masters than Little Rhody, and the southern section of Newport's Common Burial Ground was reserved for captives. Well . . . the northern quarter was reserved for freemen. Now, in the aftermath of liberty, the latter is more crowded, less comely, than the former. Still, not to make a federal case from this thing, everyone's a slave to something, to the grim bloody reaper, for example. (Clara was historian enough to take the long view, to know that places aren't by their nature evil or innocent. She believed, she told herself, in evolution. Although she had feared from the time of their courtship that she'd be returned to this backwater like a trophy of war, a hostage of her husband's loyalty to his beginnings, she was now drawn to Providence's dark history with an outsider's piquant attention, a voyeur's dank focus. But damn it, she did not wish to finish here, the widow Dwyer, the leftover Dwyer.)

The Dwyers failed to keep pace with the new technology. James DeWolf, a go-getting slaver, bought his own sugar plantations in Cuba, and when the price of Negroes dropped, he put his cargo to work there, cutting out all but one middleman, in Africa, and once human nature took its fruitful course, and his fecund stock bred and increased, he might have eliminated that one too.

Were it not for Abolition fever. Way back, as early as 1650, Providence had put into law a bill disowning slavery:

Whereas there is a common course practised amongst Englishmen to buy negers to the end that they may have them for service or slaves forever, for the preventing of such practices among us, let it be ordered that no blacke mankinde or white being forced by covenant bond or otherwise to serve any man or his assigns longer than ten years. . . .

This law, passed before the provident recognized a main chance about to be thrust in the cargo holds of their ships, was soon enough ignored, and then repealed. Think how compact was the commodity! (Remember, this was before the invention of cocaine.) Imagine the bulk of horses, wheels of cheese, barrels of tar required to equal the value at market of a single human being. Still, the Dwyers felt queasy about the use of the "negers" they traded. Let others take slaves as house servants, the Dwyers would not. Other families, notably the Browns, divided bitterly across the question of slavery. Among four Brown brothers— "Nick," "Joe," "John" and "Mo"—the two latternamed, John and Moses, fell out in 1774 when Moses, a Quaker altruist, freed his own chattels and set up his house as a stop along the Underground Railway.

John, meantime, was the greatest of Rhode Island's guinney traders. His Georgian house at the corner of Benefit and Power streets was said by John Quincy Adams to be "the most magnificent and elegant private mansion that I have ever seen on this continent." Unlike Moses Brown, who suffered from vertigo and pacifism, John relished heights, liked to muscle his way through obstacles to his will. When the Crown passed the Sugar Act in 1764, levying duty on sugar and molasses imports, putting a serious crimp in John Brown's principal line, he took to arson as a means to his ends, organizing a party to burn the custom's ship *Gaspee* to protest the tax. The crimp was uncrimped; good morning, prosperity.

His descendant, John Nicholas Brown, when he reached his majority at Harvard in the 1920s, was apostrophized by tabloids as the richest man in the world. The Browns spread their interests beyond the triangle trade. In Colonial times, despite differences with the Boss in England, the Browns were privateers, licensed pirates. (Sort of like today, like Providence Public Works employees. Back then the prizes were merchant ships flying foreign flags; today the booty might be snowplows, manhole covers, asphalt.) When it became clear even to John that Abolition was a cresting wave, he led his family into the China Trade, outbound with cannons from Hope Furnace, back with tea, gunpowder, silk, and Canton. Values change. The *Ann and Hope* (an East Indiaman christened for the wives of John Brown and his son-in-law, now the name of a discount chain in Pawtucket, Warwick, and Seekonk) used Canton as ballast, as her sisters might previously have used "negers." Well, fishermen once upon a time used lobsters as chum. Now, come to think of it, a lobster is worth more than a black man to many a white in Providence, but substantially less than Canton china.

There were race riots in Providence in 1824 and 1831. The Hard Scrabble Riot at a black dancehall was followed seven years later by an episode a few hundred yards from the place Roger Williams had called Providence Plantations (sweet farmy name) and established as a haven for the oppressed. It seems a drunk white sailor troubled the peace of a black man sitting on his Olney Street stoop, and the black man threatened the white sailor, who shouted, "Fire, and be damned." The black man did and was. Retaliation spread across the fetid canal to Snow Town, and climaxed in a bloodbath, a reading of the Riot Act by the Providence Sheriff, backed by the First Light Infantry at the Smith Street Bridge, and a town meeting called to deplore the State of Things Today.

It was a pain to have free blacks around, and a nuisance to have to remove their freedoms. The Dwyers felt pretty bad about all this, especially since they had lost their shirts bringing from Zanzibar two shiploads of pricey East Africans, meant for Savannah, a few days after Abolition became law. (It might have struck those thrifty traders to sell passage home to the liberated myrmidons—it surely would have occurred to the Browns—but the Dwyers suffered their heavy loss stoically, if sullenly.)

Just as they had endured the loss of vessels in the fog as near as Point Judith, in storms as far away as Surinam, indeed in Providence's Great Gale of 1815, a September storm sent up from the West Indies at full flood tide that made mock of vessels docked at India Point, plunging the bowsprit of the Dwyer's *Warlock* through the third story of Trade House. Now the bustling docks at India Point are long gone, sunk in mud. At low tide the hulks of wrecks uncover, and a desultory trade in smack and stolen household appliances proceeds unremarked.

And all that remained a hundred fifty years after the Dwyers quit their initiatives as would-be Browns, would-be merchant princes, or were dismissed by circumstances from them, all that remained to Adam Dwyer was an office high in the Turk's Head Building, named for a bearded, turbaned, wild-eyed totem, a figurehead salvaged from the *Fury*. And models carved by painstaking craftsmen, with much time on their hands as laid-off coopers and shipbuilders. It was foolish, no doubt, for a Dwyer generations removed from the prosperity as well as the shame of that enterprise to sag beneath its factual, undeniable weight; but to recognize a thing as foolish is not to know how to deny or forget it. Did Clara feel shame? She was a modern woman, could repudiate reflected responsibility. Yet she was drawn to this pretty town's ugly history as to a compulsion. She knew the peril of *Schadenfreude*, the smug nastiness that kept it company. She didn't believe in jinx. Did she? And Adam? Let it be noted, merely, that Adam Dwyer did not, in 1963, drift willy-nilly into the federal practice of civil rights law in Mississippi in 1963, or later into public defense.

Adam's mother was baptized Marguerita, in the time when it was a fashion to give daughters Spanish names. She was the first Rhode Island Dwyer willing to avow she had voted Democrat. (1932, Roosevelt: four years later she converted Amos to her generous, eccentric views. Time and alcohol diminished the vigor of Marguerita's opinions. Municipal history wore at her husband's.)

Even as Republicans the Dwyers were scorned as excessively priggish and milky in their hunger for power by such relentless apostles of appetite as Nelson Aldrich, "the General Manager of the United States," a grocer-to-plutocrat Anglican who knew how to lay down a bribe, and take one up, whose daughter married a Rockefeller, who befriended Charles Brayton, a Postmaster General who secured a $37,000 loan with postage stamps. Republicans knew a thing or two.

However, many Rhode Islanders voted Democratic who said they had not, provoking Republican Boss Brayton (who liked to address brother members of the State Central Committee as "fellow machinists") to remark that "an honest voter is one who stays bought." After visiting the state in 1904, Lincoln Steffens wrote for *McClure's* that "Rhode Island is a state for sale and cheap."

The market price for a Rhode Island Republican vote in those days was two to five dollars (in a laid-back contest), climbing to $15 to $35 (if the heat came on). More than today. These were complex arrangements. Many high-minded Yankees could not be bribed to vote against their beliefs, but they'd take cash to stay home on election day. Boss Brayton, quoted by Steffens, argued that "the Democrats are just as bad, or would be if they had the money." Want of cash need not hobble want. The Democrats, trying harder, would encourage voters to take Brayton's ten dollars, and come to them for another three, translating the honest among them into thirteen-dollar Democrats, the slippery into thirteen-dollar Republicans.

About fifteen minutes after Roger Williams thought to call his haven for outcasts Providence Plantations, Rhode Islanders were famous for squabbles over land titles, politics, and, of course, religion. The colony was soon known familiarly as "Rogue Island," in reference to the quality of its settlers. But say this for those citizens, they by God looked after themselves.

The State House in Providence is topped by a bronze statue memorializing The Independent Man. This had once been a statue in Central Park of Simón Bolívar, but it was removed and broken apart, thought not to look nice. The contract to create The Independent Man was given to New York artisans, and a book telling of Rhode Island's sculptural wonders, remarks as notable that in the construction "there were never any scandals or mismanagement." Believe it or not.

The Independent Man was elevated a few days before the beginning of the twentieth century. Plated with gold. Soon struck by lightning. Repaired, returned to place without that gold plate, which was said by some to be unattractively dazzling, by others, more cynical, to constitute an attractive nuisance, if you follow.

There was more dynamo than virgin in Little Rhody back when. Tell me about power brokers! Marsden Perry cornered the Providence utilities business, electricity (after buying up and driving under the local gas companies), and streetcars. My God! He bought the John Brown mansion at 52 Power(!), and it took the Browns generations to grab it back. Perry got his start writing informal, high-interest, short-term credit. Loansharking. He bullied the meek and bribed the wolfish.

Plenty of greed around. All those new cars, huge houses. Crapulence itself became an avocation. Increase. No one was immune. Not, surely, the East-Siders, that inbred inventory of begats (Angells, Carters, Browns, Dexters, Goddards, Aldriches, Dwyers) whose chatelaines, sisters, and daughters prettified the town coming on city, whose gents cut deals at the Hope Club.

Nine years after the first erection of The Independent Man the Dwyers turned to law, Dwyer and Dwyer, brother and brother, Nathaniel and Moses (named, be sure, for a Brown rather than a prophet). Those earliest years of the century, the Naughty Naughts, were all bounty and increase. Providence gave its streets boom-town names: Gold, Silver, Bullion, Ruby, Diamond, Rialto, Empire, Imperial, Progress, Prosper, Enterprise, Eureka. Savings Street had no church. Price might be a surname, or a judgment. Is Job named for labor, or a man? Gaol, a right-angle to Benefit, was renamed Meeting. There was Harmony, Concord, Justice, Fair, Amity, Clover. Cope. But there was Cloud Street, too, Grotto and Africa, Division.

In 1915 the Board of Trade bragged up its Five Industrial Wonders of the World: "Providence is the first city in the country in the manufacture of woolens and worsted, jewelry and silverware. . . . She has the world's largest tool factory, file factory, engine factory, screw factory, and silverware factory." Smoke stacks rose above church steeples. The Dwyers wrote contracts, connected (for a fee) forward-looking fellows who might share an interest in getting on. At the turn of the century Providence had six automobile and truck builders. The Corliss Steam Engine Company built an engine five stories high to drive all other contrivances, eight thousand of them, at the Philadelphia Centennial Exposition of 1876. Providence was Fat City. Fruit of the Loom started right here!

The littlest state was cozy, too. Invite the Governor to a birthday party, and he'd probably show up. Every lawyer knew every judge well enough to call in a marker now and then. The knowing wink was genetically marked on natives of the place celebrated for tolerance, and it was as natural as breathing for a man of affairs to rest his arm across the shoulder of a fellow man of affairs. Was? Is, as Clara had opportunity to observe.

In the years before the Great War the Dwyers would relax summer days at Narragansett Pier in South County, organize huge family clam bakes, sit at long tables arguing with their Newport friends about the proper spelling and preparation of johnnycakes (or jonny-cakes). With the sun lighting the crests of those long rollers coming into Narragansett Bay from Europe and God knew where, it was impossible to deny the myth of eternal progress. In town the industrial Juggernaut was driven by capital from the Browns, who built the gold-domed Old Stone Bank in 1819, the likeness of a fortress for money, walls miles thick, impregnable vaults, the place Clara's husband took his dimes and nickels when he was a kid, where they would be safe, where he could imagine interest accumulating at almost two percent *per annum.*

The Browns also built mills, and French Canadians, "the Chinese of the East," came to work them. By 1910 they outnumbered even the Irish. Quebecoise was Lisa's stock, Audette. Jews came from Russia, fleeing the pogroms of 1881. Then Italians, then Portuguese, but mostly Italians. By 1910, if the Dwyers and their friends had bothered to notice, fewer than a third of Little Rhodies were pure Yankee stock.

The next year the Fabre Line sent its first ship, *Madonna,* up the Providence River from Marseilles, Palermo, Naples, Lisbon, and the Azores. The Triangle Trade. Italians came at a ratio of fifty to three, southern Italy to northern. The shuttle was so successful that the Fabre Line named its grandest ship *Providence,* where there was an immigrant landing station till 1934, nine years after the city's population peaked at a quarter million. Now it's down a hundred thousand; from the beginning many Italians lost their affection for the place, staying a few years, going home to Palermo or Naples.

Many who made good edged out to the suburbs, Johnston and Cranston. (Now Cranston Street has the discount, high-volume trade in hookers. A schoolmate of Skippy's, a priest, parked his car on Cranston Street. "Want a date, honey?" She was maybe fourteen; he was wearing his collar.) Jews settled in South Providence and traded up, when they could, to the East Side, especially along Hope Street, out Blackstone Boulevard to the Pawtucket line, leaving South Providence and its bombed-out lots to emancipated and unemployed blacks and Latinos. South Providence got so rough Daddy's Original House of Ribs finally packed it in, moved away. Scary? A foreign car dealer sat on the

Providence Housing Authority, but he refused to drive his Jag to the projects for meetings with tenants: "Send a cab and let them come down here. My car won't last two minutes." A billboard on Prairie Avenue: "When in Jail, Call Joe for Bail."

The ethnic neighborhoods were never classy, of course. Wood-frame houses set so close together neighbors could trade insults through shut windows. Jesus, some of the colors! Greens never imagined by nature! Pink houses. Orange! By now chalked and flaking. But the yards were neat, some of them, with fruitful gardens here and there, helter-skelter.

The old Yankee families clung to College Hill, a hard climb from downtown, cool up there. That part of the East Side has more intact colonial buildings than any city. They call Benefit Street "a mile of history," but it declined into tenements before the Depression, and had to be made fit for a new kind of gentry come the boom years of the Sixties and Seventies. (The decades of spruce-up brought a cargo of rue from side-streeters. Above Clara's desk was a four-panel cartoon, poster-sized, with love comic heroines observing of the East Side's byways that "Friendship is a one-way street," that "rich folks live off Power," that "most of us live off Hope.") The Dwyer house on Benevolent, clapboard rather than go-to-hell brick or stone, never fell to neglect, but it helped drain the modest family fortune. It was big enough, fifteen imposing rooms, to swallow many pieces of fine Providence furniture, many paintings. The backyard had been a locally celebrated garden. From the widow's walk, now rotted out, it was possible to see down the Providence River and Narragansett Bay as far as Prudence Island. The campus of Brown was a few blocks uphill, the Hope Club a couple of blocks along Benefit, the Athenaeum Library (where Edgar Allan Poe was shown the door for putting moves on a shelver) a five-minute walk. The streets were safe.

Safe too (and clean!) on Federal Hill, where the Italians congregated near Acorn Street (having displaced the Irish), and later along Atwells Avenue. They worked grunt jobs, maintained a healthy suspicion of the Irish-controlled churches and schools (until control passed to them); the nuns taught schoolkids to pull the master lever for the Democratic Party when they grew up, and why not learn from the examples of Aldrich, Brayton, Perry, and the rest to milk democracy's cow?

Federal Hill Italians kept their council, celebrated the veritable virtues of blood loyalty, subverted authority imposed from outside. Southern Italians were accustomed to the perils of contingency: bandits from the next village over, despotic absentee landlords, drought, earthquakes. They put their faith in smaller and smaller units, small businesses, blood kinship. So how was it that some came to prey on their friends and neighbors, Italians scamming and brutalizing Italians? (Ask Clara. Clara would ask why Africans sold Africans.) *Want* was the ultimate loyalty. But why? Whatever the answer, it would never be made casually available to outsiders, non-Italians, "them." Providence Italians made no moves to be wicked up by those palefaces like the Dwyers who thought they'd sewed the bag shut two hundred years ago. Legend was that lookouts used to be posted on roofs at both ends of Atwells Avenue to report the invasion of outsiders.

Most Italians were lawful citizens, blah-blah-blah. If Skippy Carbone's dad tipped his hat to The Boss, and The Boss nodded a greeting in return, this was solidarity, not collusion. Skippy's dad was a baker, and if The Boss bought canoli from him, and Skippy's dad tried to give it away free, this was not an arrangement born of fear, or at least unreasonable fear. Skippy and his brother Mike grew up good boys, played football, basketball, and baseball at St. Anselm's, graduated. Well, Skippy almost graduated. He figured he got booted for quitting the baseball team. Well, spring term of his senior year he got in some trouble, but he was basically a good boy.

He remembered when he was a squirt, maybe seven. This was way back when, before windchill factors, when minus ten was what it said on the thermometer. He and another kid (this was before he started running with Baby) broke into a deserted house. Really, they walked in. The doors were wide open, windows broken. Some neighbors had taken their savings home to Sicily, and let the tarpaper dump settle on its foundation. The house was empty; there were puddles from leaks, and dust, and the rooms stunk. Skippy was scared in there. It was kind of a dare, he guessed, but when he saw a couple of books on the floor upstairs, he grabbed them. He wasn't born to this, and keeping those books gave him the creeps. He hid them in a hollowed-out place behind his headboard at home, and when he held them in his hands, they felt hot to his touch, like they had already been to hell with him. One of the books was in Italian, just words, a storybook. The other he liked to study when he was sure he was alone, a picture book about the 1938 hurricane that wiped out Narragansett Pier and killed hundreds of people in Rhode Island. There was this little girl on top of a roof in Watch Hill, and the wind was blowing her skirt so you could see her bloomers, and you could see these huge waves cresting the tops of trees.

Anyway, stealing that book made him feel bad. (The book in Italian, because he couldn't read it, maybe because it had no pictures, didn't make him feel so bad.) He felt bad till he was twelve, getting prepped for his first communion. The nuns offered some suggestions about things the kids might want to confess, low-key sins. *Father, I have taken something that did not belong to me.* Waiting to tell this to the priest tore Skippy to pieces. He felt like he was ratting himself out, and he was scared of trouble. But when he owned up, yawn. What? It made him wonder, and by thirteen he was really wondering. That year he was standing in line, waiting to go to the rail for communion, when he caught himself praying. He'd been thinking a lot about girls, and Baby's second cousin was standing behind him, looking bored. Baby's second cousin was older, and so cool and wised up, maybe even connected (they said), he never bothered to talk to Baby, let alone Skippy. But he was talking now, not even whispering:

"If you went steady, you'd get more ass."

That snotty little Julia was kneeling there, and Skippy prayed a prayer that she'd keel over dead, right now, and Jesus, she keeled over. It made him wonder again. Was anything possible? What now? The prayer was in the record! He was thinking about this when Julia got roused from her faint, so Skippy was off the hook. Later, he let himself off the hook altogether, and decided first by himself, later with his buddies, that the whole shot was a crock. His dad didn't care when he figured it out, even if his mom faked some tears. Having a kid get all priested up on you was the worst kind of luck. What good was a priest to his mom and dad?

Where Skippy broke ranks with some other Carbones was on the issue of work. Skippy's dad and uncles hung it all out for the Festa di San Giuseppe, the annual procession honoring Saint Joseph the Worker. Skippy liked to steal fried peppers and sausage over in DePasquale Square; liked to hear the *cafonis* play their greenhorn accordions; liked to hear the noise, see the bands, watch the majorettes show off their tight little white undies, listen to the politicians lay on bullshit with a trowel during that festa. But Skippy didn't like to work. He was a young guy, and there were many things he did not know. But Skippy *knew* he did not like to work.

Thirteen, fourteen, Skippy wanted a bike. He asked his dad.

"Sure," his dad said. "You need a bike. A kid should have a bike."

"Great, Dad!"

"Earn it."

So Skippy asked his brother how to get a bike, and Mike shrugged. So Skippy asked some older guys in the neighborhood.

"Steal it."

The only question was how, and that was a question that had answers. Pretty soon Skippy was trading up, and rustling for spares. Midnight Spokes, the neighborhood guys called their avocation.

These kids were eating dinner on time, at home. They didn't bunk school, and sometimes they did their homework. But they were getting to be champion finders. They found this bike, and that radio.

Skippy's mom had eyes: "Where'd you get that wristwatch?"

"I found it up near school. Whatta you think? I ripped it off? You think I steal stuff? Cut me some slack! Finders keepers."

It could have been awkward to explain away the credit cards

and keychains under his bed, but Skippy was a cute kid. Good athlete, despite the asthma, those whistling sibilants, the inhaler. Didn't smoke or drink Southern Comfort on the street. So his mom would run her fingers through his thick black hair, and give him a hug. Who was perfect? If she forgot, Skippy could remind her about the time a truck hit a Puerto Rican woman near Atwells Avenue, and while the driver bent over that woman the word got around the neighborhood, free towels and sheets from the van. Skippy's mom didn't loot the van, but she bought some thick bath towels from neighbors with tougher skin, fifty cents each, nice towels. She was gentle, easy to please. Christmas Eve she'd sit happy for hours watching the Yule Log burn away on black and white TV in the Governor's Mansion, listening to Anglo-Saxon carols play while the log crackled like static—shit, it *was* static—through the snowy reception.

Skippy was no fool. Just because something was good enough for his mom and dad didn't mean it had to be good enough for him. He dreamed of living like Sinatra, like Tony Conigliaro (before the fastball hit him in the eye). He and Baby used to piss away time thumbing through the Sunday supplements, scoping out the ads. Everything on this page was Baby's, everything on the next page was Skippy's. Baby got the La-Z-Boy, Skippy took title to that ranch house in Barrington. Wouldn't it be a dream to break into a pawnshop Friday night, have the run of the place a whole weekend, rip off a van to carry away the goodies? Skippy couldn't figure out why someone else got it and he didn't get it. He was getting ripped off. So he took it.

Here were some things Skippy took: copper wire (when copper was trading high), the fiberglass top for a Corvette, chrome wheel lugs from a Z-Car (sad surprise for some driver), Pampers (a truckload), three hundred cans of sardines, barbells, mink pelts, a set of bagpipes, a Denver boot, other things too. He'd steal the paint off your house.

If a kid on Federal Hill wanted to learn how to do something, start a car real quick (better know whose car it wasn't!), boost some slacks, grab a UPS package off a back porch on College Hill, ride off on a ten-speed chained to a streetlamp, there was always someone around to tell how. There wasn't all that much talk about jail. (Sometimes an older guy would tell what heroic sex deeds he did on break night, the night they let him out.) You know, everyone knew where it was, the ACI, Adult Correctional Institutions, the medium-security prison clear as a movie shot of The Big House, there on the right going south on 95 to the Warwick Mall, after you passed some smokestacks, Criss Cadillac, the monster chrome horse on top of Astro Bumper Sales, the blue-bottle fly as big as a Cessna mounted on New England Pest Control, right there in Cranston. But prison was for luckless fools, and sure as hell not for juvies. Besides, who could get caught?

Baby got caught. Boy, did he! He lived above a Jew drugstore on Europe Street. He turned fifteen, pulled a nylon stocking over his head, walked downstairs, hauled a piece out of his belt, and said, no shit, "Stick 'em up. This is a stickup. Hand over your money, a couple bottles codeine cough syrup, and some rubbers." He helped himself to a carton of chewing gum, and split. He wasn't dumb enough to split for his crib upstairs. He cooled it on the street for an hour before he came home. This was after dinner. It was quiet at home. Baby felt good. He hid the stuff on the fire escape, went to bed. Imagine his surprise when he woke up with a flashlight in his face. He swallowed his gum. The cops thought he was cracking wise when he answered their question (*why* that *drugstore, for Christ's sake?*):

"It was convenient. I don't got a getaway car."

Skippy came to court to watch Baby. Skippy's friend had a set of nuts on him, give him that. Sitting there in family court, waiting to catch shit from the judge, Baby cut his initials into a varnished oak bench.

"What the hell you think you're doing," the judge yelled at him. Baby looked puzzled. Baby *was* puzzled. He was cutting his initials in the bench, what did it look like?

The Family Services man smoothed everything out. "It's okay, your honor, the bench has been provided under a federal grant-in-aid."

"Jesus Christ," the judge said.

That was how Baby bagged his rep as a cuckoo clock. He had

to try harder because he wasn't Italian. It wasn't fair, but it was the way things worked. For a while the Audettes tried to fake it, called themselves Odetta, but this just made everyone laugh. It was tempting to laugh at Baby. Like the time he was a kid, spent all night stuck in this chimney, had to call the people he had come to rob, beg them for help: "Help, help me. I'm stuck." The homeowners had to summon firefighters, who laughed their asses off before they phoned the police, who told Baby they were going to lay a fire in that fireplace down there. Fact was, Baby wasn't much of a crook, but he had a set on him, and that was so.

Baby was the only kid in school who pulled strong-arm stuff, muggings. Skippy didn't know what he thought about muggings. He thought they weren't for him, but he thought they were interesting, till he knew better. As long as they were out of the neighborhood. For sure out of the neighborhood.

Baby was seventeen before he did grownup time. And that was summertime, so he wouldn't have to miss school. Like Skippy, he got a lot of bites from the apple. Peg crimes to catchings at 200:1. Twenty to one catchings to charges. Three to one charges to indictments. Three to one indictments to convictions. Sentences? Forget it. He saw Family Court on charges of waywardness, chronic truancy (except during the basketball season), malicious mischief. He was caught carrying a gravity knife, and when they strip-searched him at Fountain Street headquarters, the cops saw his underpants; they looked like they'd been stained with charcoal, and a couple of plainclothesmen came in to look, and laugh at the shit smears. This experience was not without its consequence on Baby's temperament, his attitude toward authority. He turned a nail gun on a neighborhood kid who said something to Baby in polysyllabics the young criminal could not comprehend. His father was an imperfect influence on Baby.

"Hey, kid, check the mailbox for the welfare check."

Baby's father counseled him in the wisdom of the street: "In a bar·fight, bite the bastard's armpit. As long as you've got your teeth you've got your pride."

Some people on Federal Hill, especially the older wise guys, said Baby didn't have all the dots on his dice, someone blew out his pilot light. After a lucky day at Lincoln Downs, Baby and some of his crew stopped at a roadhouse for beverages. Baby tossed a bouquet of his winnings in the urinal, ate the urinal wafer on a dare, pissed on his money, and left it. He could be wild, and he could especially talk wild. (Who else would want to say one dawn, the prettiest dawn Skippy ever saw after a night of raising hell, "the sun looks like an asshole"?) Baby watched cop shows on television, caught *Mean Streets* at the arty-farty Cable Car Cinema on South Main, where joggers and rich hippie students watched movies on these couches (cracking wise-ass remarks and asking you to get your shoes off their shoulders), and then went after to drink sweet highballs made with coffee and Mexican syrup. And after that got ripped off by Baby, who liked to say heavy things he'd just picked up at *Mean Streets*, or in magazines:

"Give me your watch and hide, shitbird. I'd as soon tear out your lungs as piss on the carpet."

At such moments, looking down the hole of Baby's piece, people didn't think to ask, "What carpet?" "What's a hide?" They guessed it was a billfold, good guess, quick learners. Everyone gave Baby a pretty wide berth, from fifteen on. Only Lisa could talk back to him. Fact was, Lisa seemed a little bored with Baby's act. Lots bored Lisa. What fascinated Lisa was to have reefer and crank in her pocketbook, plus money in her change-purse to buy some more when it ran out, plus a name in her head of someone who sold these things. The only reason she hung out with her older cousin was to be around Skippy, who was c-u-t-e, always up to something.

Lisa didn't care diddly what was legal and what wasn't. She'd pass fake tens, but not twenties. She liked to telephone people, say she was doing research for an electronics firm, did they own a television set? Yes? How about a VCR? Camera? What brand, please? *Thanks for your time, hon.* Now Baby and Skippy knew where to pay a profitable call. But she didn't like heaviosity, and especially she didn't approve of heavy crime, violence. Neither did Skippy. The older he got, the less he liked the feel of extortion, say, or armed robbery. There were things he'd do, things he wouldn't do. Sometimes, hanging out with Baby, Skippy did things Skippy wouldn't do. Like the gas station job in Pawtucket, one of those quick-off/quick-on stops next to I-95. They were in wheels borrowed from a stranger, heading for a Pawtucket Red Sox vs. Toledo Mud Hens twinight double-header; one of them figured out they didn't have money for the ducats. This was a family car, blue four-door Buick Century, fill-hole way back above the middle of the bumper. Baby told the pump jockey to "fill 'er up, Chief." Said he couldn't shut off the motor, bad battery. Big smile. So the kid went back there, bent over, and Baby gave it a good shot in reverse. The kid woke up with a bad headache and no change belt. Skippy felt bad about the whole thing, but not as bad (he guessed) as the guy in the gas station.

Baby was not a good kid. Got into yokings downtown, around Westminster Mall. If *The Providence Journal* ran a story, "Night Crime Plagues Downtown Merchants," Baby was no small part of its inspiration. Every night was payday for Baby. To be downtown past your normal bedtime, and before Baby's, was to risk feeling his arm come around your neck, to feel a long blade against your throat. The blade made all the difference. Getting into a car in one of the big parking garages, the Outlet Company's, say, or the Biltmore's, and to feel the edge against your throat: there was one for the memory book.

"Take it! Don't hurt me. Take it! Please!"

Most muggers took it, and split. Baby, especially when he did speed, liked to throw in a beating. And if there was no loot, count on that beating. *Your money or your life* in the highwayman's lexicon; for Baby, if impulses had been deeds, it was your money and your life. Sometimes, if he had someone groveling, covering his eyes with his hands like he was watching a horror show, and if this pissed Baby off, he might say:

"I'm going to have to shoot you. Shut your eyes, and count to a hundred out loud. At a hundred I'm going to have to grease you. If you open your eyes, I'll shoot you then."

It was Baby's idea of a practical joke.

The Providence Journal's daily "Police Log" ran a lot of stories about Baby's doings, but his favorite began: "Wearing a suit and carrying a briefcase to show he was in business, pointing a .44 magnum to show what business he was in, a young man held up a Food 'n' Fuel last night in Mt. Pleasant. Police say the young man told a customer and a salesclerk he would 'blow their ——ing heads off' if they . . ."

Bullshit. The papers always printed that the gunman threatened to "blow your [fucking] head off." Maybe a lot of guys *did* say it, but Baby liked to improvise a little. He just told the girl behind the counter to look at him when he talked to her. This was after he pistol-whipped the customer who had just paid for his dog food.

"You just said not to look," the salesgirl whined.

"Lie down."

Baby rolled her over on her belly and hog-tied her with clothesline. He ripped out the phone. She heard him go through her purse, and thought hardly at all about the $80 in there, her week's wage. She heard him pulling cartons of cigarettes off the shelves. She hoped he got a good haul. She tried not to think about the pistol-whipping she had just watched, or to hear that man's bubbly moans of grief and surprise. She heard the guy in the suit punching the buttons on the electronic register. Oh, she was scared. It was a tricky register, and if he jammed its keys, like she sometimes did, it made a shrieking noise, like an alarm. She was so scared. The register was empty; her boss had just cashed her out an hour ago, about midnight.

"Got any root beer?"

"In the beer cooler."

"I'm looking in the beer cooler. Where's the Hires?"

"We just got Dad's Original Root Beer."

"Shit," said the man in the suit, removing a six-pack of Dad's, as much of it as he cared to drink in the immediate future.

Then it was over, and he was gone. She tried to explain to the policeman, and the reporter on the telephone, how it was. The part that interested them was the guy's fancy suit. That was one didn't come along every couple of hours.

Not everybody knew where Baby got his nickname. Most people thought it was upside-down for "cuddly." Actually, as Skippy knew, the nickname was "Bee-Bees," and it came from his friend's arson bust.

Where to begin? There was this tavern in Warwick, the kind that calls itself an "inn?" This was a place Baby and Skippy fenced cigarettes, booze, various consumables. Now, down Post Road about a mile, across the street, was another tavern, and this one called itself an "inne." The inne was doing better business than the inn, and the owner of the inn, driving past his competitor's parking lot every afternoon, seeing in there all those Camaros, Firebirds, Toronados, 'vettes, Trans-Ams (and even Bay Em Vays!), could not leave off brooding about this.

This was where Baby came in. To make the inne disappear. Skippy did not know this was their mission when they pulled into the inne's lot a couple hours before dawn, Skippy at the wheel, and the next thing he knew he was watching a fire. Impressive fire. Loud noise first. The next thing after that he was driving fast. Baby told him to slow down. Skippy was pissed, and telling Baby this when a red light pulled behind them coming down the off-ramp at Wickenden Street. Oh, shit! The car had been stolen two hours ago, and wasn't even missed yet, let alone listed. Baby said to cool it when the siren crooned at them, just a little bit of siren, no big deal, no need to wake the citizens, terrorize the driver.

Tom pulled the Riviera over because its tail and plate lights were off. He had a dog in back with him, K-9 patrol shepherd, but there was no need to bring her to the driver's window. He saw the Rhode Island inspection sticker; he had seen a Vermont license plate. Oh.

Skippy was about to show his license, valid, his legal name, when he felt something heavy hit his right leg. This was a pipe bomb, an extra for the inne in case one wasn't enough. He also felt Baby's hog leg between them, that monster magnum he liked to show off. Skippy had a hunch his friend wished, at this anxious moment, to put some distance between himself and his arsenal, to share those formidable weapons with his St. Anselm's teammate.

"Officer," Skippy said. "I'm really glad you stopped. I'm lost, and I wonder if you could straighten me out."

"Well," Tom said, "that's not a great idea, because I'd really prefer to ask the questions."

Skippy looked at the policeman, and he didn't at all warm to what he saw in those lazy, cocky eyes. The cop was grinning. Skippy had too many times grinned the same kind of smirky grin not to feel it for what it was. The cop was about to do something to Skippy, whether Skippy liked it or not, and Skippy figured he was *sure* not to like it. The cop might even reach for his piece and blow Skippy away. In fact, that made a lot of sense to Skippy. He could put himself in the cop's place. So Skippy shoved the .44 magnum right in that policeman's face. He was so pissed at Baby, so pissed. Skippy said all the things they say, *do this* and *don't do that* or he'd *do this!*

Anyway, Skippy told the cop to get in the back seat, and the cop did. Baby was saying "oh, man," and "shit, man," and "heavy, man." Skippy was telling Baby to shut up, and trying to think. It was a complicated couple of minutes.

Tom said: "You don't want to wreck my kid's Christmas, do you?"

True. It was a few days before Christmas.

Baby said: "What the fuck does he care? He's going to blow a hole in your dumb fucking face."

Skippy went: "How many kids?"

Tom said: "You don't want to pull Murder One on a lousy car theft beef. Look, pull the mike out of my cruiser. Shoot the dog if you want to. Take my piece away. Cuff me to my wheel. Let's all walk away from this one. Word of honor, I'll let it go. I don't want to die."

So they talked it over, right in front of Tom. Skippy talked
Baby out of it. Skippy said, like he was putting a half wheel in a
blind beggar's cup: "It's not your day to fall, Officer." They
cuffed Tom to the steering wheel of his cruiser while the caged
dog slobbered and barked so furiously the neighbors screamed
from their bedrooms at the cruiser, and finally called the police
to complain. Some people thought it was all kind of funny. Tom
got his name and face in the paper as a Great Talker. Then he
and another uniform picked up the boys on Christmas Eve.
Skippy didn't even think to remind the cop of his promise to let
bygones be bygones.

Anyway, Baby went to the ACI, night-night. Tom was satisfied. The youngster was convicted of carrying a concealed
weapon, assaulting a police officer, grand theft auto, and arson.
The mastermind had contrived to steal a stolen car. His nickname, Bee-Bees, came out of the arson trial. That firebomb was
made from sand, vodka, soap suds, lighter fluid, and bee-bees. A
mix of napalm and bullets, sort of. A spic cellmate at the ACI
switched the name to Baby.

Baby was technically a juvie when he came to trial. But the
juvenile justice system of Providence Plantations had seen
enough of the kid's act, so they waived him to the top of the cal-
endar, right into Superior Court, passing District Court without
a glance. Baby was a big-timer now, an adult offender. And he
still stuck his thumb in his mouth when he slept. Which was
why "Baby" stuck.

Skippy got his hands slapped in Family Court. Grand theft
auto could get an adult two years. Skippy got twenty-three days,
suspended. The court believed he was innocent of arson. Such a
low-key, smiley, cute kind of boy. Assaulting a police officer got
six months, remanded to the custody of his mom and dad, some
contact with a juvenile parole officer.

Tom figured it wasn't quite enough. Tom had pissed his gab-
ardines back in that stolen Riviera, and while it was Baby who
noticed this, and laughed, it could not be denied that Skippy's
finger on the trigger of a .44 magnum was the proximate cause
of Tom's embarrassment. This worked to Skippy's disadvantage

when Tom and some off-duty colleagues found him after the
Family Court trial in an after-hours club. What happened next
to the young parochial school scholar was not entirely clear, except Skippy was discovered next morning smashed up good, in a
dumpster whose lid was weighed shut with concrete blocks.
Tom arrested him, and charged him with resisting arrest after
threatening a police officer, without provocation. Tom explained that after Skippy assaulted him and his colleagues, the
juvenile delinquent ran to the back of the after-hours club, and
must have "jumped in the dumpster, your honor, and enlisted a
confederate to weigh down the lid to throw me and my colleagues off the scent."

This charge did not lead to an indictment.

Now all this was in the way-back time, maybe ten years gone.
Several predawn hours in a dumpster provided the occasion for
Skippy to reflect on his circumstances, his ambitions, his limita-
tions. He would never, he knew, throw long on third for the Pa-
triots. A point guard for St. Anselm's was not, at five-eleven, a
point guard for the Celts. A schoolboy shortstop riding the pine
seven innings out of nine was destined to join the Red Sox family
as paying rather than paid kin.

Okay. Providence was a small town, he had just learned from
Patrolman Cocoran, a man he had never seen until that night of
bad luck on Wickenden Street, and of course tonight. Skippy
figured he could give up the street life. (Perhaps become a brain
surgeon? Ambassador to the United Nations? A baker, like his
dad, laughing at dumb jokes, passing the time of day with every
tedious moron who decided to buy his bread instead of someone
else's bread?) He could find a job. Work for the Department of
Public Works, like Baby's dad, and show up two days out of five,
and those were overtime days. You had to be connected to get
on the tit of DPW, and it was ugly work stealing curbstones and
manhole covers, artificial turf and bucket loaders.

Down there in the dumpster, with about half a load of the
stuff they put in dumpsters, Skippy conceived a kind of philosophy of life. Skippy's philosophy of life was that he wanted what

he wanted, and wanted it for free. And he wanted to be wearing nice clothes when it was delivered to him. Skippy wanted a clean cop-proof hustle. He wanted the street to come to his office. He aspired to give rather than receive commandments.

"I want," he told Lisa, "to be a management."

What he would in fact be—grandee or piece of shit—was contingent upon the will of The Boss. The Boss could elevate Skippy to a corner table at Camille's Roman Gardens, or make him wish he had never been emancipated from that noisome garbage bin in an alley at the hind end of Rooster's Tap.

8

▲ ▲ ▲ ▲ ▲

THE BOSS

I F you lived in a jerkwater that outsiders bombed past on their way to Cape Cod, if you lived fifty miles south of a city that called itself The Hub, if you spent time telling people you chose to live in Providence because who needed the hassle of a big city, who needed to spend an hour looking for a parking place, who needed the pressure—well, if you lived in Providence it was difficult not to feel a shiver of pride when you were reminded (and you were reminded) that the whole New England mob got run out of a laundry on Atwells Avenue. That's Hartford, New Haven, Portland, and the fucking "Hub" too. That's New England, no exceptions.

Like Skippy, reading on the front page of the *Journal* that Providence led the nation in car thefts. "Hey," he shouted to Lisa, "go for it! We're Number One!"

A place doesn't just get to be Number One by accident. Providence didn't send America her best boosters and slug manufacturers because it just happened to happen that way. To run the New England rackets—call it "this thing of ours," call it any damned thing you want—took leadership, vision, respect, appetite, a reputation for surprise, a reputation for inevitability. To command fealty from "The Snake" and "The Doctor," to be liege lord of "Baron" (who was coarse) and "The Gent" (who once said "please" when he held up a payroll clerk), to kingfish "Apples," "Tony Ducks," "Trash," "Baby Shanks," "The Moron" . . . why, this was to be The Boss, and no shit.

The Boss had had a nickname, way back in the Thirties, when the end of Prohibition turned him briefly to safecracking. He

had acted one night with an uncharacteristic failure to deliberate, and closed a National Safe Deposit door on two fingers. He
wanted to leave that place immediately, and so he removed the
second and third digits of his left hand, just below the first joint,
with a cold chisel. The cops, recovering fingers as well as prints,
made a nice match, and for a few months The Boss was called
"Three Fingers," but during his short time in prison, his first of
two visits, during the couple of months it took to "reach out" to
the Governor for a pardon ("I guess I just felt the Christmas
spirit," the Governor explained), he managed to persuade most
people that "Three Fingers" was not his name, and after that
even the police officers who hounded him, who called him
Rhode Island's Public Enemy Number One, let the nickname go.
Why climb to the top of a lightning rod during a thunderstorm?
Where was the percentage?

The Boss, post-war, looked like Frank Nitti on *The Untouch-
ables*. Cigar dangling from the corner of his pouty lips. Huge
camel-hair topcoat, with lapels you could cut a sport jacket
from. Sharkskin high-tide slacks, with deep pleats, wide cuffs
breaking over his buckled loafers. Such neckties! Garish silk
bibs, really, and a gray Borsalino. To see The Boss betting nags
at Lincoln Downs, or fighters at Providence Auditorium, or the
Rhode Island Reds at a hockey game was not to misapprehend
his profession. This was a gangster, by God, though decades
later, in the Seventies and Eighties, he'd whine if anyone accused him of wickedness.

But now we're talking late 1950s, Kefauver's Senate Racket
Hearings. Who was the one and only mobbed up witness whistled into that circus who didn't take the Fifth? Listen:

"Let me tell you something. I'm proud to be an American. I'd
rather spend twenty years in the can in America than twenty
years in a Palermo villa. So why do you guys keep picking on
me? When my dad died, and he died from work, let me tell you,
making shoes, and not in some shop he owned, in some factory
owned by people he never met, people who couldn't make shoes
themselves, but knew how to make him make shoes, so when he
died I did some things, and I got punished. So be it. I took that

punishment like a man. So why am I here now? Why am I always the goat, the newspapers' bad man? Do you know some of
the things I've done for my people, for kids?"

The Boss was interrupted by a question, from Jack Kennedy's
little brother!

"Is it true, that when people don't do your bidding, sometimes they are discovered stuffed in a trunk?"

The Boss was not at home as a wit, but they still quote his
question about the question:

"Trunk? Car, or steamer?"

"Answer the question, sir. Is it true, when people don't do
your bidding . . ."

"You guys never mentioned anything about bids when you
told me to come here. I'm just a little guy, runs a laundry."

This was true. The enterprise was called Brite-Matic, but
strangers didn't get their shirts washed at that storefront on
Atwells Avenue, or their stains removed. Now the irony—and
these matters are frequently filigreed with irony: This same hot-
shot mob investigator, Saint Bobby, arranged with The Boss to
have Fidel Castro terminated with extreme prejudice. By that
time our padrone was the occasional guest of many top politicians, I mean top, out of Washington, but The Boss agreed to
handle the Castro contract for two reasons: He was a good
American, and he was promised payment in H. Uppmanns. (At
Christmas he'd have a couple hundred boxes of cigars in his
closet. But if you paid a call to his office at that season carrying
two cigars in your hankie pocket, he'd take them from you.
Both. The Boss had short arms, never popped for a check. He
was a lousy tipper. Took money seriously, called dollars "dollars," bucks was bush, never used "dough" or "bread." Money
was solemn, *money*. But tight as a Scout knot, wouldn't pay a
nickel to watch an earthquake.)

But he *was* a good American, and a good Catholic, of course.
When an abortion clinic was opened on Federal Hill and a
priest called that place "sinful and shameful," who had it fire-
bombed?

Of course they called him "The Godfather," when that became a big deal. And it was true: he did favors. If someone's car got stolen, and that person was uninsured, and The Boss was asked nicely to look into such a circumstance, the car might be returned, or a later model car appear in your driveway, simonized, with a full tank of gas. Let a father die before his time, from causes natural or controversial, and an envelope would sprout among the lilies delivered to Berarducci's Funeral Home. (So the orchestra played "The Godfather Theme" when he showed up for the occasional wedding, like it was "Hail to the Chief," and he was The Boss of Bosses. But it was wasted on him; the last movie he saw was *Gigi*, because he thought Katharine Hepburn, who had class, was in it. When he saw Audrey Hepburn instead, he quit going to movies.) There were legends, mostly true, about The Boss's "scholarships," anonymous payments for tuition, room, board, fraternity membership, walking-around money. Well, not absolutely anonymous. The beneficiaries—today's doctors, judges, city councilmen, parole officers, what have you—were not unaware of these benefactions.

But don't confuse Good Works with inexorable self-interest. The Boss got a letter from an Indian kid, not even an American, the kind who believes in cows. The boy wanted money (of course):

> My parents are not living again and I'm a poor Calcutta boy desiring a Higher Education. The tuition to this college is about $1200 per year in U.S. dollar. I will be too glad if you do for me with half this tuition or atleast $500, or $400. Or any amount you can afford over $300. I would except hundred dollar.

The Boss figured Sister Teresa, but he also figured maybe he was too cynical. He liked to say, "I don't trust nobody. I don't trust my right hand with my left hand." (Talk about sinister dexterity. Does the left hand know what the right wants?) But he was a sport, too, so he wrote the kid back and told him if he guessed right, heads or tails, on a coin The Boss had just flipped, $3000 would come his way. If he guessed wrong, forget it. The kid wrote "heads," and it was heads, and he got $3000. If he'd written "tails," forget it. The Boss didn't call the chief executive officers of New York's Five Families by their first names because he made promises (or threats) he didn't honor.

Jesus, he was rich! When the Feds wiretapped the Brite-Matic Cleaners after they forgot what they'd asked him to do to Fidel, a noise kept interrupting the jabber. It sounded like applause, angry applause. The investigators in earphones couldn't figure that muffled bang. Transcribers couldn't transcribe it, tried to put it in parentheses: (Slap), (Smack). An FBI agent, leaving his office for the weekend, unpuzzled it: This was a drawer slamming. That was the scrape of the drawer sliding open, then the fluttery sigh of an envelope falling against other envelopes, now the slap shut. Every five minutes, less.

So how much? Who knew? He lived simply, with his wife, son, and daughter. Not for him the tomatoes and silk suits, Rolex, junkets to Vegas or Atlantic City. Oofa guys in pointy-toed shoes wore cashmere and Banlon, drove fast noisy cars, lost respect for home-cooked food. The Boss ate his wife's food, drove a Buick, paid for, full price at retail. This wasn't a question merely of style. This was at the heart of his matter, deception, a shield to hide his meaning. He had two extravagances: toy soldiers and hand-made shoes. The Boss suffered from gout, and valued comfortable feet. He was interested in history, too, its great leaders, and especially military leaders. But *how much?* Okay: let's just say that drawer swallowed twenty-five thousand a week from a single Boston underling, a loan shark who borrowed at one to two percent from The Boss, and put that money on the street at three to four percent. Yearly, a million two and carfare. And this was only an indirect interest of The Boss. Let's say that twenty men in the Providence area were multimillionaires, unemployed men wearing seven-hundred-dollar suits, driving El Dorados. So what would you guess? Enough?

You'd be wrong. Enough was never enough. This was why he glowered, never grinned, oh maybe sometimes, around little kids. He was pure want, hundred percent gimme. Storytellers like to imagine likenesses between the mob and GM, organizational charts, a Great Chain of Being from God to inanimate objects, from The Boss to a pistol, a corpse. A little down the chain come board members, counselors, referees, legal advisors, *caporegimes*, noncoms, soldiers. It wasn't like that. It was like an open-air market, like the Istanbul Bazaar. Shouts and elbows, wheedle and bluster. He'd tailgate beef, take a hot stove if it fed the drawer. Confusion. An outsider can't appreciate how helter-skelter it would seem to anyone but an insider, and it was supposed to seem that way. To insiders, too! There was supposed to be *one* insider, Himself. He knew everything; they didn't. All they knew was he better know what they knew. If they knew they had twenty thousand cases of shoe polish, hijacked off a truck passing through West Hartford, they also knew he had a claim on five thousand cases of shoe polish that had never entered his calculations before just then. The drawer opened; the drawer took; the drawer shut; a hijacker and fence lived to eat another breakfast.

You think these things just happened? He fucking made them happen. He made everything happen. When it rained? *He* clouded up. When an apple hit a scientist on the head? When a guy lived to eat another breakfast. The Boss talked in curves; it was labor to puzzle out his meaning; it was meant to be. You could be fooled by the *dees* and *dozes*, the *boots* for *booths*, into imagining that guy didn't have a VisiCalc upstairs, didn't know every street, alley, *cul-de-sac*, and grave in New England. When The Boss said, "I embrace you," when he tipped his hat and said, "Salut," you could misunderstand. When he mumbled his favorite catch phrase, "Bet your life on it," it was almost possible to misunderstand.

Skippy misunderstood. He thought he was special. This was his point of view, like most points of view partial. He knew The Boss's name, so he thought The Boss knew his. He was right: The Boss knew his name. He knew everybody's name. But just because Skippy gave a shit about The Boss didn't mean The Boss gave a shit about Skippy. Skippy, looking for a clean scam, looking for a line where cops like Tom wouldn't take batting practice on his pretty face, was the last guy on earth to figure someone didn't care about Skippy. Lisa cared. Boy, *Skippy* cared! The Boss said "salut" to Skippy's father. The Boss had spoken to Skippy, when he was a kid, riding his Big-Wheel on the sidewalk, Atwells Avenue. Two guys had climbed out the front doors of a black Buick Roadmaster, and one of them opened the back door for Him. What did Skippy, at four, know about Him? Skippy pumped those pedals; make way. Well, he ran over The Boss's shoes, his *cuffs*! There were gasps, whispers of outrage. The Boss glared. Skippy said he was sorry. The Boss cut him dead. To be cut dead by The Boss was to wish you were dead, which you probably were. But this time He decided to grin. Skippy's dad saw all this, and told the story again and again, until Skippy utterly misunderstood its meaning. How The Boss reached down, messed Skippy's hair in a benediction, said:

"Kid, you're cute. You're a doozy. You're okay. Worry about nothing; I like you."

So why didn't he have a place in the office? Why was he still a dime-a-dozen freelance? Why didn't The Boss tell people he was a "good boy"? When The Boss called someone a "good boy," that boy was in clover. Why didn't he even have a real nickname? What was he, Skippy "Ten Fingers" Carbone? Well, fuck that. He'd squeezed rubber balls and massaged those ten fingers with Vaseline to become a tender-handed booster, and he couldn't even get a meeting with The Boss. And if this grated his ass, you should have heard Baby on the subject of being left out of the action. It wasn't fair; they'd paid dues; they were hang-around guys; they knew their way around. And what they knew should have made them look sharp, look this way and that like deer hearing a twig snap. If they'd thought about it, they would have figured that freelancers were tolerated, if they fed the drawer. Or until they weren't tolerated. Say they took a little safari around the northeast, switching diamonds at the wedding ring counter, boosting Hart, Schaffner and Marx suits, hanging paper, uttering and publishing. Say they asked The Boss's non-com what would be an appropriate tribute, and did they maybe step on their dicks somewhere along the line. Then they were tolerated, or maybe laughed at, a couple of pussies scared of their shadows. The line was thin, thin. Say on the other hand they tipped over the wrong place in the wrong neighborhood, say Johnston (where The Boss lived in what the disappointed newspapers complained was just a "modest ranch dwelling"), say Federal Hill. If they extorted from a mobbed-up restaurant owner. (Shit! Even Baby knew better than that!) If they brought down the heat. So spunk and resourcefulness had everlastingly to be measured against prudence, and it was not difficult for wise guys to make dumb choices.

Especially at the time we speak of. Now The Boss was holed up at home, an old fart in his peejays, with diabetes and a crummy pump, vegging out on *All My Children*, *As the World Turns*, refusing to watch or even think about *General Hospital*. Some hard guy, according to Baby. Outsiders began to wonder about The Boss when he took out a full page ad in *The Providence Journal*:

Since my release from prison many years ago, with a full pardon from a great Governor, after a minor crime [armed robbery, safecracking and murder] when I was a youngster, my time has been continuously and assiduously employed in honest endeavors. This is the result of my resolution, made in prison, to mend my life. This resolution has never been broken. I challenge anyone to prove by competent evidence that I have since, to any degree, deviated from that resolution by my engagement in any illegal or criminal enterprise or activity. The tranquility of my family has many times and oft been rudely disturbed by the rehashing of my criminal record in your news columns. I, more than anyone, deplore that record. How bitterly I realize the truth of a great poet's words: "The evil that men do lives after them; the good is often interred with their bones." Your newspaper seems to take a fiendish delight in parading in its obituary columns the peccadilloes of many former decent Rhode Island citizens, including a great Governor, whose family can only be hurt by my mention of his name, Joseph Delamater.

Was that weird? Of course, he had always hated the ProJo, and now especially this eager-beaver, Ann Hutchinson, four years out of the University of Missouri Journalism School, easy on the eye (which made her dangerous), humorless (which made her difficult to charm), brave (which made her unilluminated), ambitious (which made her a pain in the ass). She was everywhere, in court, on Federal Hill, at Fountain Street headquarters, pestering this mouthpiece and that D.A. The Boss had said it all: "A chone with a typewriter can murder you."

But what did Skippy know about publicity? What did Baby? Skippy read the newspapers, mostly for sports, sometimes to keep up with Lisa on current events and show business. He read what Baby made it his business to hear: The Boss was sick. Some of this sick was pure scam, of course, because the times the old joker would get really sick, laid out on a stretcher with tubes stuck up his nose, coincided again and again with the night before he was served with a subpoena, the Tuesday before a Thursday indictment. Heartache? Tell me about it: angina, erratic heartbeat, blocked arteries, chronic depression. At first everyone believed the medical reports were bought, paid for by The Boss's scholarships, years ago. And if that was the only way to have got a note from Mommy excusing him from school, that was how he would have got it. But it wasn't necessary. Finally, a Superior Court judge had The Boss examined at Harvard Medical School. The doctor made it clear: "To determine how serious is this man's physical deterioration, the State will have to conduct an experiment. If he is put on trial, has a heart attack and dies, I will have been proved right. If he is put on trial and does not die, the State will have been proved right."

So they questioned him at home. The papers said he was hysterical as a broad. Sobbed at anything. Any question. A memory. Mention of a dead friend, such as the brothers machine-gunned six months apart in the same phone booth of a Federal Hill grocery store. (They should put plaques on the great crime scenes of Providence, if only there were brass enough.)

It was too easy to misconstrue the consequences of The Boss's chronic sadness. It was unhappily easy to believe that because he'd lost his teeth, he'd lost his teeth. It was Baby's unfortunate blindness that he could not see The Big Picture, did not accurately estimate the value of his own anger, virility, youth. When

he finally managed to steal a few words with The Boss, during a
by now rare visit to Atwells Avenue, Baby asked for a job:

"I'll do anything."

Baby must have figured he was owed, for a favor he'd done
one of The Boss's subordinates, the kind of employment that
came to a Canuck from time to time. But just now The Boss,
flipping through his databank for the file *Baby*, found it, and
frowned:

"You're a junkie. Be a man; rob a bank. Then talk to me on
the street, if I look like I feel like talking to you. Now get out of
my way. Oh yeah: throw away those suede shoes on you."

Independence Day of this year a few items appeared in the
"Police Log," third page of the *Journal's* Metropolitan Section:

> In related incidents this past weekend 150 railroad ties and
> three AMTRAK bridge supports were stolen from the yard at
> Union Station. Police apprehended Albert Read, 55, of 14
> Wayne Street in Cranston, together with his son Bobby, of no
> fixed address, as they allegedly were in the act of winching a
> magnet—four and a half feet across and weighing 4000
> pounds—on to the back of a flatbed truck registered to Mr.
> Read. The weight of the magnet, valued at more than $10,000.
> by an AMTRAK spokesman, broke the axles of Mr. Read's truck,
> according to police. Mr. Read is alleged to have explained to
> police that he was removing the equipment, and had removed
> other railroad property, because he "thought it might come in
> handy sometime."

> Also:

> "'Ghost' with Knife Tries to Rob Woman"

> PROVIDENCE—A man in a white sheet and a mask, who
> knocked on the door of Carol Thompson of 186 Benefit Street,
> and announced he was there for trick-or-treating, removed a
> butcher knife from beneath his sheet and demanded money.
> Mrs. Thompson slammed her door in his face, and telephoned

police, who failed to locate a man fitting the assailant's description.

But not:

FEDERAL HILL—A pair of silver candlesticks were stolen last night during a break-in at the home of Patricia Bianchi. During the course of the home invasion one of the perpetrators climbed to the second floor of Mrs. Bianchi's dwelling, where he discovered her in bed with a man considerably her junior, who was not her husband. The burglar, armed with a .44 magnum, laughed at the sight, and said, "Wipe the cum off your moustache, bitch, and give me your watch." Examining the inscription on the timepiece, he then said, "Keep it; it's a piece of shit."

Mrs. Bianchi's wristwatch, like her candlesticks, were wedding gifts from her father, Mr. M———, also known locally as The Boss. Though police have not been advised of the crime, or Mr. M———'s feelings, he is said to be irritated.

Skippy didn't know whose house it was. He'd been on so many jobs with Baby, he didn't even ask anymore. Baby would rob anyplace. Once, drunk, he tried to push a laundry sack full of silver out of a federal judge's bathroom window. The sack was too heavy to lift; dragged clanking like chains down the hall it awoke Your Honor, who called the police, while Baby locked himself in the third-floor bathroom awaiting them by taking a dump. Baby would rob anyplace. But not *that* place! Skippy should have figured. He wanted to get out of there as soon as Baby climbed the stairs. It was too unguarded, as though this person lived in the world's only house, or crime hadn't been invented.

Besides, Skippy had come along only because he was bored. Lisa had been working later and later at the Biltmore, doing coke with the busboys. Sometimes, it made Skippy wonder. Busboys ran escort services. Someday, he told himself, he'd have to look into that little matter. He wasn't sure how he felt about Lisa doing escorts, coming home beat at breakfast, clean from a fresh shower. What was he supposed to do while she was "working late"? Get a payday, go out with Baby and drink like heroes.

Fencing the candlesticks that afternoon, the candelabras, whatever the fuck you call them, was easy as pie. Skippy couldn't believe it. Good price, too, couple hundred, and he had thought they might be plate. It should have made him think. Baby didn't even call about his cut. It should have made him wonder.

The Boss had had his differences with his only child. He'd wanted her to go to college, why not Brown? He'd wanted her to marry a gentleman with an interest in military history, maybe a professor, or a military officer, with medals. Instead, she'd married a wise-ass car dealer. When the wise-ass fooled around, she'd begged her father to have him killed. The Boss told her never to ask such a thing again. So she took care of things herself. The second time her husband fooled around he came home to find the trousers of his suits altered, legs cut off above the knees, snip-snip, Bermuda shorts. A little later, the married couple was parked at a light on North Main Street when a jellybean walked in front of their Jag.

"Hey, honey, it must have been a bitch getting into those jeans. How you going to get out?"

"You'd have to buy me a drink to find out."

The teen was heading for Allary's. The husband of the daughter of The Boss began to put in hours at Allary's. One night he came home too late from Allary's, smelling too funky. So The Boss's little girl Krazy-Glued his pecker to the side of his leg.

The Boss wished his daughter had turned out different, but he also liked the way she had turned out. Now someone had ripped her off, had ripped *him* off, *his* personal gifts, and for the first time ever The Boss lost control. He went up and down Federal Hill yelling that he wanted those fucks nailed before the end of the week. No whispered malediction, no arched eyebrow. He went ape: "Kill them! Kill them!" It was generally believed that a man thought to be competent to whack Fidel could seriously alter the futures of a couple of guys called Baby and Skippy.

9

▲ ▲ ▲ ▲ ▲

THE COURTHOUSE
GANG

MIDSUMMER of that year, Donny and Marie Osmond came to
the little city to do the Warwick Musical Theater. They put up
at the Howard Johnson Motor Lodge, Jefferson Boulevard, Exit
15. Hoping to treat themselves right that afternoon, brother and
sister headed poolside to zone out before the night's pressure
screwed down on them. HoJo's staff treated them right, as
though they were just another couple of customers, and not *People* coverpersonages.

Imagine the Osmonds' surprise that sweltering forenoon to
find no swimmers in the pool, no fans pretending not to stare. I
mean, how blasé! Okay, Providence had given birth to its own
entertainers: the radio personality, "Salty" Brine, not to mention Nelson Eddy and Frankie Carle, who liked to come home in
his golden years to tell how a kid who took piano lessons at five
as a punishment for smoking cigarettes grew up to join the
Horace Heidt band, and become sort of a legend. ("What keeps
me going? I look at pretty women, and go to the races. Also, I
don't worry about anything.") But now the *Osmond* siblings
were poolside, and poolside was deserted. Surprise soon yielded
to enlightenment. The Cranston City Council, meeting next day
in emergency session, would call it a "thick, sweet odor," and
blame it on Warwick. The Warwick Sanitation Department
would call it a "mysterious smell you could cut with a knife."
Newporters, paddling water thirty miles downwind at Bailey's
Beach, or balls at The Casino, said "yuck" and inquired into
flights to the Hamptons. Skippy, trying to cop zees with Lisa on

College Hill till the crack of noon, woke her with a question: "Do you smell shit?"

For the management of Howard Johnson's, Jefferson Boulevard, Warwick, this was over the line. It was mortifying, another provocation for the great world to scorn Little Rhody. While the Osmonds ran for cover, and asked (urgently) why their air conditioner couldn't be programmed to condition their air, the management raised hell. Called the ProJo's "Action Line" reporter. Don't think *he* couldn't smell it! Everyone was pissed. The afternoon paper headlined the crisis:

"Mysterious Odor Invades Providence"

Investigative reporters dug to the bottom, but not before the Osmonds had checked out of motel, town, and state resolving this was the kind of wrong turn you didn't take twice. It developed that Cranston and Warwick were both having a spot of trouble with their ca-ca. Warwick liked to store its sludge outside, drying in the sun to reduce its weight before it was hauled off. To Cranston. The Plant Manager in Cranston admitted that just about the time Donny and Marie hit poolside, he got a phone call from his wife:

"Ron, your plant stinks."

Ron told the press: "She was right. There was an upset. There was definitely something out there. I'll admit we had our problems. But we took care of them. This week has been a crummy week for us. The wind went northwest. Hey, it's a sewer plant. You're going to smell something."

Granted. But should Donny and Marie have to smell it? What good's a million if you have to toot Cranston's night soil? Face it, the problem of bad smells and ugly sights was general that summer. "Mysterious Odor Invades Providence" wasn't a patch on a subhead from the *Wall Street Journal*: Providence is just "a smudge beside the fast lane to Cape Cod." And how about the headline from the mighty *Times*: "Sense of Rot Gnawing at Providence."

Maybe the conceit was muddled, but it bruised to have New

York finally notice you, and no sooner notice than cover their eyes and clothespin their noses. *Sixty Minutes* had placed some preliminary calls to Area Code 401. The problem, frankly, was corruption, and in the middle of a summer when the courthouse should have been ticking over on idle, the place had never been busier, hotter, tenser, more remunerative for defense counsel willing to leave to those with more temperate appetites beach, cottage, links, cutter and fighting chair.

The scene in front of City Hall, a squat Beaux-Arts edifice at the west end of Kennedy Plaza, was too San Salvador for words. Federales, SWAT Team varsity bearing state-of-the-art ordnance. The order of battle was first to throw an off-switch on the shredders. Then change the locks, photocopy the records, see who bought tickets for Honolulu. The bad news just poured down. After decades of sweet deals, pay for no-show, overtime for no time, goodwilled extortion, embezzlement, theft, fraud, kickback, ghost bills for ghost materials, ghost payrolls for ghosts, tax reductions for contributions to tax auditors, expense vouchers for about a thousand lunches per civilly employed chow-hound per year, scams their perpetrators forgot were illegal . . . after all that good easy dough, now everyone's bones were rattling. *Doctor, my Valium seems to have used itself up.*

Over at Superior Court the indoor astronauts had to bump passengers from the elevators, they were so jammed with civil servants caught in the summer's jackpot and come to testify, answer indictments, beg to cut deals, wear the wire. Plumbing licensers had been caught selling master's licenses, or the answers to the master plumbers' exams. (And you wondered why your faucet dripped.) A Civic Center exec had just been caught with five rolls of tufted polypropolene, artificial turf, valued at a piece apiece, five grand's worth. (And Ringling's elephants wondered why it hurt so bad to stand on their trunks in Providence.) Asphalt for sidewalks went astray. Snowplow contracts were sold to people who forgot to plow snow. Snowplows were driven in the front door of the Department of Public Works garage with the city seal on their doors, and came out belonging—

check it in the transcripts—to the Busy Bee Construction Company. On the *Bible*, "Busy Bee."

Not just snowplows, either. Bucket loaders, jeeps, payloaders. Wheelbarrows. Fire extinguishers. Manhole covers. And when the indictments came raining down just after Independence Day, the Providence River began to take a tide-raising load of heavy equipment. Name it Caterpillar River! Manhole covers! (Made in prison!) Now divers were searching the river for the dull things. They cost Providence about $125, weighed 451 pounds, were worth, as cast iron scrap, $6.75 each. Hey, there to be borrowed. People had put in hours stealing manhole covers, and yonder truck-mounted crane with its huge magnet, within sight of the courthouse, was set to retrieve them. Why throw them in the river, you ask? Call it conditioned behavior. What would a Master Felon do with a body he didn't any longer need? Flow on, big muddy. A miscreant with a hot manhole cover got that cover wet.

Now official scavengers had already grappled to the surface some shopping carts. Would they dust them for prints? The heavy equipment was thought to be in deeper water, and there was the detective in charge of scuba police, sitting in a van with his wet-suited divers, waiting for the rain to stop: "Why stand around taking rain? Those snowplows aren't going anywhere."

On the subject of wet: one public works supervisor got burned by his oldest friend, who wore a wire to the Jack-in-the-Box where they cooked up their story. From then on, after the publication of those mortifyingly ungrammatical tapes retailing mortifyingly complex schemes to extort eighty bucks here, $81.24 there, many civil servants were saying to their own closest colleagues:

"Let's take off our clothes and talk."

One rat shorted himself out in an athletic club shower, and an hour later woke up dead.

Taps were strung from Federal Hill to Silver Lake. Federal agents wore headsets that messed up their 'dos, and watched the tape reels spin, and transcribed the inside skinny:

"What're you doing?" asked Heather Cappricio of her friend Kenny.

"Watching TV," said Kenny.

"So what are you watching?" asked Heather (noted the federal agent, taped the recorder).

"Gilligan's Island."

"That's a cute show. Dana says she thinks Justin's really cute."

"Yeah?"

"That's what she told Julie."

"Yeah."

"Does Justin like Julie?"

"How am I supposed to know? She's just a fifth-grader."

"So am I."

"Yeah."

"Well, do you care how old I am?"

(The reel spun, recording silence. The federal agent figured Kenny for a dumpster, Heather a dumpling.)

"Kenny? Are you there?"

"Yeah. I got to go to dinner."

"Don't hang up. Do you care how old I am?"

"My mom's calling me to eat dinner. She sounds really pissed. I'll call you back."

(Sure you will, Ken. The moon's made of blue cheese, and the check's in the mail.)

The panic pissed off connected guys. It was an election year. When they were asked, and they were asked often those sweaty weeks, the advice was always the same:

"Keep telling yourself: 'I ain't done nothing wrong, and I ain't going nowhere, except maybe Florida, when I feel like it.' "

"Low-jinks in high places" was the sad assessment of a local university president. He said everybody bore a share of the blame for the neglect of rectitude and selflessness. Come off it! We're talking Providence, a piece of the flag, a little piece of the action, little piece of the littlest state. *Double sawbucks, get thee into my pocket!* Crooked? Well, at an exhibition game back in

1927, with Lou Gehrig and the Babe (who had played for the Providence Grays), the contest was terminated midway, after the fans stole all the baseballs. We weren't talking extraordinary when we talked crooked public servants.

But some of those officials were indignant. It was ignominious to have some wispy-bearded DA plant his brogans on the courthouse steps and talk into a camera about how you stole this and lied about that. Frankly, it was a pain in the ass to look down the road at maybe a dime in the can, fourteen months to serve. To speak up for their sullied reps, a couple of the Busy Bee's executive officers, coincidentally high on the payroll of the City of Providence, charged with who knew what all, pumped themselves full of margaritas and invited themselves on a phone-in radio talk show.

So this listener phoned in, said she was curious how a fellow, a laborer, could afford a two-hundred-thousand-dollar house on Warwick Neck, and a Mercedes.

"I save a little every week," said the laborer, called Frog by his friends, and sometimes Mr. Frog.

"I find that difficult to imagine," said the call-in listener.

"What's your address?" asked Frog. "Maybe I'll visit and explain how it worked. I'm only kidding."

"Seriously," asked the host. "All that smoke. There has to have been a little fire."

"I wouldn't say so," said Frog's superior in the Highway Department. "Where there's some smoke, it could have just been a lit cigarette burning in the ashtray."

This, then, was an incendiary analogy. Because, as it happened, the principal indictee haunting Superior Court that busy summer was no one less than Hizzoner, groaning beneath the load of some heavy felony weight, not least of it a charge of assault with deadly weapons, to wit one (lit) fireplace log, one (lit) cigarette, one (heavy) ashtray. Adam was counsel for the defense.

Sometimes a person pauses, marks an X with the toe of his shoe, looks over his shoulder toward the horizon back there, and won-

ders *how did I get here?* That summer, waiting for the dime to
drop on him, Adam often looked over his shoulder. You wouldn't
think a fellow with cells banging around like corn in the popper
would feel time drag, but Adam felt time drag. He was almost
willing to call the sensation "boredom," but he wasn't so far
gone that he knew just how to define boredom. He made lists, in
court he made lists: women he had kissed, women he thought he
could have kissed had he tried, stupid names of boats (*Tee Mar-
toonis, At Last, About Time, Finally*), smart, simple names of
boats (*Petrel, Nimrod*), jazz pianists, World War II airplanes, the
people who might have stolen money from his pocket at Fence
Club twenty-some years ago. The next thing he did after he
made lists was wonder what was the next thing to do. It was
weird: watching Ike's goldfish laze around their bowl irritated
Adam. He went to a death counselor about that, and about another thing. Not his fear of dying, but his wish that others die
too, lots of others, maybe everyone on earth save Ike and Clara.
(Would she despise him for taking too long to leave? He could
see how someone could hate someone—put love aside—for
stretching it out.) The counselor helped, but Adam quit going
when he looked down at a kid sitting in the waiting room with
his robust mother and wasted father, drawing a family picture
that included a kid and a robust mother. Sound counseling, to
encourage the boy to accustom himself to a family of two. Ike
didn't know yet. No counselor could help Adam figure how to
tell him. That was a news story to be unriddled solo, or so it
seemed to Adam.

Sometimes Adam felt special. What teachers like Clara called
"gifted." Picked out for something. Mostly Adam felt bad.
Lethargy, dry mouth, no appetite, sore shoulder. He bruised easily and couldn't look at those purple stains on his pallid skin. He
puked bile. There were spinal taps, and after them migraines.
Intravenous remedies were beasts: his skin was knotty now, and
his veins rolled under the needle, hiding from it. Sometimes
Adam's genetic event took a holiday, and gave him one. At such
times he almost felt himself again, could believe it would all go
away. But then it came back. And then Adam felt bad. Bad bad,

from those fucking cells. But also bad the way people sometimes feel bad. Down. These weren't the change-of-life blues;
these were the end-of-life blues. He knew that. Boo-hoo, he told
himself, don't hang crepe (he told himself), and bore up. Some
things surprised him that didn't surprise Clara. That he didn't
break the rules, tell people fuck you. You'd think he'd have broken the rules, but he didn't. Adam just wasn't a *carpe diem* kind
of guy, and that was the truth. Adam's friends didn't know they
were watching him check out, but Adam knew what they were
watching, when they bothered to look. Oh, Adam wanted to die
well.

He invested time in his files, ridding them of anything that
could hurt Clara or Ike. He imagined them thumbing those files
to find papers that would bring him a little to life for them.
Well, he'd clipped some dirty pictures from a magazine, *Beaver
Hunt*, an anthology of pictures of amateurs—housewives and
schoolteachers and barmaids, all sorts—who'd felt the itch to
show themselves. Adam didn't know what had made him buy
that magazine, or why he had looked at those pictures more
than a few times, or why he paused more than a nano second
before throwing them away with a pack of rubbers he'd kept
seven years in his desk drawer. But he knew that those pictures
could consequentially alter the course of his son's life. He also
knew this wasn't just, but maybe he was a criminal lawyer because he kept forgetting life was just.

Standing on the X, looking back, why *was* he a criminal lawyer? Back there, at Columbia, in Mississippi, the prospect had
been different. Civil rights law had taught him trial law, of
course. He had defended long-hairs busted on spurious drug
charges, the usual. After Nixon's election, when Government
work felt like diminishing work, he stayed in the south—New
Orleans, his compromise between ideals and comfort—as a public defender. The pay was awful: it worked out to maybe twelve
dollars an hour, often less than half his out-of-pocket expenses,
but it saved having to talk to clients about money. Money talk
gave Adam the willies, back then; he liked the salaried pursuit.
He liked too the suspense, the variety, getting cases assigned al-

phabetically, so depending on "Dwyer's" place in the alphabet
he got a couple heavy murders, or a prolonged bad-check melo-
drama. But time came, with Ike ready for school, when it wasn't
enough. So home to Providence. This petri dish. Another compromise: some public defense, some private defense. Credo:
Adam told himself it felt better to free people than put them
away. That's what he told himself, because it made sense. That's
what he told himself less and less.

The hairy truth was, criminal law was fun. Well, it was interesting. The combat got his pump going. He liked a license to
fight, and it felt noble (in a silly way) to fight fair, inside the
bounds, and to know the game's rules like a . . . like . . . like a
lawyer. Before Ike squinnied into his birthday microscope,
Adam liked to take on bizarre, catchpenny cases, oddities nobody smart would touch, sideshow cases that gave Adam a laugh
when he remembered them, gave Clara many a laugh, when he
violated lawyer-client confidentiality, which he often did, to
make Clara laugh.

Remember, Adam: the gunman who slathered tartar sauce on
a bus driver he had just held up. ("I don't know what got into
me, sir. This imp, I guess.") The sullen kid, adjudged sane, who
set fire to a peacock at the zoo, and said he'd like to do it to another peacock, because NBC had canceled his favorite wildlife
show. Adam convinced a jury that the lad had put paid to the
pretty bird because he couldn't bear to see it caged, that he
would have killed it some more merciful way "had he the
means." It amazed him what juries will believe. No laughs from
that case, but it made Adam scratch his head, and what reminded him he didn't know everything, reminded him also he
was awake, alive.

That was before, of course. If then was now, he wouldn't have
invested time in the wealthy man accused of stealing a can of
tunafish and a string of Polish sausage from Star Market. A
twelve-year-old girl who stole two dog biscuits and four bottle
caps (Pepsi had a bingo game going) from Star Market. A RISD
student who stole a canned ham from Star Market. (The store

detective chased her through the parking lot; when she tossed the ham under a car, he tackled her. Nice counter charge for undue force. Sweet case.) In fact, Adam was known as the Star Market adversary; he found the establishment crabbed and mean to drag into court every shoplifter they caught. Oh, maybe he had waged a vendetta against the store for refusing to refund Clara's money for a dozen bad eggs. Why do law, if not for justice? If not for fun?

Adam defended a man charged with stealing a telephone booth. Another who ran off with four flag poles. Two brothers who removed a picnic table from a highway rest stop, and were caught for erratic driving on I-95 when the wasps attached to its trestle began to circulate angrily through the brothers' station wagon. How about blue shoelaces, twelve gross? ("They sharp. Look bad," was the word next day at Chad Brown Development, word of mouth, blood to blood, until the alleged thieves were apprehended. "This is a case for Dwyer.") Wedding presents, from Villa Romano, a convention palace at Warwick Mall where bride and groom could be photographed on a 10 by 16 white sand beach, with rubber coconut palms in the background and a mural-sized photograph of the sea on the rear wall. Two hundred fifty folding chairs from the basement of the church where bride and groom were wed? Same Saturday? Different perpetrators? Same defense counsel? How about gold teeth, from the cadavers at Brown Medical School? Two hundred railroad ties? Ten pounds of pennies? A burglar alarm? Pots and pans? A golf cart from the Agawam? (". . . last seen driving south on Massasoit Avenue . . ."). A doghouse? Thirty-six pairs of socks, from the dryer at a coin laundromat? Fifteen pounds of silver dust (alias, $3400)? How about a set of barbells and three hundred pounds of weights? Wouldn't a reasonable man like to spend a few hours alone with the "accused intruder" who was captured "running along Lloyd Avenue" carrying such physical fitness equipment?

Adam, in the old days, defended a couple of grown men who broke into a beach house in Narragansett, expensive house on

Ocean Road. Took no booze, no stereo, no silver, no television, no paintings. They stole a garden rake, three bathing suits, and a collection of authentic sombreros. Were arrested at the Twin Willows, ten miles away, wearing a couple of sombreros.

"That's why we liberated them, man. To wear. Aren't they a gas?"

Oh, they also stole some wind chimes. Jesus, what next? Adam loved his work.

There were things about his work he hated: having always to look smart. He hated the sound he made arguing with Clara, or explaining to Ike, his instinct for the opening in the line, the way he ran through it, not running, as they said, for "daylight." Running for the first down, merely. Running for field goal position, calculating averages, figuring the score. So trained in the rules of argument and evidence, Adam would hear himself object to his wife's supposition, his son's notion. Adam issued writs of mandamus commanding Ike to clean his room. He wondered, did Adam, if he might not be a small print artist. He also wondered if Clara wondered the same wonder.

"Yo, Adam, you've lost weight! Looking good, my man, lean and mean! Running?"

The observant one was Providence Plantations' Medical Examiner. Forgive him, Adam did look impressive these summer days. All that character etched in his face. Even he could see it, could almost puff with vanity. Pounds were coming off, nothing crazy yet, so far a dignified leaning. See his collars noosed comfortably rather than slackly. And Adam was "running." He said yes to cases he once wouldn't take. The more he said yes, the more people asked. Hizzoner, for example, who was said to have gone nuts after listening to a tape—we're talking audio, low-tech, *essence de Providence*—alleged to dramatize the rapture of his estranged wife calling his alleged best friend "Oh Christ! Oh Baby! Oh Jesus!" Charged with assaulting his best friend with all those outré at-hand weapons. Charged with asking his best friend (in exchange for his best friend's continued existence) for a million dollars, which was the only million dollars his best friend owned.

Crime-watchers raised their eyebrows, some of them, when His Nibs hired Adam, who wasn't Italian, who sometimes lost cases, who didn't cabaret with wise guys, who wasn't blown dry, whose fashion sense could use some invigoration from *GQ* ("He dresses like a DA."), who was thought to be standoffish, maybe a snob. The mayor's ass was in a crack. There were witnesses to his maybe true bill of particulars. This mayor was maybe thinking appellate, helpful writs, delicate stipulations, bond motions (Adam was toasted for the elegance of his bond motions), maybe parole. This mayor was maybe considering the value of Adam's rectitude, his connections, in the sense that connections were cited at the Hope Club rather than on Federal Hill. Hizzoner was maybe thinking long-term, God forbid, five to seven.

Adam was thinking short-term, five to seven months, and Adam was thinking cash, estate planning. Adam was "running."

Adam had been showing good moves lately in his wrongful death actions. Just now he had a pip on the burner. Some facts were not in dispute: A certain man was frightened of dogs. Walking home every evening from his bus stop this man was obliged to pass a neighbor's yard. The neighbor owned a wire-haired terrier, and the dog got a boot from chasing the man as-keered of it. The man would run home, feeling nips at his heels, nips at his cuffs. Safe in his living room, out of breath, he would call the police. Not once, twice, half a dozen times. Not a dozen times, or a score of times. More often. So the man became fabled among the dispatchers, who could be counted on to send rookies to the dog's address. Time passed. The terrier remained vigorous, a student of acceleration, the propulsive principle of fear. The dog cared about the frightened man, and the frightened man about the dog. They were the only beings in their universe, otherwise unremarked, especially by the police.

More time passed. The terrier-pursued man reported a break-in. Red-haired burglar, with a red beard, armed with a meat cleaver. Sirens, police officers. There he was! Stop! Witnesses agreed the bearded man turned toward the policeman there on the stand. He had to have turned, because he got gutshot.

The ill-starred idiot was wearing a red wig, with a red beard from his kid's costume kit pasted to his cheeks. Riding to Miriam Hospital in the ambulance, he tried to explain to his wife, that gentle widow-in-the-making, why he had been apprehended breaking into his own house.

"They never come when I call. I was clocking their response time." The man was hooked up to portable electronics, and lighting bulbs red, ringing some serious alarms. "I was teed off." The man was dead.

Now these days, Adam took his fees on the front end, a reasonable doubt at a reasonable price, as long as the check cleared. He had the rationale buttoned tight; he was a very Jesuit of casuistries; answer Adam, you of principle, was not an attorney who discriminated among clients like a physician who would not treat boils because he liked not pus? Not that Adam would call his new self a shyster, one of those latrine lawyers, but if someone stiffed him, stiffed Ike and Clara, he'd find that deadbeat anywhere in town, any time of night, and roust him. This lawyer was no altruist. Adam's persistence in the matter of prompt payment for services given had attracted the attention of the kinds of debt collectors who gave vigorish to The Boss.

But Adam had this case on contingency, on behalf of the angry, dead man's dependents, suing Providence. Tom Cocoran was in the audience, curious to observe the unraveling of such a tangled skein of rights and wrongs, sympathetic with the hard situation of his fellow officer, watched Adam question, refute, accuse.

Adam listened to the Medical Examiner yammer: "Of deaths, there are two general kinds. Natural and unnatural. If unnatural, we have accidental, suicidal . . ."

("Shut up," Adam thought.)

". . . and homicidal. Now an autopsy, of which I have done no fewer than a thousand these past fourteen years, may be considered surgery on the dead . . ."

Adam thought about the victim. He never thought about victims, any more than he asked clients if they did or did it not. He never thought about victims, any more than he told clients, "Don't! Thou shalt not!" (*Says who?*) Adam thought about the victim, hounded, dying under his wife's eye, dead wearing his kid's paste-on beard. How the ex-man had eaten some sausage, as the court was currently learning, and maybe wondered what TV would show him that night. How he had spent his evening on a slab, taking elective "surgery for the dead." Adam "running" indeed, on empty, thought about being dead.

"I object, your Honor!"

Tom Cocoran thought he knew Adam, a little. He nudged a goggler beside him, a regular at interesting cases, and at uninteresting cases when no interesting cases were being heard.

"What's with Dwyer?"

The rubberneck nodded, animated. "Ain't he something? Ain't he pissed off? Ain't he *just!*"

10

▲ ▲ ▲ ▲

LOVEBIRDS

IN the earliest weeks of that hot summer she copped rooms at the Biltmore in the early a.m., when she came off shift. The rooms were "comfy" (Tom caught himself using Lisa's word; he thought it was cute), one like another, every bit as restful as the bedroom at home in Cranston. She had associates at the hotel who fixed her up with keys. That Lisa had friends, it figured, and Tom didn't ask questions. She wouldn't take the bit, didn't choose to be grilled; besides, what was to find out? The woman had a million dollar personality. The rooms were free. Everything was free. Tom liked the set-up.

He liked Lisa. She made him laugh. Didn't phone him at home, didn't at work. Sometimes, rising from street to heights in the hotel's outside, glass-walled elevator, seeing the city at his feet, he wondered if it could see him. But she didn't demand anything out of the way, at first. It was handy for them, he reckoned, no strings. They could meet each other, or not; either way was jake by him, but he tried to connect with her every night. So in early July, when Tom began to call during the lunch hour, inviting her five minutes after she showed up for work to meet him for an extra "brief conference," "overtime," he was willing to put up with the unmade beds of just-now-vacated rooms. She told him they were lucky to have a place to meet on short notice, and he saw her point. He didn't much care for the smokes in the ashtrays, and the television blasting some game show at them, and the wet towels on the floor. But like Lisa said, it was free.

And later, when things began to change, and he had to buy

their rooms—cash, no VISA, Deirdre paid the bills—Tom understood. Lisa had called in too many markers that summer. The maids and bellhops and house detective were running out of hospitality. And if Tom was paying in other ways? Of course, who believed in free lunch?

That was later. Now was a blast. She wore flimsy cotton skirts, no panties. ("They're a hassle.") When he reached under her skirt to feel her generous hips, to manipulate her even before they lay down, she was wet. She walked around wet.

"Have you been thinking about me?" he asked, smirking.

"Sure. I guess so. What do you mean?"

"You're wet."

"Isn't everybody?"

He waited for her to giggle, to show that set of pearlies as perfect as a dental assistant's, that practiced smile, chin tucked down, eyes angled up, opened wide; but she was asking a question that almost had her full attention. She gave sex her full attention. She was athletic, Jesus, tireless. But hushed. No yapping. Tom liked a quiet woman. She always brought a candle, waxed it to an ashtray, lit it before they drew the curtains shut, switched off the lights. Lisa wasn't one to shut her eyes when she kissed a guy, or moved on top of him, or sucked him. She could seem shy, but she wasn't shy. On the other hand, when she was done, she liked to turn her back.

"Don't watch me sleep," she said, later, after she stopped bringing a candle when they met. "I don't like it."

"I'm just waiting for you to wake up," he said, surprised how whiny he sounded. "I want to do it again."

He wanted to do it forever. *Tempus fugit* and all, but he *wanted* it. It wasn't that he was superhombre, Tom the Sportsman, laying pipe like an outlaw, shooting his wad again and again just to go for the record. Sex with her was a fucking drug; he wanted to lie with her, basted in sweat and greased by their funk, wrung out, flying out of himself. She'd let him keep it in her after they finished, as long as he liked, till she wanted sleep. Then she'd go under like Maisie in diapers, no leg-over between awake and asleep. Then time would run out, and she'd pop awake—"Shitski, I'm late"—and jump into her clothes like Maisie almost late for school, and bomb out of the room ("Cheerio"), with Lieutenant Cocoran's voice trailing after her, "When? Tomorrow? Maybe later tonight?"

Not that it mattered to him all that much. Hooking up with Lisa wasn't life or death for him. It was just that she had "awakened feelings" in Tom, as he told himself, wondering even then where the words had come from, maybe the movies? Perhaps he should say she'd rattled his cage? He was cruising with his partner a June afternoon, trying to explain. His partner had told Tom he seemed off his feed, asked what was eating him.

"Look," Tom said, maybe too quickly, "I haven't talked to anyone about this."

"You don't have to get into anything with me, Tom. It's none of my business."

"No, I want to talk to someone."

"There's no need."

"I met someone."

"Let's forget I butted in, okay."

"I think she's special. Goofy, but special."

"No need, Tom."

"I love Deirdre, you know that."

"But this is different? You've never known it could be like this? She makes you feel alive again? You only live once? You owe yourself a life? It isn't just the sex, but you've never had a beejay like that? You laugh till you cry? She's amazing? You can take it or leave it? No strings?"

"Let me tell you how it is."

"I just told me how it is. Once is enough. Let's talk about sports."

Sometimes they did things besides fuck and suck. They teenaged: played grabass, acted up; he stared moonstruck. He had to be careful where they were seen together, didn't want to hurt Deirdre, if it could be helped. One night—this was a blast, he wished he had a Polaroid—they went out in the country, up near Lincoln. She wanted to smoke some reefer with him, and skinny-dip in a reservoir. The dope made him antsy, but he wanted to show her he had a life out of bed, so the adventure was worth the risk. They adjusted their consciousnesses; he felt out of it, sort of unmanned, really, and it didn't help that she seemed same as ever. (Maybe she was always stoned?) Anyway, they passed this roadhouse, a few cars parked in front. The Main Event: it made her laugh. "Live Act," the sign promised. She wanted to see the show, and he wanted to make her happy. This was like the bar in *Star Wars*, but with a few sullen workers sucking draft Bud, George Jones on the juke.

"When's the show start?" she asked.

"Hold your horses," the bartender said. "Have a highball."

So they had a couple highballs. Played Dr. John: "Such a Night." He tried to tell her how he felt about getting his gold shield, but the words tripped one another coming out. He tried to tell her he wasn't as fucked up as he sounded. That he was a weighty man. He was talking like a barber, but he wasn't making all that much sense. She motioned with a toss of her pretty hair toward a guy at the end of the bar: "He wants to jump my bones."

"So what?" Tom asked, blushing, pissed. "I'm trying to tell you about my wife."

"I don't want to hear," she said. "I don't even know the lady. You know her; you worry about her."

"I meant life," Tom said. "I meant to say life."

Lisa pouted. Tom was telling her about rewards for merit, the way the system worked ("it's not what you do, it's who you know"), how he used to have to moonlight construction jobs, directing traffic, how the bulletproof vest wasn't really bulletproof, "don't even talk to me about Teflon slugs," about Street Survival, about Street Smarts, who skates and who falls, about wondering every morning if this was the day you got taken out of the game, about the good feeling it gave him to help someone with a problem. . . .

"Hey," Lisa said to the bartender, "is the show ever going to start?"

Behind the bar, beside the bottles, a curtained window. The roadhouse was a concrete bunker, a little below grade. Soon as Lisa asked about the show, the bartender nodded at the lip-licker end of the bar. The guy uncoiled his horny self and disappeared through a back door. The bartender stood by the curtain pull at the window. There was a rap on the window, and the bartender pulled the curtain open to reveal a black pane of glass. Another rap on the glass, and he flicked a switch. There was the show, just the other side of the window, where the guy from the end of the bar had tipped over a garbage can. Two raccoons, scarfing scraps. It was a joke, sort of, but it wasn't the most boring thing Lisa had ever watched. The most boring thing Lisa had ever watched was . . . Jesus, she couldn't remember, something at school, or in church, or the motion of her dad's lips when he talked at dinner about getting fucked over at work, or the sincere look on that cop's face while he talked about how good it felt to help someone with a problem.

Thinking about her, night and day, he carried more than half a husk in his pants. He wore out his pocket thinking about her. He felt love like a lottery prize. He found himself short of breath, like he'd been popped in the chest. He tried to imagine what she saw when she looked at him. He tried to remember whether she ever looked at him, except when she was on top, and there was no other place to look, except at the landscape above the head-board. He tried to talk to his partner.

"I can't figure her out. She's an enigma. I think she likes me, she says I'm a hoot, but sometimes she acts like she doesn't give a shit about me. How do you figure it?"

"Figure what?"

"What makes her tick. How her mind works."

"I don't think about it."

"Come on. I'm asking for input. You owe me."

"That's true, but I've never known you to check the books on who's ahead."

"I'm sorry. I just can't figure her out."

"See that parking meter?"

"So what?"

"You know how it works?"

"You put coins in it, you empty coins out of it. So?"

"Maybe if I made my living emptying parking meters, I'd want to unriddle how they worked. I mean, there's a mechanism in there that makes them do their thing. You know?"

"Yeah, but . . ."

"Don't interrupt me. I'm telling you something. I don't make my living emptying parking meters, so I don't give a shit how they work. Something else, don't tell me how you're thinking about running away with her to Mexico."

Tom imagined how it would be in Mexico. How they'd rent this little hacienda near the ocean, in a town with a marketplace and an old white stucco church, a little cathedral. How they'd lie in bed days at a time, doing all the good deeds he was learning to get used to. How he wouldn't have to make appointments to see her, or sneak away from home, or off his shift, because there wouldn't be any home, any job. He'd be happy, or at least too busy wrapping his legs around her to be sad. They'd break for dope, and it wouldn't matter if he acted like an asshole, because there wouldn't be anyone but her to judge him. Without the badge to make him feel guilty, why not toot some coke, keep his pecker going with Black Beauties? Where was the sin in having a good time? Not that he needed drugs. A frosty would make him happy, lying beside her drinking a Carta Blanca so cracking cold he'd need mittens to hold it.

Okay, so she wanted to better herself, like she said. He'd buy her a camera. She could learn to take pictures of the church, the marketplace, the peons dressed in straw hats, riding around town on donkeys, whatever they called them, "burros." He'd be home in bed, waiting for her to come back, and she'd be late. When she got home her hair would be wet. She'd just come out of the shower, or the sea. He'd wonder about that. He was too smart to fight. He knew he didn't have a lien on her. In a couple of weeks the phone would ring. When she answered, she'd say something in Mexican; it meant *wrong number*. When he answered the phone, it clicked dead.

He'd call home. Deirdre would hang up on him. Maisie wouldn't cry. She'd say, "Don't call us again, Dad." Those were Tom's Mexican dreams.

He was lying beside her, wearing a pair of novelty briefs, "Home of the Whopper," they said on the fly. They made her laugh, even harder than the last pair, with a yardstick down there. Tom was thinking about his daughter, her face scarred from the burns. He was thinking how it was when the phone didn't ring for her. Kids at school weren't cruel to Maisie; they were careful around her, and she got invited to the prom by the nicest boy in the class, who was going steady with someone else, and wanted to be friends, he said.

"How was it for you?" Tom asked. "Growing up. How did boys act? Was it rough?"

"It was easy. Great. Had to beat them off with sticks."

"I caught my kid giving this guy a handjob in the den. She said it was the only way she could get him to ask her out."

"Oh-oh," Lisa said. "Did you rubber-hose him?"

"No," Tom said, "I didn't. I told him to go home. It's an old story. He's a jerk, but so was I. I wonder sometimes how she feels."

Lisa was doing something under the sheet. "Feel that?"

"Yes."

"Like it?"

"Yes."

"Will you cop me some coke?"

"What?"

"Just for recreational use. So we can have some fun together? How about it?"

He stole it from the Evidence Room. It was easy. It didn't even make him feel that crummy. Lisa joked him out of his bad mood, said she couldn't afford to buy it and wasn't quick enough at addition, multiplication and conversion tables—dimes to zees, grams to keys—to sell it. She just liked to put it up her nose. Her drug of choice was Percodan. Well, maybe thrusters. "I've got a yen for that Darvon-N." Actually, Lisa told him, there was nothing on this earth like laughing gas. Redlining on wake-ups had its qualities, but to take hits from N_2O, nitrous oxide, the stuff that pushed whipped cream from a can: cloud nine, welcome to Cuckooland. Trouble was, she wound up with a whipped cream jones. Now 'ludes were always fun. And a little hit of industrial strength Valium could rub down the edges of acid flashback. So, sure, Valium, if Tom could get it.

"You're a sweetie," she said. "You're cute as a button."

She was *Merck's Desk Reference* with long, soft hair, wet lips, wet everything. He'd never met anyone who knew as much about anything as she knew about drugs. She was healthy. She laughed a lot, when she didn't sulk. Drugs made her happy, no drugs didn't.

"Back off," he said. "Let's back off. There's a limit. Eat this sandwich."

"Chow flattens a high."

"Why not take one? You don't need all three now."

"One? I've never heard of taking one of anything."

"Save some for later."

"Why? I've never owned anything I like more than a few hours."

"You're going to burn out your lobes, Lisa. Think about it."

"What a drag."

Thinking, he knew, did not make her happy. Toys for the mind made her happy. Goofballs, little violet friends. Herb made her happy. Devil dope. Leper grass. Killer buds. Mojave blond. Drying home-grown in her GE Toast-R-Oven, and not burning it black: that brought satisfaction. Rummaging in her purse for an alligator clip, and finding it. A whack attack made her sad, but Tom copped good goods from the Evidence Room; this made him "good people." Lisa called him "Kiddo" and "Ace," and that put steel in his unit.

She told him about the cute bong Skippy had "bought" her, shaped like an old-timey telephone. "Just Say High" it said on the mouthpiece.

"He's a pismire. You should cut him loose. You're too good for him."

"He's good to me. He's cute. He doesn't hassle me."

(In fact, Skippy had been porky lately; he was pissed someone was beating his time. Served him right for missing her gig at Goddard's that night. Skippy could be demanding. When Lisa forgot to take her baby medicine, he wouldn't wear a rubber, claimed it messed up his blowjob. But he was wicked funny, called his thingamabob a trouser trout, a Johnson. Named hers a peach fish. Where did he get all the words?)

"And I do?"

"What? I wasn't listening."

"Hassle you."

Lisa shrugged.

"What's he do for a living?"

Lisa was smart enough to play dumb. "He cleans his teeth and blow-dries his hair."

"Jesus, a conversation between the two of you must be like listening to two pecans in a bowl. Why don't you let him shoot 500 cc of Thorazine right in your heart, get it over."

She stared at him. Shook her head. "Guys are such babies. Such awful goddamned fools. I wish I was a dyke. Women could never get away with the shit you guys pull."

"If women didn't fuck, there'd be a bounty on them."

"Get your hand off it, Tom. Don't touch it."

"Okay, I was kidding. You want a toot?"

"Sure."

They shared a toot. Well, she did three lines, and he did the other.

"What would your wife say if she knew about this?"

"Sometimes things get beyond you, choices are taken from you."

"Wow! That's what they all say!"

"I don't want you to talk about Deirdre."

"Who cares about her. I don't even know her. You're the one who knows her."

"You've said that before."

"So?"

By August, there wasn't much left. Tom wanted to patch it together. He wanted so bad to please her. One night she knocked on the hotel door, and found him in his clown get-up. She almost had to laugh. He kept begging her to sing the songs she'd sung the night they met at Goddard's, a million years ago. How was she supposed to remember that far back? He was scaring himself with some wiggyness brand new to him. Not just the coke. He figured he was still wrapped tight enough to keep that under control.

It was his marriage. Marriages were going belly-up all around him, and he didn't want that for him and Deirdre. He hoped they'd end up rocking on a porch together, wise, maybe even dull, but friends, hanging in there, both of them understood and forgiven. But that was down the line. Now he had something going, and he didn't want to turn it loose.

At a police picnic in Narragansett, Fourth of July, he'd heard Deirdre talking to another wife, a stranger, for Christ's sake!

"My Tom used to eat lunch with me every day the first year we were married. It was real cozy. Till the bees came."

"Bees?"

"Bees in the park where we used to eat lunch, and when the weather was fair we might even make love. Roger Williams, near the zoo? The bees scared him away. It's never been the same after."

"Let's go home, Deirdre."

"Don't use my name. I don't want you using my name."

"You're drunk."

"No, I'm not."

"I know you're not. Let's just go home. Maisie's waiting."

"Excuse me," the stranger said, a little late for Tom's taste.

"I'm not sure I don't hate you," Deirdre said, before the stranger walked away.

Tom tried to draw a bead on his wife's point of view. This made him feel punk. So he tried to see things from his point of view, which was a lot easier. He really liked to lie down with Lisa. His point of view. But he didn't want to hurt anyone. That was why he tried to be considerate. For example, one night early in the summer he didn't roll up the driveway till 6:30 in the morning. He didn't want to hurt her with confessions, so he undressed in the car, down to his skivvies, hunched in the car waiting for the paperboy, knocked on the front door reading the headlines, cool as you please.

"Sorry. Locked myself out getting the paper."

Now he lay in bed beside his wife, thinking how to betray her. In fact, he was too tired by Labor Day to puzzle out the logistics of betrayal anymore. He figured that was *tired*.

By then he felt like the butt of a joke. He didn't want to be alone, and not being with Lisa was being alone. Say they'd never met . . . Say what? It was time to get off the dime. That was her phrase. "Get off the dime, Ace." He thought he might cry. He'd caught black cord fever, seemed to spend his life punching the touch-tone. The last time he'd phoned her for a meet she'd been gelid, dense, hard, monosyllabic. He had talked about drugs, and right there at his desk on Fountain Street—did she know the risks he ran!—and even drugs seemed to bore her. He told her he'd heard about new paraphernalia, Apogee, "the Rolls-Royce of bong technology." She didn't even laugh.

"You wouldn't recognize love if it bit your underwear," he said.

"How do you know?"

"Talking to you is like talking to my forearm. You haven't got a serious worry in the world."

"How do you know?"

He told her what his partner had said about parking meters, and he wondered if she was too slow to catch the drift of the parable.

"I know what he meant."

"No: you don't understand." He was afraid he was making her

feel even dopier than he had meant to make her feel when he
wanted to hurt her. What the fuck was going on? He didn't understand much of it. She wasn't a moron; she was bored! How
dare she be bored! She was an enigma.

He said so: "You're an enigma."

"I'm just a waitress, Tom, and I have to get back to work."

"But I want to see you."

"Find someone else."

"See me Monday."

"It's Labor Day. I'm off. I'm leaving town."

"With that shitbird Skippy."

"Tom, I've got to hang up."

"Tuesday?"

"Maybe."

"I'll call you."

"No, I'll call you. I guess I can't call you."

"Call me. At work. Home's fine. Either one. If work doesn't
get me, call me at home."

"Bye, Tom."

"I think I love you."

"Yeah. Ooo-la-la. Bye."

Oh, no! He followed them. He wanted to bust the little fuck's
eyeballs, but the convertible Bug was hers, clean, he had it put
through the computer. He followed them from her apartment
near Thayer Street (he'd never seen it inside), an hour south to
Scarborough State Beach. He staked them out all day, tailed
them to What Ales You in Galilee. Sat in the parking lot, listening to A Roomful of Blues, playing a movie in his revving fancy
(the candy-assed dancers in there wore freebie Moosehead caps),
feeling not a day over eighty. He wanted to kill one of them. He
wanted to dance with Lisa ("bounce," she called it), kiss her tits,
make her smile at him. He fell asleep in the car. A state policeman, young and nervous, woke him Sunday morning, recognized
him, tipped his hat at Tom.

"On a job, sir?"

"Yes," Tom said.

"Tough duty for Labor Day."

"Dark and lonely work, someone's got to do it."

Why couldn't she laugh like that? The state policeman knew Tom was a good guy. Tom had earned good people's respect. Why didn't she see him as he saw himself? What was wrong with her?

No sooner did he find their car back at the state beach than he cobbled together a plan. Tom thought it was a good plan.

So it fell out, bang at noon, that a Cessna swept in low over Scarborough Beach. It trailed a banner: *LISA SEE ME I LOVE YOU TOM*. The first pass, everyone cheered: "Go for it, Tom! He's okay, Lisa!" Lisa laughed out loud, what a hoot! The cop was nuts, but okay. She'd had good times with him, why not have some more?

On the third pass, quite a few people had quit watching the plane.

Fifth pass, it was irritating to have Buffett and the Beach Boys drowned out by that fucking engine.

Tenth: what an asshole! "Lisa! Tom's an asshole! Kiss him off!"

She sure saw their point. Skippy was lying on his hard, tan belly, studying *Car & Driver*. He hadn't noticed the airplane. He was wicked cute, him and his honeybuns. She ran her hand up the inside of his leg, and the minute she touched him she knew she had him hard. That was another thing about the married cop. Lately? Mr. Softie. Not every time, but who needed *that*? Guys like Skippy, you could count on them. She knew it wasn't her, especially. It was her hand. The distinction didn't interest her. She was wet, and she told Skippy what she wanted, and he shrugged, looked at a few more pictures of red sports cars, and took her where she wanted to go, because that was where he wanted to go.

11

▲ ▲ ▲ ▲

THE HIT

DRIVING home, Skippy felt punk. For starters, it was ragweed season, and he couldn't breathe right. His eyes itched, and he wheezed, and Lisa got pissed off when he took hits off his inhaler. Sometimes he wondered whether that girl would stick around for the long haul. Suppose he got sick? Forget sick, how about tap city? If she knew he was broke, would she show him the door? Nah, Lisa was okay, Skippy was down in the dumps because his asthma was acting up, and because he got burned. Ouch! They'd done some world-class fucking behind the dunes at Scarborough Beach, and then they fell asleep, and the sun burned the back of Skippy's knees, don't mention his ass. It was almost worth it; she'd shown him some new moves down there in the hot sand. Tender, was how Skippy put it. Patient. A lot slower than he was used to. He liked what she did, serious and dirty, more like checkers than stickball.

But none of this took away from Skippy's unhappiness when Baby telephoned. They could hear the phone ringing while they parked in front of Lisa's place on Meeting Street. The phone rang and rang. Stopped ringing. Began again. It gave Skippy a sort of a chill. Lisa ran upstairs to answer the call. She hadn't had a bit of good news in her life, if she only knew it, but she always thought this call was The Call. What? Hollywood? Lot-a-Bux sweepstakes? The Queen of England calling to say Lisa didn't just look like Lady Di, she fucking *was*? The phone stopped again, before she got there. Rang again.

Just Baby. He wanted Skippy, no small-talk with cuz. Tomorrow morning, he said, come with him to Logan, a doctor had ordered a new Volvo, half a yard apiece from the middleman.

"It's the day after Labor Day tomorrow. Traffic will be a bitch. The Expressway's torn up. I've got a sunburn. It's killing me. What do you need me for?"

"Company," Baby said. "Advice. Expertise. You got a slim-jim and butterfly. I need your technique. To cover my ass. To drive my junker home."

"I don't know," Skippy said. "I don't need the aggravation. My hands get greasy."

"It's a one-tape job," Baby said. "We'll be listening to Tom Waits side A when we leave Providence, and side B will still be playing when we get home."

"Bullshit," Skippy said.

"It's a chance to pick up some new wheels for yourself. Long-term parking's wall-to-wall Porsche."

This was true. Skippy needed a Porsche. He had been devoting much time lately studying how unfair it was that he didn't own a Porsche.

"If I liberate a car, what'll we do with yours?"

"Dump it. I don't care. I got no sentimental feelings about somebody else's Reliant."

"Okay. I deserve a good car."

"Of course you do."

He'd never seen Baby so squirrelly. Skippy drove, while Baby lay in the back seat, jabbering. He said he was coming down from coke, but Skippy figured speed. Cruising up North Main Street, past the Cheater's Club and What's Your Beef, boss hangouts for someone hunting pussy, Baby's noise hurt Skippy's sunburn. The Reliant's air conditioner was on the fritz, so it was hot and stuffy, difficult to breathe. Swinging off Branch Avenue to 95 north, toward Pawtucket, Baby was in full cry back there, drowning out Waits, "Small Change Got Rained on by His Own .38."

"You know what? You think you know me. You know what? I've greased a guy Not just *a* guy. Guys. You don't believe me? I did it because they asked. The Boss. Not The Boss, exactly, but The Boss, if you see what I mean. I went to his office. Invited. It was like going to the White House, or shooting the bull with the Pope. Would I like some coffee? Polite. Now he didn't ask for the favor personally. That's not how it goes down."

"Tell me about it," Skippy said, bored.

"You know what," Baby said, "you think I'm bullshitting you. You never give me credit, man. It's a mistake to underprice me. I've got weight. You don't know my history. You think you're smart. You don't know shit about me. Let me tell you some things."

Baby told his old friend some things. Skippy drove; Baby talked; Skippy listened, wanting to believe his friend was just bugs, wanting to assume his antenna didn't pull in all the channels. Baby told about a recent trip to New Jersey, how he broke some guy's arms and legs with a pool cue because someone in New Jersey had a daughter whose tits this guy had touched, and her father had a friend on Atwells Avenue. Baby didn't even know the guy's name, the one whose arms and legs got bust up by a pool cue.

Baby told about another guy, just a Providence citizen. This was recent. He was a doctor, and someone in The Office had pulled some sweet moves on him. Told the doctor if he invested a thousand to put out on the street, he'd get back two grand in a month. From someone who didn't report interest income to the IRS. Sawbones invested, sawbones got back his two thousand. Pretty soon the citizen was climbing the walls to invest more. This was just a Ponzi scheme, the oldest sucker game there was. The medico finally came up with two hundred thousand, mortgaged his house, his Bertram, his future. End of the month telephoned someone at The Office to collect his four hundred. He even got through to the exec he wanted. The guy he wanted said: "You wanted to fuck; you got fucked. Don't call me again." The doc called again, talked heavy, talked law. Now Baby was on the case. Put a blow-torch to the surgeon's eyes. Practiced first at home, burning paper.

When Skippy remembered, considered what his boyhood

friend had done, he reminded himself to have a care. Skippy drove slowly. He saw something funny, a man sitting in an MG, dressed for the office, suit and overcoat, hat. Another man, got up like a laborer, pushed the dead MG along the break-down lane, not just a few yards, but far, like he planned to push the rich guy to Boston. Skippy mentioned this drama to his old friend, but Baby was preoccupied with personal history.

He told about his first hit. How he and another knockaround guy ("never mind who") had welded a third person ("the surgeon I was telling about?") inside an oil drum in Barrington, thrown the drum into the Bay, and shot it full of holes while it floated south. ("A dragger recovered the barrel before the peckerhead rotted. I heard he looked like he'd gone through a paper shredder.") Baby said he'd used a Luger 9-mm on that job. ("Boss weapon. Awesome muzzle velocity. Projectiles slid through that oil drum like shit through a sick cat.")

Baby said, speaking of Bertrams, he was kind of a water-sports specialist. The Office had had a beef with a fellow who skimmed some numbers money in Manchester, New Hampshire. The crook felt the wind shift on him, and hid out in Canada for a couple of years. Met a cook in a ski lodge whose dad owned a restaurant on Block Island. Married her. Moved to Block Island to run the restaurant. Modest ambitions, a pipsqueak without a nickname to his name. Easy man to forget. Eight years had gone since the trouble in Manchester. The question on Atwells Avenue was one of credibility, so Baby went out to that island with a guy from The Office. It was October, almost a year ago. Freeze your stones off. Capped him with a .44 magnum, Clint Eastwood weapon. ("Fucking flipped him right over. He was fishing for bass. Tracked him to the water's edge, and he never heard us. Had the wind in his face. Impressive, believe me. Blew him right into the water. I had to check him out. Stuff dollar bills in his openings, like in his mouth and his ears. In his ass even. He wanted money so bad, he got money. I ruint a good pair of shoes. But I made friends. I'm a comer, Skip, a made guy.")

"You know the Moron? Got the schnitz last spring? Yours truly, baby: Baby. Now there was a world-class dipshit."

This was so. Skippy's travels through Providence had brought him together from time to time with the squirt everyone called the Moron. Ugly as a hatful of assholes. Who else would stick up a gas station wearing a shirt with his name monogrammed on the pocket? Who else would rob from two black men at a game of dice ("African golf") what the victims would tell their friends was a "valuable collection" of something, the collection being a first-rate collection of cocaine? Who else would the following evening shotgun that couple of spade coke dealers in a South Providence liquor store, get away clean, and show up when their remains were loaded into the meat wagon to spit on their body bags and curse them ("Hell ain't half full yet, shitbirds!")? Who else would go ape like this in front of thirty, forty Africans, no small amount of niggers, while the cops watched? (No one? Maybe Baby.) There had been talk on the street that the Moron had mouthed off about The Boss, how he might snatch the old geezer, hold him for ransom.

"The night I dropped the dime on the Moron he was raising hell at the Penalty Box. Jesus, Skip, his clothes sense! Karate gear. High-top sneakers. Nunchuks. Some old guy had been blubbering in his beer about how nobody loved him for the real him, and the Moron had driven home in his Charger . . . wouldn't you guess: a Charger? . . . to get the crybaby a pit bull. 'He'll love you. Keep him. From me to you. My dog. He's your dog now.' Oh boy. The dog got snarly, and scared the old guy, and this pissed off the Moron. Moron suddenly yelled: 'I declare KA-RATE!' Cleared out the bar. I'll tell you the truth, Skip, he even scared me. Kicking the drinks off people's tables. Tossing karate stars into the walls. Doing these screwy grunts and chuffs, gross-out! So he cleared this path, just a little bit of an asshole, no more than five-seven, five-eight max. Went out back to relieve himself. So here comes Baby from behind. Hush now. Good night."

Now Baby told how he and another—he named the other—loaded the Moron in the back of the Moron's van. The other man, well-connected (Skippy wished he hadn't heard that exec-utive's name), drove, told Baby to search the body for ID. The driver heard something back there crinkle, a crumpled twenty. ("He could hear the sound of a twenty in the dark, above the noise of the engine. I had to give it to him. Gratitude, huh?") The Moron had made a sighing noise.

"Shut up, you dead fuck," Baby said he said.

Down by the river embankment they had prepared to dump the Moron. It stunk bad in the van. The other guy told Baby it was poop, how they go moolie in their pants when you clip them.

"It only hangs in your nose a couple days. Boil sugar to neutralize the stink. Can't you take it?"

"You kidding?"

The Office bigwig stabbed the Moron in the belly with a boning knife. More than a few stabs.

"What's the point?" Baby had asked. "He's dead."

"He'll rot quicker. The rats'll get to him quicker, and the bugs. He won't float."

This had made Baby figure his accomplice had done this kind of thing before. They hauled the Moron from the van, and dragged him by his legs to the river. Ground zero, downtown Providence. Right in front of a couple courthouses. While they dragged, they grabbed at all the Moron's gold. Chains and bracelets, wherever jewels would fit. Baby told Skippy the Moron's eyes were open, and he grinned this shit-eating grin at them.

"What the fuck you looking at, cocksucker! Who you staring at, Black Belt? Dead fucking black belt asshole!" This is what Baby told Skippy he said to the Moron. Baby said they dumped the Moron in the river, and watched him sink, and saw by lamplight his blood spread like smoke through the dark water. Then they walked away, got a cab to the important man's restaurant, where Baby washed his hands in vinegar, a specific against powder traces. Then they ate hot roast beef sandwiches, Baby said, "with lots of au jus on them."

Five miles south of the Massachusetts line Skippy said, "Why are you telling me this?"

Four miles south of Massachusetts, which was debating the

restoration of the death penalty, Skippy felt the piece kiss the back of his neck, just at his hairline. It figured. You'd never want to grease a friend in Massachusetts; the courts were tougher, and Walpole wasn't a patch on the ACI for comforts.

"Welcome to the last day of the rest of your life," Baby said. "Last hour of the last day, in fact. Last couple of minutes."

Skippy told his old friend to save the chatter, palaver was bush. Now he felt the piece in his ear. Leather gloves! A .45. Trust Baby to go for the big splash. Overkill. Baby mentioned a rest area just up the road. Skippy knew the place. They'd fenced silver there. The pull-off was sheltered by trees from the view of I-95.

"What's the price on me?" Skippy asked.

"Twenty-two fifty."

"You couldn't squeeze them for three K?"

"I'm talking twenty-two dollars fifty cents, Skip. Price of a New York strip and a clear at What's Your Beef. A Ralph Lauren polo shirt, not even. And my beloved ass."

"Why?"

"Why? Because you trusted me, came off with me to cop some wheels, get paid."

"I mean why. Why me? What did I do?"

"Stole the wrong candlesticks, man."

"That was your job! I just went along."

"I know. That's why they asked me to do this, Skippy. We both owe them. I pay this way; you pay that way."

"I'll buy her a set of diamond fucking candlesticks."

A truck downshifted into the pull-off. Skippy looked in the mirror, watched the trucker study a map. The diesel rumbled. Didn't the driver want to stretch his legs? Check out the scene? The truck shuddered, lurched, climbed whining through the gears, past them, around the curve, north, gone.

"Welcome to the last day of the rest of your life."

Skippy figured Baby had rehearsed the speech. He wasn't that smart. Maybe he'd heard it somewhere.

"You've said that before. You're an asshole."

"Who isn't?"

"Yeah. Well, shoot me then."

Baby also said well, and then said he was going to light Skippy up. It was show time. Then he told Skippy a shit-storm was coming. Then he said the shit-train was due any second at Skippy's station. It began to dawn on Skippy that he might not die, that the front of his face might not get painted against the shattered windshield of a Plymouth Reliant this first Tuesday after Labor Day.

"What can I say? I needed candlesticks. It seemed like a good idea at the time."

"I got no choice," Baby said. "They screwed down hard on me."

"Everybody's got a choice," Skippy lied.

"I'm going to shoot now. Should of dumped you last week. I gave you a free week. Who lives forever? I got orders. I got orders about the Moron. I wasn't even mad at him. I done it. I got orders; he got dead."

"So he did," Skippy said.

"I'm going to kill you now."

Skippy thought if someone tells you he's going to kill you, someone maybe doesn't. There were limits. Always. Like Lisa would pass funny tens at the shopping centers, but not twenties. This but not that. Skippy wouldn't hit Baby, for example.

"We go way back," Skippy said.

"Fuck way back, buttwipe. Fuck you!"

"Let me turn off the engine, okay?"

"You're cashing in, man. What do you care about the energy crisis?"

"We go back, Baby."

"Yeah? Then answer me this. I got a question."

"Shoot," Skippy said. Baby didn't laugh.

"In the Saint Joe's game? I was down court, clear. Wide fucking open, man. You passed to Vince. How come? You knew me. Like you say, we go way back, Skippy."

"He scored."

"Why not to me?"

Skippy sighed. He remembered their only bank job, Industrial

National, East Providence branch. Skippy made it to the sidewalk with a gang of greenbacks. Baby was the wheelman and
lookout. Skippy hit the bricks to find Baby pointing his piece at
three passersby lined face to the bank's wall. He was lifting their
wallets. He'd noticed one of the businessmen wearing a tank
watch he admired. Skippy had had to run his terrified ass way
down the road to save it.

"Yeah, I know you."

"Then why?"

"That's why."

"Why?"

"Because I knew you'd choke."

Then, Skippy just opened the car door and climbed out. He
didn't know what to think, that he'd take a round in his back
pocket, maybe. Walked just so, not fast enough to spook Baby,
or slow enough to let him think. He figured Baby to try something fierce, try to run him over. Skippy was halfway across the
median strip. Here came Baby, tearing up the grass, coming at
him, nothing Skippy couldn't dodge.

"Hey, fuck you, Skippy, you're dead meat."

That was it. Not much, really, not much conviction in it. Baby
stopped the car. Skippy was beyond range of anything but a
lucky shot. They looked at each other. Baby shot him the finger
and swung north again on I-95. Skippy wasn't surprised. He
wasn't not surprised. He'd done what was left to do. Baby? He'd
dropped another ball.

Skippy walked south on the highway, his wet briefs chafing
his thighs raw. Then he quit walking. Stuck out his thumb.
Grinned. Got a ride lickety-split.

Now Baby was another story. Before they packed him into the
trunk of that Volvo at Logan they sure must have sent some serious volts through his gourds. He wasn't anything you'd want
your picture taken with. Nobody, not even Ms. Hutchinson of
the *Providence Journal*, would have wanted to see Baby after
they retrieved him from Massachusetts. What Baby looked like
now the cops didn't want to talk about. Oh, did somebody put

his feet in Baby's ass! Munched on that boy. Oh, did they give Baby the natural blues! They didn't leave his engine running. Comer my ass. Has-been and never-was. Goner.

Requiescat in pace, you sorry sack of Canuck shit.

12

▲ ▲ ▲ ▲ ▲

BREAKING IN

NEEDING an expense advance, Skippy decided to do that
house on Benevolent Street he'd tipped over last spring, if he
could recognize it after all this time, three months? There.
Empty driveway: that was good. Maybe the fat cats were
stretching Labor Day weekend. Oh, now we got security, pre-
cautions. Burglar alarm stickers on the windows, most of them
fake, the kind they bought at Benny's when they couldn't hack a
full-dress system. Floodlights, unlit. Citizens lit their yards for a
month or two after they got diddled, till the electric bills pissed
them off or they couldn't sleep with all that light bouncing off
their bedroom walls. Greased sills. (The rain had worn down the
slick; Skippy could tap dance on those sills.) Bars on the windows. (Most of the windows.) There had to be an alarm, but it
wouldn't be sonar: Mine Hosts kept a beast. Deadbolts, natch:
leadpipe cinch for the old Skip. His glass cutter excised a pane
in the Dutch window of that side kitchen door. Reached in—the
key was in the deadbolt lock, as he suspected. Snap. He was in.
Found the security system humming in the front closet, where
he usually found it. Now came a choice. Four numbers, written
on the wall. Dunderheads just wrote out the code, so they
wouldn't forget. Cunning dunderheads wrote it backward.
Skippy remembered the automated teller card he'd lifted from
this place. Backward. He punched in the numbers: 1137, probably a birthdate; it was usually a birthdate; people couldn't remember their anniversaries. Someone had been born November
of 1937.

Now he tensed. This was a silent system, so he had to wait for

the cops, if he had figured the number wrong. Here came the
adrenaline, but he wasn't jumpy. Shit, he about took the whole
shot not twelve hours ago. Stood right up to it, impressed himself. Skippy had this confusion, that because he wasn't scared
crouching at the kitchen door, he was brave.

Waiting, listening for security guards or cops, he heard gar-
gling. The dog. Growling, but without much conviction. There
he was, looking away embarrassed. This time Skippy might have
to kill the pooch; this was Real Life tonight; this had to go
smooth. Big trouble out there for Mr. and Mrs. Carbone's little
boy. Good boy, Fido, wag that tail! Jesus, Skippy *loved* that animal; he'd put that canine in the dog Hall of Fame; that dog was
his friend. So why was Skippy sweating? It was hot, was why.
Skippy heard a sweet loud moan upstairs, a window air conditioner, music to a thief's ears. Except oh-oh, someone was up
there.

In the great harbor of Salt Pond, boats rocked in the gentle
surge. A few halyards rattled against their masts, but Block Island was quiet. The night was warm; a zephyr pushed *Warlock*
from her anchor. Adam slouched against the cockpit coaming,
his arm around Ike. They smelled the mud flats uncovering.

"I always liked low tide best," Adam said. "I like to see what's
under there."

"Not me," Ike said. "I like high tide. It's cleaner then."

Adam watched the anchor lights arc through the clear night
sky. Ike's head was angled higher, at the stars.

"Do you know which stars are which?" he asked his father.

"I used to, I think. My father taught me. From this cockpit. I
should have remembered. Should have taught you."

"Why don't I learn about them, and teach you?"

"I'd like that. Ike, I'm dying."

"What do you mean?"

"I mean, it's time you knew."

"I don't know what you're talking about."

"I'm trying to tell you what I mean."

"Is the tide coming in, Dad?"

"The tide isn't."

It was copacetic. The security system was off. Skippy breezed
through the house, hunting for silver. He needed valuables, easy
to pack and carry, liquid. Ah, *shit!* Where was some stuff? Just a
pissant camera and family junk. The ship models reminded him;
they'd pretty much cleaned out this place. He saw the photographs on the piano, cheap wood frames. He remembered the
picture of that sweet piece of work wearing the bathing suit and
a monster rock on her finger, sticking out her tongue at her kid.
Okay, he'd looked at that picture more than a few times. The
woman was tasty. Well, he'd admit it; he'd come for that, too.
Maybe.

The breeze was dead. Block Island's heaped bluffs were gone, or
there on faith. Clouds rolled in, snuffing the stars. The dinghy
hunted aimlessly on its leash, bumping *Warlock's* transom,
bouncing back. Far off, at the head of the harbor, a man begged
a woman to come below.

"Another thing, when you go to Exeter . . . You'll like Exeter,
good school, better than when I was there, tell your mother
you're glad to be going to Exeter. Anyway, it's important to start
well. First impressions matter. If teachers think you're lazy, or a
wise ass, it's difficult to make them unlearn that. Another thing,
be careful about friends. Don't shun geeks, they are the interesting people, the kids other kids laugh at. Don't be cynical, either,
keep your innocence."

"I don't understand," Ike said.

Adam laughed. "Jesus, I sound like Polonius."

Ike said, "Who is he?"

"Champion adviser."

"I don't understand."

"I don't understand either," Adam said.

"Then why are you telling me?"

"We've got to try to understand."

"I don't want to know this," Ike said.

Adam held his son. His son was stiff in his arms, but his hair smelled like a kid's hair. His son didn't cry. The boy was rigid. Anger? Fear? Don't ask.

Upstairs, behind the shut bedroom door, alone, Clara slept naked, tangled in a sheet.

Downstairs, pacing aimlessly, Skippy had run out of choices. There was nothing left to steal. Skippy didn't like to pace aimlessly. He was a straight-on guy, as drawn to direct paths as piss rattling down a sewer pipe. He climbed the stairs flatfoot, distributing his weight close to the edges. No creaks now. Past the landing; he was deep in. This was a new frontier for Skippy, the upper invasion. He had promised himself, no upper invasions. Well. Now he was there, upstairs. Open door. Kid's room. Red Sox banner on the wall. (Bums!) Celtics banner. (Go, Celts! Who's Number One?) Empty bed. Tidy. Where was the kid? This was a school night. Divorce here? So who was behind that shut door? Daddy or Mommy? Revved as he was, new to this higher altitude of risk, heart whacking his chest, Skippy understood the distinction between a sleeping daddy and a sleeping mommy.

They were below, in their berths. Adam lay on his back, arms tight against his sides, attentive. He held his breath, listening. The air was still. Ike, on his stomach, made a sound Adam couldn't understand. Not weeping. Not snoring. Teeth grinding?

"Ike?"

"Can I sail *Warlock* single-handed?"

"Sure you can. Tomorrow."

"Suppose there's a storm?"

"I'll take charge."

"Suppose you're dead?"

"Ike. I won't be."

"How do you know?"

"I know. Believe me."

"Why should I?"

"Have I ever lied to you?"

"Yes. You didn't tell me you'd die."

"Ike."

"I'm sorry."

"I know you are. So am I."

"I don't believe you."

"Don't believe what?"

"What you told me in the cockpit."

"Ike, listen to me."

"I am listening. What?"

"Ike. Listen."

"What?"

"Ike."

"What? Dad? Are you alive?"

"Sure. I guess."

The dog licked her awake. She heard a wheeze, a thin whistle, slushy inhalations, the sound of slippers shuffling across a polished floor. She saw him right away, backlit against the window. She shut her eyes tight. Couldn't breathe.

Skippy's asthma had kicked up again. He thought he'd like to just clean out the cash and bijoux and burn rubber. Now the fucking dog was rattling its collar, licking her face. Skippy watched. Wisps of hair stuck to her pale shoulder, veiled her flushed cheek, kissed the corner of her lips. She had to be awake now. She was faking sleep. So this was it. Skippy walked to her bedside. Eyes opened wide. Mouth wide. He couldn't let her scream. He slipped the boning knife between her lips, tenderly, didn't want to hurt her. He didn't cut her bad. Just a little nick on her lower lip.

"Okay?"

She nodded. He could see her clearly by a streetlamp's yellow spill. He touched her forehead as another man might comfort a feverish child. She sat up, with the sheet bunched at her throat.

He wanted to put aside the knife, but it was practical to let her terror work for him, so he showed her the knife. It was her knife. She used it to cleave chickens, slice through their bones.

He saw she was beautiful. Total class. Blushing, maybe shy. She licked her dry lips. Nothing cheap, of course, just because they were dry. Still, Skippy hoped she'd do that again. He took a handful of hair. Held it tight. The bedroom door was open, and heat was pumping in, taking hold against the air conditioner. Her face was damp.

She had thought about this, and reminded herself not to look at his face. It annoyed Skippy that she wouldn't look at him. He rubbed the back of his hand against her warm, damp cheek. These were his best moves. They came from the heart. He could smell her sweet breath, he was that close.

"Please," she said, wanting the word back the instant she uttered it. It was just the wrong word.

No, he understood what she meant. "What do you think I am? I'm a thief, lady, not a creep."

The dog wouldn't leave. Sat there happy, watching them, wagging its tail. Skippy was attracted to this lady. Liked her, wanted her to like him. He told her about himself. His philosophy of life, what Dr. John liked to sing: *If I don't do it, somebody else will.* How he had long arms, always popped for the check. Never walked a check, and if he did, left a cash tip, so the help wasn't stiffed. How he was boosting records at Discount in the University Heights Mall, and heard this beautiful classical song, Pablo Casals playing solo Bach partitas, but he didn't know what he was listening to, so he had to ask the clerk, had to buy the thing, for Christ's sake. Had she ever heard that record? So fucking beautiful, he'd send it to her, wait and see, he kept his promises. She'd love it. He'd seen that guy Casals on public TV before he died, an old guy, nothing to look at it. But it didn't matter. The noises he got from that big fiddle.

"You think a thief can't groove on the sunset? You think that, you don't know me, lady. Hey, what's your name? I'm telling you my life story, I don't even know your name."

Clara told him what he wished to know.

"I'm human. I like to ride a waterslide, shop the malls, play miniature golf. I wonder how far away are the stars, just like you. Married?"

Clara told him. She hoped it didn't irritate him that she was married.

"Okay. I can dig marriage, long-term relationships. For instance, once I stole this mailbag . . ."

"Why did you steal it?"

"Huh? Oh, because a uniform left it beside a mailbox for a couple minutes. It was there, you know?"

"Uniform?"

"Mailman, then. Don't interrupt. I'm telling you something. I stole this mailbag: some cash in a few envelopes, a bunch of credit card numbers, a negotiable bond, trash. But there was this letter in there, some chick telling some guy she'd changed her mind. 'If you still love me, write me at this address by the end of the month, and I'll marry you. If I don't hear from you, I'll know I changed my mind too late, and leave you alone. Your move, darling.' What do you think I did with that letter? Most guys would have laughed. I forwarded that letter. I even wrote something on the envelope: 'Write quick, you sap!' I'm not how you think, Clara."

She stared at him. Stared at his knife. He put down the knife. The dog wanted to play. The dog wanted to go out for a walk.

"Get out of here, Bozo," she said. "Get *out!*"

"Don't call me names, bitch. I'm in a funny mood. I was in a situation today. Don't fuck with me."

"The dog," she said. "Bozo."

Skippy was suspicious. He frowned. Then, what the hell, who could make something up so fast? Skippy grinned. Clara did not smile.

"Look," he said. "I like you. A lot." Skippy came down hard on *a lot*. It had done some good work for him in the past, *a lot*. "Just let me kiss you. If you don't like it, I'll take the jewels and things, and split."

Clara didn't shut her eyes. Clara didn't debate her choices. She offered her dry shut lips. Skippy didn't kiss them. He lay

beside her, talking. Told her how he liked to walk in the rain.
How he cried when sad things happened. When a kid died, or an
animal, in the movies. Had she seen *Raging Bull*? How about
Elephant Man? He understood, he thought movies were crap,
too, a waste of valuable time. Anyway, in *Elephant Man* it had
made him cry like a baby when the plug-ugly got hunted down
by a posse of citizens, and trapped in the crapper of some railroad station. "I'm not an animal!"

"That's what the poor guy said, and I felt for him. Raging Bull
said something like that, too. Different doesn't mean bad. Like
I'm not a freak just because I make my living stealing. You understand?"

Clara nodded. She sat with her back against the headboard.
Her fists clenched cramped around the sheet. He rested his head
against her breasts; he must have thought he seemed gentle.

"I make the best spaghetti sauce you ever tasted. No shit. Let
me make you some. Maybe not tonight. I'll send you some.
When I get settled, that's what I'm going to do. You think Paul
Newman makes good spaghetti sauce? Bullshit. Natural tomatoes, that's the secret. No chemicals. Organic. I'm sick of this
life. Who needs it? What do I need? To get found by some
money. Couple hundred a week to pay for clothes and cocaine,
something left over for Happy Hour, get someone to sit on my
face, I'm out of there. I'm entitled, you know? I'm a white man.
Hey, don't look so sore. I've got a rough way of talking, that's
all. No bite, just bark. How about a kiss?"

Clara offered her shut dry lips again. He didn't kiss them
again.

"Don't get me wrong, lady. Clara. I'm not looking to get my
ashes hauled tonight. I just feel friendly about you. Why can't
you feel the same way? Maybe you're scared about herpes.
Everybody is. Jesus, am I? I boil my hands before I beat off! Pardon my French. Have I asked you if you're clean? I trust you.
Trust me. You think I'm going to rape you? Is that what you
think? Let me tell you about rape. Say you're jumping some
broad just under the line, say she's sixteen. Say you're just over
the line, eighteen. That's rape? What: you scared of the knife?

I'm not holding the fucking knife. Suppose another thing. Suppose she lets him kiss her, if he wants to, and then she quits letting him do what he wants to. Piss you off, right?"

Skippy touched her. Not intimately: he touched her as though they were together on a hayride, junior high schoolers, blind dates not quite working out, but what the hell, he retained faint hope, fate had thrown them together. When he touched her gently, she stiffened. Skippy was annoyed now, reached for the knife, tapped its tip against her huge emerald ring.

She misread his meaning, let the sheet go. He blushed.

"Cover yourself. I want that ring."

Clara twisted the ring round and round. It would not slip down her finger. She had read about another woman in this city, a similar dilemma. He had removed her finger. The ring would not slide. He told her to get out of bed. He thought she'd wrap the sheet around herself, but she just got out of bed, bare-ass naked. He didn't give a shit about her anymore. He was a businessman; this was business.

"Don't cut off my finger?"

Jesus, he thought. *Jesus Christ*. Used the terror for leverage.

"Let's go to the bathroom, lady."

She led the way. He opened the medicine cabinet. Bingo! Adam's painkillers. Demerol, Talwin, Dilaudid.

"High times!" Skippy said. "Dillies! Let's get down! Let's party!"

He popped some Demerol, and offered her a couple. She looked so scared. Maybe thought he was about to do some surgery. Wow! There it was, some KY jelly that would grease the fellow down her finger.

But it didn't. Finally, Skippy had to take wire cutters to her square-cut emerald engagement ring, Marguerita Dwyer's ring before Clara's, other Dwyers' before Marguerita's. Manipulating the wire cutters brought them close. Skippy had to touch her. She recoiled like he was a hot wire. It turned him off the way she jerked back from him. He made her wrap herself in a towel. She led him to everything: boss jewels, a Kilim, whatnot. No cards, she said. She was apologetic: they didn't replace them after the last time. He commanded her back in bed. All the time, the dog watched, followed them. He made her sit up in bed, with the sheet gathered again at her neck. He used a pillowcase to carry what she had given him. He put another over her head.

Clara thought: Now. He stood quiet. She said: "I won't call the police."

He said: "I forgot about that."

She heard him cut the phone cord.

He said: "Look, I had no choice. Forget you ever met me. Okay? What the fuck's the matter with you? Can't you even say okay? Okay. We'll do this professional. Don't move. Don't leave that bed. Don't touch that pillowcase. Be good and live a long life, lady. Tomorrow you'll forget you ever met me. You'd better forget you ever met me. I'm going to kill your dog, to show I mean business."

She heard nothing then. She didn't hear him. She didn't hear the dog. She sat still. Her husband and son, home from the sea, found Bozo on the front steps, curled asleep. They found Clara in bed upstairs, the early afternoon light blasting in. The air conditioner hummed its hum. The room was hot and close. Adam saw his wife wrapped in a sheet, with a pillowcase over her head. He shut the door before Ike came in, but Ike saw, too.

An hour later, Adam thought he knew everything. Adam didn't know. Except about someone's whistling wheeze, an asthmatic sibilance. And that Clara stared straight ahead, rocking back and forth. And that she wanted the dog given away, put down, whatever.

13

▲ ▲ ▲ ▲ ▲

BREAKAWAY

S H E telephoned from a pay booth at the International House of Pancakes, a block from her place on Meeting Street. Deirdre answered the phone. Three a.m., Deirdre felt she had an interest to express, prepared to unload a thought or two on the excited young voice down the wire. Tom had promised it was over. Just this morning, at breakfast, he had promised to give her back her life. Tom was as good as his word, before. Deirdre wanted to tell the girl these things.

"Give me your husband. I'm not screwing around. I want Tom. Tell him Lisa."

Tom said what, and heard a mess of words. He nodded, reached for his notebook. Deirdre couldn't believe it. The son of a bitch was pretending to take notes, like he was on the job. Enough of him, his bullshit, the piety. Enough of his fake, cheery questions (*How did it go today? Feeling okay tonight? Hey, good lookin', what you got cookin'?*); tomorrow, the lawyer.

While he dressed, slipped into the shoulder holster, checked the chamber, spun it, his wife stared at him.

"What can I say?" he said.

Deirdre couldn't imagine how to answer a question like that.

Tom was impressed. Here was dread, the bona fide jimjams cowing Miss Trank of metropolitan Providence. Lisa was trembling when he found her in a booth at the IHOP, not even eating strawberry waffles; she had been drinking water and asking for more water. He tried to wrap his arms around her: comfort. She recoiled: smothered.

"That's what pissed them off."

"What?"

"You. Seeing me with you pissed them off. You've got to fix it with them."

"Who?"

She stared at Tom like he was an extraterrestrial, like she'd never noticed before he was a greenhorn off the boat, no spikka too good da ingels.

She'd come home from the Avon, *Last Tango in Paris*, couple of blocks away, the midnight show. Saw from the landing her open door. Thought maybe her boyfriend had forgot to shut the door.

"Skippy?"

"None of your business, officer."

Tom was surprised how neat she kept her apartment. Bed-clothes stretched tight, quilt folded square, dishes put away, trash empty, ashtrays clean. Tom thought of his orderly wife, the life-changing mess waiting at home. No chaos here, no evidence her place had been tossed.

"So what was taken?"

"Nothing. That's what I'm trying to tell you. They sent me a message. They don't like policemen, rollers."

"Who? What message?"

Lisa, at her bureau, back to Tom, responded with a moan of woe. She held a picture frame in her hands, and looked at other pictures, snaps of her with friends and kin, beach shots, party shots, first communion. She turned, gave Tom what she was holding. Tom said oh. It showed her standing with a guy, Tom guessed. Hard to tell, because the picture had been cropped before someone returned it to its frame.

"Skippy?"

"It was Baby."

Someone had cut Baby's head from his body. Someone had also altered every likeness of Lisa, razoring cuts through her cheeks.

"Who did this?" Tom asked.

"Who do you think?" Lisa asked.

"Skippy."

Lisa shook her head. She seemed amazed. "You're a dope," she said. "Just like he said. You really are."

"He's jealous," Tom said.

"Of you?" Lisa said. "Maybe your wife did it."

Tom thought he had let love turn him into a chump. Thought? Knew. What could he do? Then he saw the saddest sight he ever saw. On the kitchen table, his letters to Lisa. Long letters, careful. He'd used a thesaurus, double-checked his spelling, looked up quotes. He'd said things he meant, how he didn't want to be her prison, how he didn't want to be a problem to be overcome, how he wanted to be good for her. He had promised in those letters never again to congest her nights, if she would just be his friend, if she would just ... She could be what she wanted, ladylike or bitchy, jokey or sulky, whatever she wanted. If only he could see her now and then. The letters were stacked, in their envelopes. The topmost envelope had been torn partly open, as though Lisa had had some spare time to check it out before hitting the flicks, but something had distracted her, as though it were too much a pain in the ass to read a love letter. The other envelopes were unopened. Tom did better with his bills, with circulars addressed "Occupant."

Tom felt like the butt of a long joke. How had such a nice little thing turned to such a big awful thing? He didn't want to believe what he believed now.

"Let's go to bed."

Lisa said what. Maybe she hadn't heard right.

"I want to sleep with you."

Lisa stared at him.

Tom said again what he wanted to do with her. He said other things, how he'd protect her, how she shouldn't worry about a thing. How drugs were no sweat. How he'd fix everything for her, unofficially, carefully. No reports would be filed. He knew how to handle things.

"If you knew how to handle things, they wouldn't have sent me this message."

Tom said he wanted to sleep with her, just once more. Now

he was begging. Now she was so pissed off she forgot to feel scared. Oh no. No sir. Not that she thought her body was sacred, or that she believed in love. She'd hang on the crank of a perfect stranger if it seemed like a good idea. But to hear him beg like a TV junkie pleading for skag—wow, what a turnoff!

"Okay," she said, a minus 40 Fahrenheit okay. "Do whatever you want. You've got five minutes."

"Lisa . . ."

"Unbuckle your pants, lieutenant, the meter's running."

"Lisa . . ."

"You've got four and a half minutes to get it hard, husband and father. Wouldn't take Skippy forty-five seconds."

Tom quit begging. He promised to protect her. He told her to phone him anytime. Then he begged again, she had to stay put. Not run away.

"Promise?" Tom asked.

"Sure," Lisa said, looking at a photograph of her smiling face. "I promise."

They busted out of Providence laughing, armed with drugs. Lisa was scared, but hid it. She wasn't a patch on Skippy for scared, but he didn't show it. Hey, life had its sunshine. They'd used up Providence; it wasn't big enough to hold them. They were on the move, no shit.

"I'm going to be special," she said.

"You are, baby."

"Fuck you. Don't call me baby. I'm nobody's baby. Something else, quit saying I'm a good girl."

"Lighten up! I'm one of the good guys, remember? I've got a sneaker for you."

"Okay. Just don't talk to me disrespectful. I won't stay still for talk like that."

Skippy shook his head. Wasn't she a pisser! Sometimes he couldn't help himself, he thought he loved her! Wanted to marry her! He reached into the side pocket of his new suede jacket, felt that monster emerald ring down there, wondered if this was the right time. Squeezed her hand. Pretty soon she squeezed back. Why not let the ring ride?

Oh, speaking of ride! Guess what was carrying them up I-89 to Canada. A Bimmer! Ice blue 321i freeloaded last night from Davol Square, especially for his main squeeze. Red leather seats. Came with Madonna already loaded in the deck, quarters, dimes, and nickels stacked in film canisters to speed their way through toll booths. Whoever had owned this car was Skippy's kind of car owner: he had had his shit in order, didn't have things all raggly-ass. Couldn't hold it against him that he neglected to use his Chapman-Lok the very morning Skippy, needing wheels, happened to cruise Davol Square.

The coins reminded Skippy of his first regular business. Some guy on Federal Hill owned a print shop, kept a boat in Newport. The Newport Bridge tokens were worth a buck each, easy to sell in South County for ninety cents. This guy went through a lot of tokens, more than he needed. He didn't lock his car. (Federal Hill: you know, he was Italian. . . .) Kept his tokens in a film canister, just like this BMW ex-owner. The nice man would buy them ten at a time, and Skippy would steal them six at a time, always leave at least one. It lasted all summer. Skippy imagined the token-supplier scratching his head, blaming his kids, wondering if his wife was cheating on him with someone lived in Newport. Finally, later than you might think, the bell rang, and the fellow locked his car. So Skippy let the air out of the man's tire, right front, always the same tire. The man got a portable tire pump. Skippy ice-picked the tire, right-front. The man must have complained to the cops, who must have laughed. Maybe he tried to complain to The Boss. Whatever, the man who owned the print shop, having replaced a couple of Pirellis, left his car door open, with two tokens on his front seat. Skippy got used to getting those tokens, and the man must have got used to leaving them, till he disappeared. Sold the shop, put Skippy out of the token business, at what? Thirteen?

Bye-bye, New Hampshire! Hi, Vermont. Bound for Montreal. It was easy to disappear in Canada. Lisa had the names of great discos in Montreal, and maybe she'd find a market for a pretty chanteuse who knew some French, but first they had to register the Bimmer, translate it into a legitimate stolen vehicle, get it in Lisa's name. Vermont was laid-back about registrations, as long as you showed up with cash sales tax and a "bill of sale." Lisa's smile wouldn't hurt. Word was the clerks in Montpelier wrote down what you dictated to them, VIN number, serial number, what have you. It was told that they'd sell vanity plates—*STOLEN*—if vanity plates were a driver's wish.

"Let's call it *XRODES*" Lisa said.

"You ought to be a writer," Skippy said. "You got a good imagination. I like it. *XRODES*."

When they got to the DMV, it was closed for lunch.

"Mexico north!" Lisa said.

They headed up Thunder Road to Barre, "Gay Baree" Lisa's brother called it. He worked the marble quarries with a mess of other French Canadians. Gravestones. Lisa wasn't sure about the name of the place he worked, but she was pretty sure she could find him. Pete was a hoot. She thought Pete and Skippy might be crazy about each other. She also thought Pete might know where Baby had disappeared to. Once upon a time her brother and cousin were tight, till Pete got out of Providence. Lisa looked through the phone book for Audette, but no Pete. Fuck him; he was a disagreeable bastard. She and Skippy were hungry. They pulled into the Colonel's, and sucked a couple bowls of weed. Good weed! Chiba pokes a stick at the chow monster; now they scarfed a Banquet Bucket. They drove back toward the State Capitol; next door to Bowl-er-Ama they found a Polynesian motif kind of place. The sign was made out of this bambooey stuff: THE ORIGINAL TAHITI TRADER. Looked good. They checked it out, worked right down the Delicious Specialty Beverage menu: Navy Grog, Pooey-Tooey, Go to Hell Punch, Zombies. Speaking of Zombies! Shitski! They'd forgotten what they'd come for! Now it was after five; the DMV had shut for the night.

Never mind. They had a bouquet of blank credit cards.

Checked into an EconoLodge, smoked some reefer, watched dirty movies on the box. Skippy wanted to try some of the positions they were seeing on *Babylon Pink*, but Lisa was too wasted to figure out where to put her ankles. They took some dillies, and giggled awhile, and then logged great rack time.

Next morning they were an hour north of Montpelier when they remembered again what had brought them to Montpelier. Screw the registration! Skippy was pissed at the hassle, the ceaseless duplicate-triplicate-quadruplicate-sign-here bureaucratic nibshit regulations they threw at you every time you wanted to take a car for a run around the block. He stole a plate off a wrecked Bronco dumped behind a Top-Gas. Who'd miss it? Report it? Look for it? Find it? So Lisa's Bimmer wasn't clean enough to sell. Who was perfect?

Within sight of the Canadian border, they pulled over. Skippy figured they should get rid of their stash. Jesus, they were carrying much good stuff, too much to use in a couple of weeks, let alone a few minutes. The substances Lisa and her boyfriend carried were fun to think about, and lots of fun to use. They didn't hammer you like acid, just smoothed out what was wrinkled. Nice and sneaky. Lisa decided drugs made her feel good, terrific in fact. Healthy and happy. If she had to give up those drugs, she'd probably feel just the same, she thought, healthy and happy. She guessed she was the kind of person who felt good, with or without. Still, throwing away drugs went against Lisa's beliefs. Skippy said this was their "moment of truth." They hugged each other. Fortified themselves with some hash oil. Thought about the movies they'd seen, families escaping Russia, crawling through all that concertina wire to get to some shit creek. On the other side of the creek was America or Switzerland or some other place where everything was Free. They'd dragged their asses through the snow, all that way, and here came soldiers, pulled by these vicious dogs. Now the soldiers saw them, got the machine guns to their shoulders.

"Who needs it?" Skippy asked, gesturing through the smoky passenger compartment toward the Vermont-Canada frontier.

"Where to?" Lisa asked.

"New York," said Skippy.

"You're a genius," said Lisa.

Now, Skippy needed new plastic. At a rest area south of Hart-ford, near a burg called Wallingford, he opened the trunk of the BMW, his office door. There was his police scanner, and such handyman's implements as a slim-jim, glass cutter, bolt-cutter, ring of skeleton keys, key copier, credit card embosser. While Lisa soaked her tootsies in a pond and quacked at ducks, he set his embossing machine on a picnic table, cobbling advantage from thin fucking air. Blanks. Diner's. Carte Blanche. The Great Gold One, Amexco. Easy-peasy. The hard part was dreaming up names. They also had six hundred cash. The Bimmer. Jesus, their wits! What were those worth? And Lisa didn't even know about the ring. Skippy was studying the future of that ring. The future of that ring required Skippy's concentration.

Two hours later, NYC. Left the wheels on the street. Skippy couldn't believe what they got for parking garages! In fact, it sort of pissed off Lisa the way Skippy kept telling her how much less the same thing—an hour parking, a burger, a mimosa—cost "back home." Passing through the Bronx, in fact a little lost, they had had a chance to watch the Sox mishandle the Yankees, but Skippy wouldn't pop for the scalper's price. "Outrageous," Skippy said. To tell the truth, it showed her a side of him she'd never noticed.

On the other hand, here they were, upscale, at the famous Plaza Hotel! Lisa had heard about it from guests at the Biltmore. In fact, she'd dragged Skip to a movie, *Plaza Suite*. It made the Biltmore look pathetic. Their room looked over Central Park, and it had this great old-timey bathtub. Skippy was staring out the window; Lisa, soaking in that tub, could see his face all scrunched up. It was hot out there. Chickies were prancing around in short shorts, and Lisa knew what was on Skippy's mind. Pussy was what. Made her smile. Men were such assholes, such babies.

Looking out the window, thinking, Skippy figured they had about two days, three max, before the reality of their credit situation dawned on the management. What then? He'd worry about then then. For now, he guessed The Boss was not looking for him up and down the corridors of the Plaza Hotel. At least he hoped not. Skippy couldn't believe the fucking pigeons out there. He was checking out the carriages, figured he and Lisa could get a horse ride through the park. He'd seen it in the movies. A couple of swells huddled under a fur blanket, with the snow coming down on them. He'd like that, but forget the snow. It was about a hundred out there. Maybe he'd lay the ring on her then, lock her up. He liked her, even if she acted like a spoiled brat sometimes. He'd almost smacked her face when she bitched about those tickets to the ball game, called him tighter than a ten-year-old. She was coming out of the bath. She looked like a beautiful painting on a record album, all pink and wet, sweaty face, hair long and straight. No shame. Just standing there, smiling at him. Sticking out her tongue. Oh, Lisa! Come here.

Later, after the buggy ride, they ate dinner and drank tasty rum mixtures at Trader Vic's, in the basement of the Plaza. Where were all the poor people? It made that dive back on the Barre-Montpelier Road look pitiful. Skippy and Lisa agreed they were ashamed even to have seen that place on Thunder Road, forget they got shit-faced there. It was hard sometimes to admit their mistakes, but they took it as a sign they were growing up.

Later, after Trader Vic's, they watched television, and fucked each other, and watched television. They kept at it till the last dog was hung. They watched the Zone, and smoked weed. Lisa wanted to watch *Gilligan's Island*, which Skippy thought was dumb. But later, when he watched Tom and Jerry cartoons, she said those were dumb, and left for a walk. It was just after sunrise. Skippy called the house doctor, to have his consciousness altered. Damn straight it was an emergency! Hustle. Then Skippy ordered a monster breakfast, every breakfast thing he had ever wanted, eggs and pancakes, toast and English muffins, ham and sausage and bacon, all three. The Diner's Club would have wanted him to order a big breakfast. A couple hours later, Lisa came back to the room and found a mess. Skippy was wasted on something. He couldn't figure out how to get the room service cart through the narrow door, hadn't heard of retracting table leafs, had figured the way they did it was tip the table forty-five degrees while the plates and platters heaped with unused chow were still on that table. Lisa forgave him; he hadn't had her advantages, spending those nights in the Biltmore, learning the ins and outs of room service.

Later, the maid banged on the door, pushing it against the chain. Some bigwig called from downstairs, asking if they wished to have their room made up, how long did they plan to extend their stay, the rooms were much in demand. Skippy was in her when the nabob telephoned, and he didn't even break the beat. The manager or whatever must have heard something fishy up there, because he pressed Skip hard, what *were* their plans, exactly? It wasn't too cool that Skippy told him none of your fucking pees and ques fuckface. Maybe this bird wouldn't fly. Maybe New York was for after, when Skippy had made a million off his recipe for spaghetti sauce, and Lisa had cut some recordings of standards, like Linda Ronstadt, except Lisa was easier on the eye than Linda. Hey, this wasn't just Lisa's opinion; other people had said so. Of course they were different looking. You couldn't really compare the Jodie Foster/Lady Di look with Linda's. Lisa admitted, it was basically a matter of taste.

Later, lying on his back, Skippy asked if she remembered Mike.

"You mean your brother Mike?"

"Yes."

"You mean Mike who used to plant people?"

"Yes."

"You mean the one who disappeared when we were little?"

"Yes."

"Who went to Atlantic City?"

"Yes. Remember Mike?"
"Nope."

Mike had worked at a Providence funeral home. Moonlighted as
a lugger, carrying people to high-stakes poker games. Did some
debt collection for the winners from the losers, easy-going, like
painting the front of a deadbeat's house a color that deadbeat
might not have chosen for his house, say black. Mike had left for
Atlantic City with a hundred thousand cash, or so the story
went. He was known as a stand-up guy. Went against the con-
ventions of the funeral business. Said "died" instead of "passed
away." Was said to tell widows to save their money, go for the
simple casket, let another sucker pop for bronze. He did all
kinds of favors for people in trouble. For example, it was rumored that when The Boss's people got in trouble holding an
extra stiff, an important dead man, Mike buried that man in the
grave dug for someone's unlamented granddad, and dumped
granddad in the Providence River, where no one was looking for
him even if he did float to the top, which he didn't, because you
could count on Mike.

So Mike showed up in Atlantic City with a hundred K, and
much important goodwill. Christmas and birthdays he telephoned Providence, sometimes sent boxes of grapefruit from
Florida, traded jokes with Skippy on the phone. It hurt Skippy
that Mike had never asked him to Atlantic City to visit, and
sometimes it pissed Skippy off to think why, that maybe his own
brother was ashamed of him. To tell the absolute truth on this,
Skip wasn't one hundred percent sure Mike would pull through
for him, but he was in a jam now, right out of options.

Finding the Bimmer gone ripped it. Skippy and Lisa had
walked their check at the Plaza, traded their clothes for a
shower curtain and electric shoe-shiner. (Skippy had wanted to
rip off the original oil paintings, but Lisa, who knew the hotel
business, said they were repros, worth squat.) They had headed
down Fifth to where they'd left the BMW on Fifty-fifth, and no
more nice ride. In its place was a Sir Speedy delivery van, and

Skippy was just whipping the shit out of its tires, kicking that van to fucking death, when the driver came out, stared, and pulled at his dreadlocks.

"Oh mon," said the Rastafarian. "Please don't."

"Let's split," said Lisa.

They worked up a plan in the Mayflower Coffee Shop. Here was their plan: Lisa would call the cops, and ask if the car had been towed. If the cops said yes, they'd discuss what to do next; if the cops said no, they'd figure out what next.

The cops said call this garage. Lisa called from a pay booth, Avenue of the Americas the street was called. Skippy liked the sound of that name. It was an important street-name. The car was at the garage. Lisa heard voices in the background. Skippy thought license plate; he thought trunk, burglarious tools of the trade; he agreed with Lisa: they were out a car. He phoned the casino where Mike hung out, and got right through to him. Mike sounded weird, like he was putting on an act for someone. Friendly, but not. Skippy hated to say this, but his brother sounded like he was faking affection. That wasn't Mike's way. It made Skippy wonder, but what could he do? Mike said sure, come on down, he'd meet the bus. Mike had also asked Skippy if he needed anything, and when Skippy said no, he was loaded, Mike seemed relieved. That was definitely not the Mike Skippy used to know.

"I stepped on my dick in Providence," Skippy said.

"Yeah," Mike said. Not even a question mark. Talk about jungle drums.

"Well," Skippy said, "how do you feel about that?"

"You're my brother," Mike said.

"Yeah?" Skippy said. "Mike: thanks."

"Yeah," Mike said.

"I'm bringing Lisa," Skippy said.

"Baby's cousin?"

"Sort of."

"The airhead?"

"Come on, Mike."

"There's a bus every hour. I'll be at the station six. If I'm late, wait for me."

"Mike, I've missed you."

"Don't take off. Wait for me."

"Mike, listen . . ." But the operator wanted more coins, and Skippy was tapped.

Mike lived good but tight, in a condo next door to Bally's. You couldn't exactly see the beach, but you could smell it. There was one bedroom, and Lisa and Skippy got a pull-out couch. It wasn't ideal, but they were excited. Up all night gambling, seeing the floor shows with Mike and his lady. Well, not exactly a lady. Even Lisa said Bonnie was a dish, but what a grouch! Wouldn't smile, forget laugh. Even with a snootful, watching Bill Cosby do Fat Albert at The Sands, she looked the other way: out windows, through doors, at other tables, her fingers, people's jewelry. It tickled Skippy to watch Mike's woman looking at somebody's shitty little ring, and then to finger the emerald in his pocket. It almost made him give it to Lisa, so she could blow Mike's girl out of her socks.

Mike had always been close-mouthed, but when Skippy asked what he did to put food on the table, Mike gave his brother such a look!

"Hey," Skippy said. "I've been around. I didn't think you were a brain surgeon, or a corporation lawyer."

Mike looked hard at his little brother. "I'm into debt collection. I make out. Not great, but okay. I've got respect in this town."

Skippy wasn't stupid. He caught his brother's drift. "I don't want to piss in your soup, Mike."

"Don't worry," Mike said, "I won't let you."

Frankly, Skippy and Lisa got loaded that first night there. Between the coke, the reefer, and the booze, it got sloppy. Here's how sloppy: Mike introduced to Skippy and Lisa his boss, a man about fifty, maybe sixty. Whatever. Older. Believe it or not, this guy Mike called Joseph Somebody from Philly actually said to Skippy and Lisa:

"My friends call me Dago Joe."

And Skippy actually said: "Put her there, Dago Joe. Call me Guinea Skip."

Now, from Mike, we were talking *looks*! Even Mike's pussy got interested. Joseph Somebody studied his palms for quite some time. He looked at Skippy, and put an arm around Mike's little brother, and said:

"You got a nice sense of humor. We all got a good sense of humor. Without it, what have you got, am I right? Of course. You know, I didn't want to meet you. I don't need to meet people. I know people. This is something Mike should think about. And now listen to another thing Joseph wants you to know."

The man named Joseph was looking at Skippy, but he was talking about the person Skippy was thinking about giving a valuable, square-cut gem.

"This is a girl she's got a great built on her, and that's no shit. I'll give her—what is she, a Lisa? I'll give your Lisa five hundred dollars in cash bills to look at her tits."

"Say what?" Skippy said. How did they operate down here? Did you lose loved ones in card games, use them to pay debts, give gifts? "Listen to me," Skippy said. "Where I come from . . ."

Mike laid his hand on his brother's hand. Lisa was what? Grinning! Unbuttoning. Right now, the top of her dress. There they were, right there. Joseph Whoever looked at them. A long look, but not so long you'd have to call it fascinated. Maybe respectful was the word. Now Mr. Joseph My-Friends-Call-Me-Dago-Joe was peeling bills off a roll. The money had just materialized, like it was part of the man's hand. The moneyclip was gold, with a happy-face of bitty diamonds. He gave the bills to Skippy's fiancée.

"I want to say, it was worth every buck."

"Thanks," said Lisa.

"No," said the guy. "Thank you."

———

So it fell out that Lisa and Skippy became the houseguests in Margate of Joseph Mire, pronounced *meeray*, mispronounced at the mispronouncer's hazard. This house was immense, what filmgoers expected to see in Miami or LA. Rooms for this, rooms for that, rooms for nothing but to take up space. The floors were marble, some of them, or tile, or pale hardwood. The furniture was white, extremely tasteful in its execution, Lisa said. But the standout feature of Mr. Mire's house had to be his collection of pets. There was a white poodle he said ran off with Mrs. Mire's diaphragm a year ago, and Mrs. Mire was still "out there somewhere" (Mr. Mire pointed past the dark, moonlit lawn, to the seawall, and beyond) looking for it.

"Cuckoo," said Mr. Mire. "My wife was a cuckoo clock." He made a circling motion around his ear: nuts. "She drove me crazy. Not the kind of crazy I like to be drove, either."

Lisa laughed. Mike gave her a look. Skippy was getting fed up with Mike's looks. Mike's Bonnie acted bored, except on those few occasions when Mr. Mire glanced at her before he glanced away from her.

The pets that interested Skippy were the peacocks on Mr. Mire's lawn, the parrot asleep in a cage beside the bar, and an indoor pool filled with goldfish. Huge goldfish, big as trout. Fat, and deep, deep orange.

"Your goldfish are a real trip," Lisa said.

Mike and Bonnie said they were tired, had to get to bed, Mike had early work. Mr. Mire maybe waved them out the door, and maybe didn't notice them leave. It was hard to guess where he was looking.

"They're koi fish, Linda."

"I'm Lisa."

"I'll give you that round. Lisa, I never forget a name."

"What do you mean by 'coy'?" Skippy asked. "They seem to be regular fish, in their attitude is what I mean."

"*Koi* is a Japanese word, Lisa. They're carp."

The host and his guests stood around the pretty pool of tiny mosaic tiles bedded in what seemed to be gold caulking. A fountain jingled water up through ferns, down through clean pink stones. It was like a dream standing there. Where was Providence?

"How about that," said Lisa.

"I know what you mean," said Skippy.

"Here's the real part," said Mr. Mire. "Guess how old they are."

"The fish?" Skippy asked.

"The koi fish, Lisa. How old?"

"Twenty years?" Lisa had a worried face on, like she was writing up a complicated dinner order, was anxious not to fuck up on who wanted to eat what.

"Wrong," said Mr. Mire.

"Let me guess," said Skippy.

"These fish live two hundred years. They cost me how much you think, Lisa?"

"A hundred each?"

"They cost me a thousand each some of them. I got a Jap comes from Princeton, where Princeton University resides, sells me these fish, and takes care of them."

"How do you know," Skippy asked, "some of the fish he sold you aren't a hundred ninety-nine years old?" Skippy laughed. He had a point there, if he said so himself.

Mr. Mire seemed worried. He looked hard at his fish. "Let me tell you something," he told Skippy. "There are degenerates right here in this part of New Jersey who buy these fish and eat them. Cynical people, got no sense of history, serve them to other cynical people at dinner, cold, with mayo. People like that, no vision, deserve to drown. I keep these fish because I want something that will outlast me. I don't keep these fish to laugh at them, or listen to other people laugh at them."

"I'm sorry," Skippy said. "I didn't mean anything."

"I know that," Mr. Mire said.

"I didn't think," Skippy said.

"I know," Mr. Mire said. "You think nothing. You mean nothing. You don't dream."

"Hang on there," Skippy said, and then said nothing.

"I had a dream," Mr. Mire said, looking at Lisa.

"To have something outlast you?" she asked.

"No, honey," Mr. Mire said. "To own a thirty-room beach house, and I do."

Let's face it: they got to stay there because of Lisa. This made Skippy uneasy, even angry. But he felt safe with Mr. Mire. Mr. Mire was something. The Boss would get out of Mr. Mire's way, it seemed to Skippy. He was a gentleman, too. Put no moves on Lisa, just talked sweet to her, and taught her things that bored the shit out of her, things about military conflicts and the history of painting. Cultured? Yes and no: when Skippy asked him if he had Bach's partitas for viola da gamba, Mr. Mire didn't seem to know who the fuck Bach *was*. It made Skippy wonder.

After a time, couple of weeks, hosing up Mr. Mire's cocaine and eating his Philly steak hoagies, charging clothes to him, driving his Seville, in fact freeloading, Skippy wanted to make some dough and clear out with Lisa. He wasn't sure she felt the same, but how she felt wasn't the point.

He walked the Steel Pier with Mike, and told him how he felt. Mike told him he was lucky Mr. Mire didn't dislike him.

"He likes Lisa."

"Whoever."

Skippy asked Mike for a stake. He wanted to go into business, spaghetti sauce. He didn't need much to get over. Mike looked at his little brother like Skippy had said he wanted to borrow a moon rocket for the weekend.

"What, spaghetti sauce? Jesus, you know anything? *Anything!* What are you saying? Borrow from me. What you think I got? I'm a working stiff."

"The hundred grand . . ."

"Bullshit the hundred grand. Gone."

"You got that condo . . ."

Mike bought some taffy. Led Skippy to the edge of the pier. They watched the waves break against barnacled pilings. The rollers drove in from some storm way offshore, hurricane for all they knew, and snaked through the hidden supports down there. It was sinister. Mike offered his little brother some taffy. Skippy remembered way back, when he'd stolen that book from that deserted house, the book about the Great Hurricane of 1938. How he thought he'd go to hell. How he finally screwed up courage to tell his big brother. How Mike came through for him, absolved him, gave him the whole rigmarole, the whole nine yards of confession and absolution, and fed him candy in communion with the spirit and flesh of their Savior. Some savior.

"I rent the condo. Or Mr. Mire rents it for me. Bonnie? He rents her for me, until he decides again he's rented her for himself, again. Let's say Mr. Mire rents me, you get what I'm saying? I don't belong to myself."

"Mike, you had a hundred grand."

"I did. Then was then; now is now." Mike rolled up his sleeves. The wind whipped them. Skippy shivered. "I wasn't prudent." Mike tapped inside his left elbow with his right fingers, as though he were working a bad vein. Skippy saw what he saw. "Hey, here's my Keogh Plan." Inside his right elbow, same sorry sight. "And here's my condo by the beach. So you see, I won't be investing in the spaghetti sauce business. I haven't got the talent. Now Mr. Mire, he invests. He's as patient as Chase Manhattan, more. Until he isn't. That's where I come in. And where he tells me to go in, I go in. Right up their assholes, if that's where Mr. Mire urges me to visit. What do you think goes on down here in the world? Fifty percent return on a thirty-second investment? You got debts. Debts are a serious concept, Skippy. Be a serious boy. Pay your debts. You're the kind of guy comes to town, hits the roulette table at Caesar's, before the wheel spins says *What do I owe? How much did I lose? Can I play some more? Gimme credit?* Never borrow what you can't afford to pay. Water over your head? Too deep for swimming, no shit, Skip. You're not the tallest guy I ever met, no disrespect intended. You're a little guy. Act your size, Skippy, it's better that way. Now I got to go, check my traps."

"Hey, fuck you, Mike! Hey, brother, thanks. You junkie fuck! Hey, don't walk away from me. Who the fuck you think you're walking away from? You *shrug* at me, junkie. Shame on you, you fuck. Hey, Mike! Wait till Mom hears. I'm going to tell Mom, big Mike, the standup guy, like a son to The Boss. My ass!"

But Mike was gone, and the waves smothered his little brother's angry sorrow, as well as the holiday shrieks of sightseers, who gave this distraught young man a wide berth. So when he turned his attention to strangers passing this way and that in rolling chairs, asking them collectively what the fuck they thought they were staring at, no reasonable response could be imagined. The Steel Pier at Atlantic City had weathered graver blows than Skippy Carbone's disappointment in his brother's opinion of him.

That night they were alone in the big house, and wandered from room to room. Lisa gave Skippy Mr. Mire's cocaine. It was the night of the Miss America Pageant, and they watched it on television, looking for Mr. Mire beside the runway, wondering if he bothered to peek up the contestants' skirts. They quarreled about the Pageant: Skippy figured it was fixed; somebody fucked somebody, and one of those somebodies became Miss America.

"I could be one," Lisa said, and Skippy believed her. She was great-looking, and how about her voice? But Lisa wouldn't know how to put in a fix, everything was rigged. "Bullshit," Lisa said. "You're like he said, cynical."

"Remember the Magnum P.I. Lookalike Contest, out at the Midland Mall? Who won? Who should have?"

"That was different. Rhode Island's bush. Providence is. Everything's fixed."

"Truth is, baby, everything's Providence."

"I said I didn't want you to call me baby."

"He calls you honey."

"You're pissing me off. Also, I'm sick of hearing about *knockers* on *trim*. And don't pick your teeth."

Skippy thought about the ring. "I got something I want to give you," Skippy said.

Lisa pouted. "What?"

Skippy whispered what. They did it right there on the floor, with the poodle watching, as usual, those almost immortal Japanese fish, with the parrot watching them, jabbering criticism, or so it seemed.

After, they made mimosas with Dom Perignon and Minute Maid, garnished with jarred sweet cherries. Lisa said the cherry syrup was slurpy, but Skippy was busy angling for *koi* fish with a safety pin on a string, smoked salmon for bait. Then Lisa teased the parrot. The parrot made noises, the illusion of anger.

"I've got this parrot in my pocket," Lisa said. She tried to stroke the bird's head, but it struck at her with its beak. "This parrot likes me. I can tell."

"Be careful," Skippy said. "Fucker can take off your finger."

"This parrot adores me." The bird bit her, and she looked at her bloody finger in amazement. "Look what you've done now," Lisa said. I used to be able to roll out a lid faster than anyone, and now I'm handicapped." The blood was dripping on the white wood floor, and Skippy just watched, let her ride the wave right up on the rocks, if that was where she wanted to go. The parrot was nervous, prancing in its cage, spitting at her. Lisa took a fire poker from beside the marble mantel, and jabbed it into the cage, again and again. "You asshole," she said, "come here. I used to like you. Now I don't. When you've been dumped by Lisa, you've been dumped by somebody."

Listening to the Eagles, "Desperados" and "On the Border," she finished the parrot's own stab at immortality. Skippy watched. The way he saw it, everything that happened was destined to happen.

Next day was payday for the night before. For a man pissed off, Mr. Mire kept his cool. And why not? Cool was something you had if you had the wherewithal to have it. He didn't say, *I'll bust your fucking eyeballs.* He didn't even ask which of them iced the bird. First thing, he called Skippy to the telephone in his "library." (Leather books on the shelves.)

"We'd like the candlesticks," the voice said.

"They've been melted down."

"Then we'd like you."

"What if I say you can't have me?"

"What do you think? You're washed up."

Except the voice said *warshed*, which was how they said that word in Providence. When Skippy hung up, he looked at Mr. Mire, who was sitting beside Lisa, holding her hand like she was his daughter. Mr. Mire was telling Lisa about her cousin Baby, and what they found when they found her cousin. How they found his head in the trunk of a Volvo belonged to a professor at MIT. How that was all they'd found, so far. How there were nails in Baby's head, probably from a nail gun, maybe a hammer. How Baby's eyes were gone. What had happened was somebody had sewn Baby's eyelids shut over a couple cockroaches.

While Mr. Mire told Lisa about the end of her best-known cousin, she stared hard at the hand holding her hand, as though she were studying her hole cards. She said: "It wasn't even a clean knockoff."

Mr. Mire agreed that was so. "Death is a mess, honey. And I'm not even talking about my pet. I'm talking in general. If it can be done clean, so much the better. What do you think?"

This was Skippy he was asking. Skippy was at a loss for words.

"Lisa," Mr. Mire said, "your friend is in an almost death situation. I leave it to you young people to decide. But if I had been born in Providence, like your friend, I'd go home to Providence. Why don't you talk it over. And take the shoe-shine machine, son. There's nothing hot in this house, except this pretty thing."

Mr. Mire let Lisa drive Skippy to the bus station. Crying wasn't her thing, so she didn't.

"He'll take care of you, baby."

"For a while," she said.

"No, he's hot for you."

"A little. I'm a va-voom. He's looking for a va-va-voom."

Lisa! Skippy felt so choked up he almost gave her the ring.

14

▲ ▲ ▲ ▲ ▲

HOMECOMING

TRAVELING light was Skippy's way, so how come he'd already busted a sweat humping his grip across the bus station waiting room? The electric shoe-shiner was why, a hefty bit of business, a keepsake from his holiday with Lisa. Call him romantic, but a fool he was not. For example, that abba-dabba pretending to talk into the pay phone? He was calculating whether the appliance stretching the recent arrival's arm was worth a mugging. Skippy gave the dinge a look, and the kid wandered away like a rain-soaked black cat. Welcome home.

Skippy made his way from streetlamp to streetlamp, past the Fountain Street station to the Marriott, at the frontier of Federal Hill. Used to hunt beaver here. Was a loud laugher, noisy singer, sharp dresser, heavy tipper. Was a wise guy, memorable gross-out artist. ("As long as I have a face, darling, you have a seat.") Was known. Why hide? Why try? He checked in, cash deposit, gave his name, printed it on the register with precision, the kind of penmanship only the Jesuits taught these days: SKIPPY CARBONE. Address? "The Marriott Hotel."

The next morning (what do you know, alive) he bought an ad at the *ProJo's* classified desk. This was for the Op-Obit page, a *Journal* institution. On the anniversary of a departed beloved's going hence, or maybe the day of his coming-hither, bereaved survivors might run a memorial an inch or two wide and long, sometimes with a photograph, often with a message of regret, maybe even a poem. Skippy gave the clerk a picture-booth snapshot of himself ("My twin brother," he told the puzzled woman), and asked that it run with a short message, tomorrow only:

I'm home. I won't run. I'm not carrying. When I was a kid you called me a doozy. You said don't be scared, how you liked me. Everybody knows you mean what you say. I figured you meant bulletproof. I'm sorry about the candleholders. Skippy Carbone, the baker's boy, Mike's baby brother.

After all, hadn't He used an advertisement in this very periodical to clear confusion about His guilt and innocence? In fact, that ad gave Skippy the idea, not that he couldn't have thought it up on his own.

Well, that day he slept, and that night he ate dinner on the Hill, the Villa Rosa, across the street from His office. If he said he enjoyed his fried smelt, his scampi fra diavolo, his zabaglione, his half bottle of Sangue di Guida, Skippy would be telling a lie. If he said what was the worst, it was the ache at the base of his neck, from bunching those shoulder muscles, waiting for the blast. After dinner, he slept like he'd gone twelve rounds with a pro. But by God he slept, give him that. No downers, either, no dope, just the machinery he brought into the world twenty-some years ago. Boy, for someone so young, he sure felt old.

Next night, same place, Villa Rosa. People he knew—waiters, busboys, bartender, couple of customers—went way too far to treat him like always. Frankly, this gave Skippy the creeps. This restaurant had a history of people acting like nothing bad was going down when a shit tornado was blowing through the dining room.

Glancing around, listening to the warm buzz of talk, a stranger would think, "Here's an okay place." First-rate food, no bogus fountains or plaster statues, nothing but Ol' Blue Eyes on the juke, a plaque of Bambi set above the bar. The plaque should have memorialized bystanders with their fingers in their ears, or their hands covering their eyes, or the remains of Johnny "Frog" Ducato, who came in during the dinner hour drunk and spilled a drink on somebody who didn't want a drink spilled on him. Next fact about Frog, he had powder burns on his face, and the management was covering its front window with a black drape to deny the inquiring glances of passersby. It happened right over there, first table in from the bar. At first the bartender said the shooter was wearing a ski mask, but who believed that? For sure, there were five hollow-point .38s in Frog's upper body areas, and no shell casings, because of course the stranger used a revolver. Nobody saw it happen, whatever "it" was. The bartender gave the police a statement, and repeated it verbatim for reporters:

"I dove to the floor when I heard the first bang. I didn't see anything. I have deafened my ears to talk about the alleged incident. I never knew what happened, and I have forgotten everything."

That messy outburst of pique won Villa Rosa good business from tourists, but it was said to have perturbed the elders of the neighborhood. This history of rumored disapproval had in truth brought Skippy to the restaurant. Perhaps he hoped the people he had known all his life, and didn't a bit know, might become accustomed to seeing him alive, might come to cherish the phenomenon of a breathing, eating, drinking, moving, heart-beating, walking-around Skippy Carbone. Well, why not? Who the fuck knew *what* made them happy, or sad?

Nine-thirty. The chatter diminished, hissing, like a rain-smothered fire. Skippy was cutting a tiny piece of veal into tinier pieces. His mouth was dry, his face hot. His tie was pulled too tight, but he couldn't loosen it. Had to look good. There the man was. An out-of-towner, what could be worse? Okay. Skippy concentrated on doing this right; he put his hands beside his plate, palms down just so, no hint of supplication.

"Where's the asshole?" the man asked, looking directly at the asshole.

People gestured with their heads. No one, not even a tourist, could feel bewilderment at the man's meaning or intention. Skippy held his hands quiet, did not put them in front of his face. Neither did he say "please," or "don't."

The torpedo was slender, stout, short, six-six, mustached, clean-shaven. At such moments, maybe people truly don't notice the auxiliary details. The killer said, to the room:

"Watch."

The diners obeyed. He removed the piece from a shoulder holster, and aimed it at Skippy, and uttered an uninflected valediction:

"Happy trails, Buckaroo."

And then the man shot Skippy in the face, emptied a water pistol brimming with piss. So Skippy lived, sort of.

Woe was Skippy. Two hours later, Lieutenant Cocoran was at his hotel door. Couple seconds after that, Skippy was face down on an acrylic carpet, hands cuffed behind his back, the uncomfortable way to have them cuffed.

"I've come to do you a kindness," the policeman said.

"Thanks," Skippy said. "I can tell."

"Actually, I want you to do me a service."

"Officer, how can I refuse?"

"You can't."

First, Tom ran him down the road, pulled his string, said Skippy had no options, he was walking around dead. Said he wanted a clear conscience if he picked up the paper and learned they had found Skippy in the trunk of a car parked long-term at Logan.

"Uh-huh," Skippy said. "You trying to flip me?"

"I'd appreciate your cooperation."

"Fuck you," Skippy said. "I don't roll over."

A revolver was a heavy weapon. If it were swung right, a standing man would crawl. First, though, Tom had to haul Skippy to his feet, so he could knock him down. Then he dry-fired the revolver behind Skippy's ear, a serious life-changer. He wished to make an impression on Lisa's boyfriend, and he did.

"You whacked Baby. Where's Baby's cousin?"

"Elsewhere."

"Is she alive?"

"Is she ever!"

"You think you grease Baby and skate? You think a hit like that you get for free? Listen to me, asshole . . ."

"Why does everyone have to call me an asshole tonight?"

"You know what a fitch is?" Tom asked. "Let me tell you, it's an animal; I'll give you nature in fucking tooth and claw. A fitch bites through the spines of more animals than it wants just now to eat, so it can eat them later, when it feels hungry again. You got your spine nipped by a fitch tonight at dinner. You smart enough to follow what I'm saying?"

"Who's Baby?"

"I want Lisa's whereabouts. I can get you in the Program."

"What fucking program?"

"Work release. Federal Witness Protection. Whatever."

"Oh boy," Skippy said.

"I can get you favorable disposition from the DA—you need a friend at the office."

"I don't do business."

"Business. I'll give you the fucking business." Then Tom did some things to Skippy. Then he orated an Irish proverb: *If the stone strikes the egg, alas for the egg; if the egg strikes the stone, alas for the egg.* Then he fell back on the most time-honored of feckless auguries: "Steel chateau for you, son. You'll go to the joint, do a dime to fifteen straight up, year for year. I'll hang Baby's demise on you. It'll stick. At the ACI I know hacks they'll poke into your anus with a flashlight looking for contraband. That's just day one, Orientation Day. Think about later. Did I say later? Did I say fifteen years? What years? You won't live fifteen hours. They'll take you out."

"You know what?" Skippy asked Tom. "I'm tired, I'm sick of guys telling me I'm running out of luck, out of time. I've seen this movie. I can stand up to a trimming. We got no business together."

Then Tom said Skippy would fall, do a full face-plant. Skippy said he'd get right into Tom's face, and eat his fucking lunch. And so it went, back and forth, strophe/antistrophe, like their parts had been written for them, and neither would exercise what choice might be left to him, and walk out of that movie, that role, that hotel room. So Tom busted Skippy for the Baby thing. Pushing him through the Marriott lobby, he asked one last time where was Lisa.

"Gee, Lieutenant Cocoran, gonzo. Hasn't she sent a forwarding address? I *am* surprised. Is it true what she tells everybody, you got boner problems? Lieutenant Softie? The cunt-struck cop on the pad? Softie the Clown?"

In the Marriott lobby!

At the Station, Tom was cuffing him with the iron claw to the bars of his cell, hands stretched way high. Torture didn't cut it those enlightened days, so a brother officer saved Tom from himself, for the time being.

"This isn't like you, Tom! Cool it."

"Oh Tom," Skippy said, "why this just isn't you! Sure it is. I've had your number right from Jump Street."

Tom was a sport, allowed Skippy *two* calls, gave him a couple dimes even. Number one, a counselor who had enjoyed good word of mouth the past few months, the gent defending Hizzoner, that man had to know a thing or two. Number two, Skippy gave a little buzz to *The Providence Journal*, city desk, a cryptic message for Ms. Hutchinson, something about a police officer, the Fountain Street evidence room, and cocaine.

Woe was Tom.

15

▲ ▲ ▲ ▲ ▲

PRISONS

CLARA? Imagine: who picked up her tab? Woe was Clara, verily. She was in mourning, and Adam was still alive, as it were. Was it prodigal, self-indulgent, that she believed the better part of her might as well have been buried the morning after her night hours alone with the Goblin? Adam wouldn't give up asking, until he gave up asking, *What did he do to you? What happened?*

What happened? She had eaten take-out egg rolls and mooshu pork the night the Goblin came, and that was all the Chinese food Clara would ever eat. When she crawled from her bed, she scoured the walls, sent the curtains to be cleaned, burned her sheets. Now, weeks later, she was belligerent, afraid of every stranger and many friends. She hated randomly. Walking, she swiveled her head side to side, deliberately, like a submariner manipulating a periscope. Experts cautioned potential victims of street crime to walk "naturally"; to seem stiff or off balance, uncoordinated, like Clara, was to invite trouble, to present a sick fish to a shark. But what could she do? She kept her ears on, fine tuned every street vibe, pulling in static, distortion, general menace. Her best friend got a crooked look.

Unreasonable? Of course. How about the unreasonable, the unjust imbalance of consequence and attention? "Tomorrow you'll forget you ever met me?" Did the Goblin believe that? Of course: for him, an evening at the office; for her, a new life; it meant nothing to him, less to Adam than to her, she believed.

Worst of all . . . She didn't really know what was worst of all.

Probably that she got no rest. The blazing bedroom lights barred sleep, for Adam, too. She couldn't help that. She knew she was selfish. Adam's meter was ticking; to affect trust, she would put her ear to his chest (bonier now), listen to his heart tick quieter every night. Clara knew that when he went she would lose him; he would lose everyone. And now? He puked bile, refused to burden her with the choices before him: to have himself bombed with gamma rays, and probably go blind, and surely die. Or not. On the other hand, he submitted to a marrow harvest; they took his marrow when it was good marrow, mezzo-mezzo marrow, to return it when it got worse. He wouldn't break, wouldn't even bend. Well, just once, when he said with almost human self-pity that he was running on empty. She needed no reminding, yet here she was, almost out of time with him, idling in neutral, racing in *park*.

Still, she couldn't help it, couldn't endure the dark, wouldn't sleep alone. She wouldn't go to the bathroom alone, until Adam had a locksmith come—the third locksmith; Clara didn't like the faces of the first two—and make over the bathroom into a harbor of refuge. Steel door opened out; triple, interlocking, Medeco Bodyguard deadbolt, anti-jimmy bar, telephone and siren in there. She decided against a peephole; despite assurances to the contrary, she wouldn't believe the Goblin couldn't see in from his side of the door. Closed circuit television? Clara refused to see what was out there roaming that lost continent. Panic button? She knew she'd push it, lock it like a bad dream shriek, till she woke up and died. Well. Try on her skin for fit. The first couple of weeks, she had the bathroom locks changed every five days. She knew he'd come back. He'd said he would kill the dog, and he didn't. He'd come back to finish. Clara tried to think Goblin thoughts. He must know her comings and goings; he had her timed. She made Adam buy a second car, a dummy to leave in the driveway. She made Adam give away the dog. The dog knew too much. Suppose the alien who broke in set the house on fire? In the game of hide and seek, "home" was the safe base. Was. She thought to booby-trap the house, but settled for more alarms. "Living" on Benevolent Street after the night of the Goblin was living in a cage.

The shame of helplessness! The shame manured rage, which grew in her now with tropical velocity. Adam felt helpless, of course, jammed up; his anger was inquisitive; he wondered what to do. After the car was taken in the first break, his insurance had been "nonrenewed," and this worried him more than the more complex reality that he had owned some things and owned them no more, and the replacements for those things gave him no pleasure. He wondered if leukemia or a simple nighttime burglary had made him believe he would never again laugh a belly laugh, grin, wink. Now he wondered if anything he owned would be where he left it: would he return to wherever from wherever to find his raincoat, umbrella, dog, wife—any benighted thing he had ever had?

He acted responsibly, with foresight. Obliged Ike to carry mug money, ten dollars to give to anyone who asked for anything. Clara? It was difficult for Adam to put a rope around what made sense. Of course, she was obsessed with crime. Of course she was. Early in the school year she hauled her students to district and superior courts, so they would see the system at work, she said, so they could see her husband work inside the system, she said, so they could feel with her the blood-smutched miscarriage of the system, she admitted. She taught history, the principal reminded her; were not lessons in civics best left to those trained to teach them, those less likely to confuse, even frighten, the children? She avowed (too loudly, the principal later explained to the school's trustees) that she had been trained by experts, by a Goblin, by her own husband.

Her leave of absence worked a financial hardship on the Dwyers. Not for now; Adam was raking it in. But for the future, for Clara's. Now she devoted part of every weekday morning to *People's Court*, Judge Wapner's televised essay into justice in a make-believe small claims court. Did the neighbor's dog maul the Rodriguez's part-Persian cat? Judgment for the plaintiff,

$75. Did defendant have cause to prune the limb from plaintiff's avocado tree, dropping fruit into defendant's swimming pool? Not on your life. Did the car wash cause the Thunderbird's new paint to blister? Photographic evidence seemed in conflict with the complainant's assertions.

Clara retailed the cases to Ike when he came home those first couple of weekends from Exeter, before it was thought better that he visit his uncle instead; her son was bewildered.

"Your father will explain at dinner. He knows the ins and outs of justice."

So Adam would hear the truncated narratives, their squalid torts and graceless judgments, Clara's misapprehensions of law. Imagine an oncologist obliged to hear in detail why a diet of berries and rough roots, taken with weekly highly colonic irrigation, was a sovereign remedy for leukemia, which was merely a malaise of the mind and bowels.

Clara busied herself, when she wasn't paralyzed by terror, with public lectures by criminologists and philosophers of violence. Professor H. S. spoke with feeling at Brown about the thing called "The Happy Prisoner." The Visiting Professor explained a "curious paradox" of violence: that it at once heightened and deadened the "feelings" of the criminal.

Clara asked, conversationally, "Huh?"

Students sitting nearby stared at her.

In prison, the Professor explained, birds "sing behind their bars." The allusion may have been to *Lear* or to Solzhenitsyn's gulags; Clara had missed a couple of transitions. "Of course," observed the Professor, "prisons have their own grim realities, but perhaps 'jailbird' points to consolations."

The audience laughed appreciatively. Clara asked, "Huh."

A stern gentleman on the aisle pulled his beard, said "Shhhh."

The Professor wore a brown tweed suit, soft as cashmere. He peered down at Clara through half-glasses. His hair was rich and curly. He was tall. Clara could almost recall a time when she would have admired him. (Last week she got a crush on, maybe fell in love with, the Subway Man who drilled those aliens fundraising with sharpened screwdrivers. She felt they could be sweethearts, him with the gun, her with the locks.)

"The only thing wrong with prison," said the Professor, "is that you cannot lock your door from inside."

Clara, thinking of locks and their ways, began to weep, at first quietly, then not. The Visiting Lecturer, counterfeiting ignorance of this puzzling little disturbance, speculated that throughout history, as many before him had observed, criminals were the "strongest, best, most childlike. Criminals insist on their dreams, come what may," said the Professor. "Was not Christ," inquired the Visitor, "a convicted felon?"

Upon his reference to "negatively privileged logos," Clara Dwyer made a scandal. She offered no counterargument to the Professorial notions; nor did she laugh them away; nor did she leave that lecture hall abruptly, stepping on normal people's feet. She did not call Brown University's guest a "fool." She merely screamed. Later, she explained to Adam and his brother that she had been "practicing."

She made a case for herself as rational. If she scandalized a lecture hall and outraged an audience at Trinity Square Repertory Company, was this not reasonable? The dramatization of Jack Henry Abbott's *In the Belly of the Beast* ("Awesome, brilliant," said the *Times*) rubbed her fur the wrong way. Was it not responsible of her to express her opinion of the play, and its enactment of crimes and punishments?

She was *most* responsible, Clara argued. Civic-minded. She attended meetings of the Neighborhood Crime Watch, the Crime Prevention Coalition, the Greenlight Network. She gave to Ike, meant to distribute extras to his friends, decals picturing McDuff the Crime Dog.

"Did he rape you?" Adam asked, once only.

Clara, see, had shared with Adam the gross outline of her afternoon lesson at the Rape Avoidance Center. Condensed, the advice had been to tell the Goblin she was pregnant, and if that didn't work to tell him she had the curse, and if that didn't work, herpes. If none of these deterred, she might poke her fingers down her throat to make herself vomit; disgust was known as a sometimes efficacious remedy; she could urinate, or defecate. Or, she might submit.

"I counseled deference," Clara told her husband.

Those first weeks after Labor Day circled like wolves biding their feral time. Adam wished time to take its time, but not to drag like this, as though he and she were lambs leashed to a stake, their feet mired in bog, tangling each other in their leashes.

"Clara, it's not your fault. Just now, you're sick, and that's a fact."

"That's a curious observation, coming from you. I'm sorry; I'm sorry. Forgive me, I'm sorry. I'm sorry, Adam. I know how I've been. Such a weight. So awful. And it's winding down for us. I know. It's hideous. I am. Forgive me."

"Of course. We're just victims. Of different diseases. But victims together. I believe that. We're together. Don't you think so?"

"Teach me to believe that."

"I don't know how. We'll get help. Okay?"

"If you want."

"That's what I want."

"Then okay. Help."

So Clara went to a clinic on Angell Street, approved by her group health plan. There was a sign on the front door:

Please don't break in. There's no money here. No drugs. I've taken home the narcotics and prescription pads. So help me God. Be a thoughtful citizen; don't vandalize my office; who will get ahead that way?

Clara did not open that door. But she tried a group therapist, not approved by her health plan. She stayed through a session, came back for another. A woman of Clara's age inhaled an unlit cigarette. Pulling at it without gratification seemed to frustrate the woman. She told the group of half a dozen women about a new weapon developed to trap intruders. It sounded promising.

She had read about it, she said, trying fruitlessly to smoke. (Clara wondered: Why couldn't she simply light the goddamned thing?) It was a concept borrowed from the insect world, the woman explained. Trespassers would be trapped like flies in a spider's web in thick, dense foam, floor to ceiling, triggered by an alarm device. The stuff was slippery—this facet of the stratagem caused the woman to smirk—and of course the bastards would be blinded, "temporarily, of course," she said, laughing too loud. It was a chemical. Polymer foam. It was practical, she said, beyond the blue-sky stage. She could photocopy the article. "This is for real," she said.

"It doesn't seem fair," another woman said. "What happened."

The therapist was a woman, too. Clara listened to her carefully. The therapist spoke of the victim's "second wound," aftershock. The therapist said it might seem perverse to take blame for what happened, to feel guilty, but studies showed it was a healthy response.

"Self-blame can help," she said. "It puts you back in control. See, you *take* responsibility. Try to think you *gave*, he didn't *take*. Am I articulating this? Clara, you seem puzzled."

"I'd sooner be judged by twelve than carried by six," Clara said.

"Pardon?"

"I'm getting a weapon," Clara said. "I'll carry it with me, everywhere I go. I'll set razor wire around the house. Thieves will be given a fair trial, and then shot. Responsibility? I'll take responsibility."

So Clara was sent to Boston, to visit with Asa. After he used the word Adam had used, *victim*, after she declared herself unhappy with that word, and its variants—unfortunate, sufferer, toy of fortune, martyr, loser, cat's-paw, pushover, quarry, game, prey, kill—he spoke straight to her. Asa had been in Vietnam, as he too seldom (in Clara's opinion) tired of recollecting.

"What happened to you, whatever the details, had inevitability. The East Side is a natural target-area. Where else in Providence are there goods worth stealing? It was like watching them walk in mortar rounds on a target over there. First one house, one friend. Then another. Closer, then you. Nothing peculiar about it, mysterious, portentous."

Clara was standing by Asa's bookcase, staring at the spines of several books.

"Everyone speaks in code these days," she said. People don't say what they mean. I don't understand."

"What do you mean?"

"Well, what you were telling Ike when you came for dinner last month. About communications in the emergency room. Secrets."

"Oh, that. Sure. 'Paging Dr. Redman' means there's a bad bleeder. 'Calling Dr. White' is a shock emergency. So what, Clara?"

"So why did you steal these books from your brother? And shelve them together?" Clara brought them to her brother-in-law for his expert opinion. Asa shrugged.

"You're crazy," he said. "I borrowed them. Brothers borrow books."

They were about whales. Picture books, in print, dear, available. Adam had looked for them last week. Adam would have lent them to his brother, or given them. So what frenzy of indifference had caused Asa to take them?

"You must hate him," Clara said. "Why do you hate your brother? Are you keeping a balance sheet on him? Has he fallen behind on his payments? Are you owed? Enough to steal those books? Let me in on the secret you people share."

"What people? For Christ's sake, Clara? What people?"

"Criminals. Who take what they want. Who make me stay home, minding my locks."

"I can't help you," Asa said. "Take the books; I've finished with them. I just wanted to help you. You may need me someday. I'll help. You or Ike. Money. Advice. But I can't help what afflicts you now."

"Or Adam."

"Adam better than you."

"I'm sicker?"

"In a manner of speaking."

"You should be in prison. If the death penalty comes back, you should get it. Ride the lightning, Asa."

"For borrowing books?"

Clara stared at him. Clara nodded. "You know for what."

"For telling Adam he's got it?"

"You know."

"For showing Ike a good time weekends? I know what, Clara?"

"You don't know? I don't know. Where was I?"

"Look, if you want my advice . . ."

"You gave me advice once. You advised me not to marry him."

"You came to me. You didn't want to marry him. He wasn't interesting enough for you. That's what you thought then, and that's what's true now."

"You cause pain. Why did you become a doctor?"

"Not because someone brought me a bird with a broken wing and I fixed it. Not to set a raccoon's mauled paw. Because I looked at my father, and at *him*" (Asa gestured toward his brother's books), "and I wanted something else, to be interesting, like my mother, full of life."

"She was a tosspot, and she's dead."

"She was an interesting drunk."

"Adam fought for blacks, defended . . ."

"Not interesting *did*, interesting *is*."

"Less than kind, less than kin. I hate you."

Asa shrugged. "He bores you."

"You don't know anything. I love him."

"Dying is Adam's class act, his most interesting characteristic, and that's a fact. And you know it's a fact. He's good at it. Chapeaux, Adam! Hate me, fine, don't think you can gull me. All that fine fury? Too little love."

"Do you love anyone?" (Asa shrugged.) "Do you?"

"Ike," Asa said.

"Why?"

"How should I know? I don't know about love. It doesn't interest me. Maybe he reminds me of you."

"So you love me?" (Asa shrugged.) "Do you?" (Asa shrugged.)
"Then do something for me?"

"What do you want from me?"

"A marrow transplant. I read it works, between brothers.
He'd never ask."

"He asked."

"I don't believe you." (Asa shrugged.) "What did you say?"

"That there's no point to it. It's a stop-gap for the other leukemia, chronic. People dying, even Adam, they'll try anything,
if you promise it will make them better. Those promises are lies.
I won't lie to you."

"Lie to me. Please."

Asa shook his head, and shut his eyes as though to hide tears,
which almost came.

When they arraigned Skippy the week of his homecoming, for
the crime of murder in the first degree, he didn't quite sweat it.
He'd seen this courthouse before; look in the second floor crapper, third stall to the left, that was his graffiti above the porce-
lain motorcycle: "Give me librium or give me meth." (He stole
the line, but the other, beside it, was all Skippy: "Smoke a joynt
in here and you'll be in the joynt.") He was on a first-name basis
with the golf-cart paraplegic, a candy-seller, Snap he was called,
who wished all the prisoners well. Snap had a rap: "Be good, be
cool, keep safe." When some out-of-towner thought to rob Snap
couple of years back, that out-of-towner got drowned in bad
luck.

The morning arraignment was just a warm-up act, and Skip
felt loose. Loose might have been his principal problem, when
you stopped to think about it. The fellow's ratiocination was out
of whack, his hold on the quiddities. He was like a person
throwing a light switch just as a volcano erupts, thinking he has
done it. Or maybe better, a person changing another person's
life while his own mind was elsewhere, thinking he hadn't done
it. Cause and effect were just rumors where Skippy dwelled.

But he did know the drill, in and out. Skippy knew his seman-
tics, the distinction between *lawyer* and *attorney*, *burglary* and
robbery. He hadn't boned up on *manslaughter* vs. *murder* (in its
various formulations), because they were out of his depth, beyond his area of specialization. Still, he was dressed nice, jacket
as soft as the seat of a Jag. Designer jeans. A world apart from
that junkie cutting a deal with Judge Ribaud. Rather her
mouthpiece was. Skippy listened from a guarded section of
benches, a kind of corral. If he'd been of an ironic turn of mind,
it might have reminded him of the choir at St. Joe's, where he
didn't sing. Jesus, what bozos, the junkie charged with receiving
was out to lunch before breakfast, stone stoned. Skippy couldn't
help chuckling.

So now Adam, third row back in Courtroom Five, district level,
Ribaud's, finally saw him. Police had invited him to wear
chrome bracelets that clashed with his gold link bracelet. Hundred percent five-percenter, small-timer, dressed in last year's
gray leather jacket, calf, razor-cut hair, dumb superior grin. Be
cool, Adam, eyes front, on the action at the bench.
     Providence, tight as it was, every shyster knew every judge, so
there wasn't much call for the attorney copping a plea for his
client in the spiked heels to retell his life's story to Judge Ribaud, but he did; Milton—Lasky was it?—was cruising on auto-
pilot:
     "Your Honor, I'm a new boy. I've only practiced eighteen
months. That's the truth, year and a half less than fifty. Let's be
reasonable. My client, talking to her is like talking to a wall. She
is not an educated woman, hasn't had your Honor's advantages.
Stand up when I talk to His Honor, show some respect. I'm
sorry, your Honor, but I have to talk that way to my client, she
doesn't have nice manners."

That lawyer wore a rumpled suit, looked like—what do they
call it? Hundred miles of bad road? Hundred and ten? Dirty
shirt collar, frayed edges. Skippy noticed, and looked around for

his own legal counsel, and thought he saw him a few rows back, and grinned at him, and got a look back.

The junkie woman's lawyer was explaining how she was a victim, how the biggest gem guy in the east had stolen a ten-piece flame-stitched pit set ("furniture, your Honor") and hid it in her garage, without her knowing. "She's a lonely woman, your Honor." Skippy couldn't help it, he was interested. Jesus, life could be a lot worse, he could be her.

Now they were talking restitution.

"Where do you work?" asked Judge Ribaud.

"I don't know what you mean. In a laundry once. Shirts."

"And before that?"

"Never since I was born."

"Well, you have to pay back what was stolen."

"I got to do this?" the junkie asked her lawyer.

"This is sending her to the streets, your Honor. She's lonely, do I got to spell it out?"

"A dollar a week, or jail."

"She'll pay, your Honor. I guarantee."

"That's good enough for the State of Rhode Island, Mr. Lasker."

While the clerk called the next case, Lasker, District Court all the way, was inviting Adam to lunch:

"There's a place, tasty fish, unless you'd rather go local. This is a lot of fish, you look hungry, you'll got to get a doggy bag. Sometimes the fish tastes better the next day, and that's a thousand percent right."

Skippy watched the rumpled bozo huddle with his own counselor, Dwyer, got up in Ivy League rags, a bag of bones whose flannel pant hung loose on him. Oh boy, a dieter, bad luck, they were always cranky. Specs with those pink frames, not quite skin-colored. Skippy could sympathize with bad peepers, but how about contacts? Why advertise your weaknesses?

Now Dwyer was shaking his head, smiling, and the two of

them were talking to the arresting officer in the junkie case. Skippy hoped the Ivy Leaguer was thinking the right thoughts, thoughts about how to grease the skids for S. Carbone.

Adam declined the invitation to the fish house. The arresting officer made a lewd gesture with his tongue when the junkie walked past, looking at her feet. Adam hoped she didn't notice.

Lasker said to the cop, "You got no call to treat her bad."

"Is she throwing you one?" the policeman asked the bush-league attorney. "We pinched her real nice. Polite. Put her in the back seat. She says, 'You guys are cute. When this is over, I'll show you a nice time.' Not in my lifetime. Is that your cut?"

The rumpled lawyer looked confused, sort of lost in that place he'd worked most of his life.

"No. She's a poor girl. I waived my end. Her mom and dad tried. She tries. It's a tight family."

Sure, thought the policeman. Of course, thought Adam.

Currently in the pipeline was a Portuguese defendant. Police were explaining a drunk quarrel about something or other. Shotgun. Boom. Skippy had spent the night in the tank with him, never would have figured him for a go-the-distance guy. This was some heaviness, no? Skippy listened up. Charge of murder bore on his own circumstances.

The accused, after a night in the tank, as sick of himself as he was of his dead friend who wasn't dead before the accused got sick of him, terrified, thought he might as well plead guilty. Only about twenty people saw that shotgun go boom.

"I done it."

Trust a fucking guido to blurt out "I done it." Your Portugee element couldn't pour piss from a boot. Skippy couldn't help himself. He laughed out loud.

What? Adam, not much of a laugher, had to admit that had been an absurd misreading of form. The Public Defenders in the front row were on full alert, waiting for Ribaud's call. "I done it" was not what the game called for. Did a batter tell the umpire the ball that just greased past was a strike? Where was the decorum, the propriety in such a bonehead violation of the game? Not allowed, to plead guilty to a felony. His boy, Skippy Carbone, was laughing out loud.

PD to the rescue! Glancing through the shotgunner's folder. Ribaud was rushing. It was 11:30. Deliberate speed was of the essence, getting through by lunch. Whatever might be deferred, as all was deferred, was not to be deferred into the lunch hour. *I need a conference, your Honor; I'd like to file a motion, your Honor.* Next month, okay; next fall, fine; half an hour from now? Forget it. The process could stretch till the edge of doom, until witnesses wearied of it, police forgot what was what, and couldn't any longer read their arrest notes. But this part better be done by 12:15.

A few words, and it was over. They were leading away the Portuguese, and calling Skippy's name. Show time. Skippy figured bail for a hundred thousand. He figured Jimmy—this little old guy maybe five-foot-five, hundred and twenty, always wore a baseball cap—would go bail for him. Jimmy was legend, the Bondsman. Quick, knew the ropes, wandered the aisles of district and superior courts, scaring up trade. He always went to the wall for Providence clients. He knew they wouldn't jump on him. Because, one, Jimmy had friends up and down town who owed him favors. Because, two, Jimmy ran fast. Jimmy, working on his seventieth birthday, would outrun any person who thought he should run away from a court appearance guaranteed by Jimmy's bond.

Jimmy was in court when Skippy faced the judge. These things were arranged by a glance and a nod. Skippy was glancing, but Jimmy wasn't nodding. Skippy figured, okay, he'd play his hole card. He had squirreled away that emerald ring. Maybe he'd have to let Jimmy hold it. Okay, good, Jimmy's ear was to that Dwyer's mouth.

But till the lawyer spoke up for him, Skippy was on his own. He talked easily with Judge Ribaud, said he had no need of a "PD," wondered whether "CR" might not be "appropriate."

"CR?" asked the Judge.

"You know, conditional release."

"You've got the nomenclature down. At least. Bail is set at sixty thousand dollars."

"Wait a minute," Skippy said. "I got a lawyer in this room."

"You can afford private counsel?" his Honor asked.

This was a delicate moment for Skippy. What was the right answer? Where did the worst trouble lie? Too rich, or too poor?

"What's in your pocket?" His Honor asked.

Skippy looked at Joe College, huddling with a DA and that fucker Tom Cocoran, that would-be fucker, that never-to-fuck-Lisa-again-fucking lieutenant, that crooked cop. The three of them (two wanted to send him away forever, the other was supposed to want to keep him out) were, like, pals! First baseman chatting up a baserunner between pitches, while the ump nodded his head. Adversaries bullshitting about some magazine article, or where to go for legitimate veal, and the accused might have been pardoned for wondering whether some kind of fix was in.

"What's in my pocket?" Skippy said.

(What, in his pocket? He forgot he didn't have drugs there anymore, or his knife, a two-inch cold steel Urban Pal Skinner. He had once had someone else's emerald ring, but not in his pocket, up his ass, and that ring was safe now, squirreled away. In his pocket? Some fake ID and a couple of Polaroids of Lisa, bare-assed in the Plaza, and a picture of his mom and dad and brother. In his pocket? NONE OF YOUR FUCKING BUSINESS, the accused didn't say, his eyes darting toward Dwyer. Don't screw up, the accused said to himself.)

Adam waited for Ribaud to beckon him with his finger, as judges did. *May I have just a word with you*, it meant. There. Adam was on. Don't screw up, he told himself.

"Obviously, your Honor, personal recognizance." Skippy was nodding vigorously, but also keeping his eye on that bondsman, Jimmy, who seemed to be leaving the courtroom. "Ties to the community . . ."

"Bail is set at sixty thousand dollars. Let's eat lunch."

Skippy was led to a holding tank. He figured Jimmy would follow him there, and they'd cut their deal. He waited for Jimmy. Jimmy didn't come. For that matter, neither did Skippy's lawyer, who had smiled and given thumb's-up to this young man charged just now with a murder he had not done. What the fuck?

Before the lunch hour ended, Skippy was handcuffed to a metal ring set in the side panel of a van turning off Pontiac Avenue into the parking lot of Old Max, the prison you see in James Cagney movies, a hulking dungeon built a few years after Lincoln freed the slaves, with granite walls two feet thick, surrounded by fences and wire, watchtowers at the corners. If you asked a kindergartner to draw a prison, he'd give you Old Max. Guys charged with heavy "crimes against the person," or those few sadsacks without bail, got Old Max, the hardest house in the ACI, steel city indeed. Good God, the parking lot was hardass!

WARNING! Area Patrolled by Drug Detection Dogs!

You might as well have been in the Badlands. Ten minutes south of Providence, there wasn't anything to remind a man of New England, of any familiar place. No trees, for example, or grass. This was not in the least like a college campus. A rope slapped forlornly against a flagpole. No flag. Much serious instruction, don't park here, don't park there, either. Gray sky, asphalt, old granite. Remind him: the Plaza Hotel was a what? Atlantic City was where?

This was new to old Skip. This wasn't meant to be. The reception room had a poster with instructions: No keys, paper money, jewels (fat chance!), sneakers . . . And these were for visitors. No need to mention weapons, drugs. "Have You Locked Your Car?" a sign asked. Another time, another place, Skippy would have grinned at that one.

The hacks took over from the cops. Pushed him along gently. Through a metal detector. Into a holding corridor like a lock in a ship canal. Skippy had given a school report on the Panama Canal, and he used to remember best those killer mosquitoes, but now he recollected how the locks worked, how they lowered you by degrees from one sharky sea to another. This was a serious corridor. A guard stared at him from behind thick glass, straight above. Skippy couldn't see the guard, but he had heard about him, looking down, armed. The door at Skippy's back shut. Sliding steel door. They told him it "clanged" shut, but it whispered pneumatically. No need to shout in this place.

But when the door at the other end opened, Skippy heard shouting. From a distance, mind. Ahead was daylight, a tarred perimeter about fifty yards wide. No Man's Land. If you were there, without reason to be there, they'd take you down with deer rifles, from the guard towers. This had more to do with people leaving than with people like Skippy, coming. Still, Skippy moved across this strip with deliberation, not upright enough for a *fuck-you* manner in his walk, not slouchy enough to seem not to care where he found himself that autumn afternoon.

Now he was being processed. The hack wasn't nasty, exactly. He was bored, exactly.

"Now strip. Open the mouth wide. Okay. Raise the arms. Feet. I said feet, Misery! Now, bend over and spread those cheeks; you understand? Okay, that's fine. Good boy. Now step in those shorts, and dress in these clothes. I've seen all I'm paid to see."

Old Max was overcrowded. No: that did not do the circumstance justice. Old Max was barbaric. Every year the Rhode Island Supreme Court threatened to shut it down, turn the inmates out on the street. Hey, had anyone heard about the Eighth Amendment? Cruel and unusual punishment was out. So sayeth the Law. Consider Old Max: a din bin, three tiers of banging metal, blaring television, shouts of unlocated anger. Before today, rats for Skippy were mostly a rumor. I mean, he'd seen mice. But those were rats he was looking at. Right there. Down on the floor it was dank. Up on the third tier, where they took him, thirty degrees hotter. Hot. There was meant to be a fan to circulate that air, but it had fritzed out.

Now he was in a cell with a guy.

"New boys have to double bunk," said his roommate.

Skippy hadn't been to college. He didn't understand about roommates. This one seemed friendly. Maybe he was a homo?

"You're Skippy. We heard you was coming."

Skippy understood how it worked. The Outfit got to some lifer, promised to take care of his wife and kids. In return, the shank; nobody ever had to think again about Skippy Carbone. No death penalty for a lifer doing a guy in a Rhode Island prison. Massachusetts was different, Skippy thought. He wondered if he could get sent instead to Concord, even Walpole. Where the fuck was his fucking lawyer? The lawyer had promised to do what he could. What was this? Like Skippy was some doormat amateur? Some small-change punk didn't know the ropes?

"I got no beef with anybody," Skippy said.

"Hey," said Skippy's roommate. "Hey. What beef?"

Now there was more orientation. The sergeant on Skippy's tier, Block K (at least at Walpole they named them for counties, to make you feel at home), explained how it was. Outside was different from inside. Here was a cosmic ladder, the hierarchy from godhead to pismire. Warden, guards like "yours truly," mobbed up guys. (When The Boss went in the can, there was a riot. The ACI was sealed off, no water, food, communications. No one entered, for sure no one exited. So how was it every morning The Boss checked his stocks in *The Wall Street Journal?*) Safecrackers were high-ups, paperhangers, bank robbers, armed robbers, embezzlers, counterfeiters, and other greedy bastards. You wouldn't find any Orientals in there, but the best prisoners were Puerto Ricans, and next best were negroes. Bottom rung? Harps. Micks tried to tough it out, dumb micks. Even their mutts got sent to the pound. Of course, below the bottom rung were skinners and baby blasters, scum of the scum; the general prison population felt strongly about sex offenders. Their wives and kids were out there, unprotected. Protective custody was for psychos, and unfortunates marked by the Outfit.

"Are you reading me?" the sergeant asked. "Maybe you han-ker for PC?"

A bad criminal was not necessarily a bad prisoner, the non-com explained. The rules of Good Citizenship differed in and out. Out there you might have nailed a guy; in here, if you talked soft and said yessir and went where and when you were asked to go, mommy could send you a television set. There were consolations in here: books from the library, open cell doors, paid labor making picnic benches, manhole covers, or brooms for $1.25 a day. They termed this Creative Use of Leisure Time Under Restrictive Environment. It was a locution prison offi-cials found agreeable. Prison could be agreeable. You could come to like it in here.

"Brooms?" Skippy asked. "So we can make a bundle making brooms outside?"

"We can't have you fellows competing with free world work-ers," the guard said. "I forgot to mention visitors."

"I haven't seen my lawyer yet," Skippy said. "In fact, I didn't even kill the guy."

"Well, I never," said the sergeant. "There's been a dreadful mistake, then?"

Skippy maybe couldn't pronounce *recidivism*, but he knew when his chain was yanked. What had he done to earn such a monster portion of shit?

"I don't belong in Supermax, I'll tell you that much."

"It's 'Old Max,' son. You should know the name of the joint where you do time."

The two men were the same age, about. Skippy hadn't been in the can two hours. Nobody had hurt him. And already he wanted to grease someone. He stood beside the sergeant, look-ing down from on high. They stood on a catwalk shielded by one-way glass. The idea was to see without being seen, but pris-oners could sense motion up there, and some now looked up, and shouted: "Gallery! Gallery!"

"They hate to be watched," the sergeant said. "Who can blame them? Zoo monkeys dislike the cage, and the sightseers. Makes sense to me." The sergeant pointed to irregular brown and black smears, evil action painting. "That's why some of them throw shit at us."

Then the sergeant explained what was done to prisoners who threw shit. Who boiled piss with their immersion heat coils and splashed it on guards. Who cursed them. Who misbehaved. "Who disappoint me."

Skippy was sent to see the dreamwitch. He waited in a room with magazines, just like the dentist's office, or the hair stylist's. These magazines were law enforcement periodicals, prison journals. He thumbed through an article. It said the Garden of Eden, regarded just so, was also a prison. It said prison "afforded a liberation from time." Truly, Skippy was losing track of time; under artificial light 3 a.m. and 6 p.m. were identical marks on one long measure.

Skippy said to the guard: "When do I get to talk to my lawyer?"

The guard gave Skippy a green mimeographed sheet, detailing regulations for visitors at the "Intake Service Center." The information didn't have much to tell Skippy about his predicament. There were twelve rules: number seven said "loud, abusive, or obscene language" would end the visit. What else had Skippy heard? Numbers nine through eleven were relevant to chone:

"Female visitors will not visit inmates if they wear shorts shorter than mid-thigh length, tube tops, low cut or see-through blouses without undergarments, dresses with long slits. . . . Hand-holding above the table . . . A brief kiss, close-mouthed, and discreet embrace is permitted on arrival and departure. . . ."

The headshrinker was from Pakistan, he said. A wiggy smoke, in Skippy's judgment; such white teeth!

"Can you prescribe Haldol?" Skippy asked. "Some 'ludes, maybe? Val? I'm jumpy. Another thing, they crushed up my asthma medication in applesauce. I take it straight. What can you do for me?"

"Would you wee-wee in a bidet?" the analyst asked.

"Huh?"

"In a sink?" tried the doctor.

"Huh?"

"Out a window?"

"Would you?"

"No," said the doctor. "Would you bomb a train station?"

"Why?"

"You are not political?" the doctor asked. "Would you take money not belonging to you?"

"Ah," Skippy said. "Can I see my lawyer?"

Skippy chose the tweedling to represent him because Joe College didn't know him, wasn't a Hill counselor, and just might treat him straight. The pale, skinny guy across from him seemed run down, but word was he had weight with the Parole Board, if things got even worse than Skippy thought. And he was said to know how to file a writ. A guy who went with judges to the country club might even know how to reach out, as the saying went. With an envelope, Skippy meant.

"Why didn't Jimmy bail me?" Skippy asked.

"Maybe," the attorney said, "he didn't want to. Who can answer for bondsmen? In my experience, they're mysterious creatures. The music Jimmy heard in court yesterday? He didn't like it."

"I got bread," Skippy said. "I've got a gem. Worth a lot. I bought a ring for my girlfriend. It's worth plenty and then some. Hock it for me? Get me out of here? Sell it, and do my bail?"

"Where might I sell it?" Adam asked.

Skippy told him which fence.

"Where might I find the ring?" Adam asked.

Skippy told him. Clever place.

"I'm innocent," Skippy said.

His attorney cocked his head at Skippy, and smiled gently. "Of what, Mr. Carbone?"

"Offing Baby."

"That's nice," the attorney said.

"Don't you care?"

"Not really," the attorney said. "I took you on because your case interests me. It could be the capstone of my legal career, you might say."

Not really. Adam took the case because the accused—charged by a rogue police officer and a federally protected, bought-up hit man of killing another hit man named Baby—was a man who used an inhaler and whistled when he breathed. The very thing Clara called the Goblin. That gem? An unsought benison, gravy.

16

▲ ▲ ▲ ▲ ▲

JUSTICE

AFICIONADOS of crime and punishment were confident that the legal action in Superior Courtroom 9, Judge Barlow presiding, would be a pee-whistler. A button man ratting out a button man, who had clipped a button man, who had clipped a button man. Now really, an everyday case? The Federally Protected Witness, Jumbo Searle, was a retired pro wrestler who called himself the Hairy Beast because he appeared to wear a black turtleneck sweater when he was naked. Now he was popularly called the Hairy Canary because of his new calling, and formally addressed on witness stands throughout the northeast as Mr. Witness to protect his identity; he often sang his sad canary songs from inside a black cloth hood, with slits for his eyes and mouth. Some cynics believed the "Mr. Witness" and the black cloth sack were show business, the remnants of that flair in Jumbo that had made the dark and dangerous grappler good box office before he became a murderer, before he became "Mr. Witness." As "Mr. Witness" he got relocation, a late model Chevvy sedan (FBI car, in fact), a little less than a thousand a month, and license to ignore his money debts past, present, and future (until his testimony dried up, if it dried up), and a new identity, which meant that people who had never before seen the brute would not recognize him. Jumbo became "Mr. Witness" after declaring (and not even the first to conceptualize the notion!) in a light-hearted manner, while drinking a highball at the Bushwhacker, that it might be profitable to put the snatch on The Boss. Silly Jumbo; scared simply shitless Jumbo.

Lieutenant Cocoran had run into Jumbo a few years back,

hours before the hit man went off to the can on a weapons conviction, and Tom had passed along the word from Federal Hill: "Be careful." When someone up there whispers "be careful" to a convict, or a member of a jury, this is not the same as when your mom says "be careful."

So Jumbo, in return for protection, decided to come forward. This decision took longer to make than to tell; *come forward* has a special place in the Outfit's lexicon: miserable words, *come forward*, and they call for mighty protection.

Hence the commandos in black uniforms, red berets, crawling all over and around Superior Court, peering into passing cars. Just kids from Little Rhody, really, but they were just kids in Beirut, too. Rhode Island's were the Tactical Unit: riot batons were just the beginning of their story. Short-barreled Remington 870 pumpguns at port arms on the courthouse steps, and don't neglect to remark the lookouts on the roof, cradling Uzis, a few with Springfield .300 deer rifles and sniper sights, equipped to take down a person on, say, another roof, 500 meters would be reasonable.

Lieutenant Cocoran had exhorted the Hairy Canary to do his duty. The lieutenant's plot outline called for Jumbo to swear on a Bible and his good name that Skippy had whacked Baby, who had dumped the Moron. But who knew how the plot might grow subplots?—which is why any number of influential Providence residents might have longed to abbreviate the span of two fellows due that morning at the bar of justice. Ergo the Tac Team, and the metal detectors. Metal detectors! Criminy! Belt buckles lit them up, cheap tooth fillings rang their bells, grommets on your shoes, your best girl's IUD. Never mind; the groundlings weren't deterred. This was the toughest ticket in town. A lot of years were on the line here. To fall in, waiting for the lie detector to blink into business, to stand on line from eight in the morning until the trial began at ten, to stand there even in the dimmest hope of bagging a seat . . . Of course it was worth it. Hang the peril: these old reliables were tough customers. They knew what had happened at the Angela Davis trial out on the other coast. Every valuable enterprise had a price tag attached.

If The Boss wanted to bomb Superior Court to dust this morning, so be it. No question, here was where to be. Let Newport have boasting rights to the trial of Claus von Bulow, the count or prince or archduke or viceroy or excellency who was alleged to have sent his soulmate on that long journey to napland. Good draw for tourists, handsome payday for the Treadway (where the networks and out-of-state counsel bedded down), La Patisserie, the Full Beli Deli (and in fact a change of venue to Providence for the retrial had thrown electric panic into the Newport Chamber of Commerce), but that was pussyfoot felony, all those names that sounded like food in a German restaurant: near-beer naughtiness. Here was the place; now was the time.

Adam arrived early. He'd seen his share of gogglers, but this was an audience! The dependables had come, fans of the game, retired folk, gum-chewers, and serious buffs of the law. The regulars had commitment. That quahogger over there? He quit clamming when a big case came on the docket. Eighty days he gave the Bonded Vault case. Out of bed at six in the morning to bomb down from New Bedford, setting the cruise control on seventy, forget passengers, who might have to relieve themselves enroute. Such a one felt contempt for the fly-by-nights on line this morning. Regulars shared nickname familiarity, with one another, with court officers, and with lawyers, who had been known to posture for the pit.

If there were some alarming houndstooth sports jackets to be seen in those patient ranks, so too a Louis Vuitton bag, a navy wool skirt, black and white Jourdan pumps, high cheekbones. What brought them? Say an addiction, a thirst for novelty, a free show, a chance to grab a look—up close, personal (and don't forget *safe*)—at the geek. A long-ago French thinker esteemed this a rule of human behavior: faced with a choice in an open field of confronting a tiger or a lamb, a person would prefer the lamb. Put the beasts behind bars? Show him the tiger.

So the rubbernecks would hazard a quarter bet on the outcome, guilty or innocent, did Skip skate or fall? For all they cared, he could die. That would be interesting, see a man die. Most had never seen that kind of show, such heaviness.

PROVIDENCE 193

Sometimes, after a trial ended, a spectator might hope to make the early edition, or even television. He might say, "Leave me alone" to the reporter, but "leave me alone" was not what he meant. You know, the post-mortem:

"Well, I went back and forth. It was like a quarrel at the dinner table, you pull for the state, you pull for defense. You're not supposed to, but Day One I made up my mind; I mean, where was the motive? To be frank, it was a close call, in my book. The State made a monkey of that alibi witness. The defendant was framed. My cousin was his dentist, says he's a peach. I can't speak for the jury, of course, but defense counsel made a poor impression on me. He was a showboat."

Adam sailed past them. No collegiality in him. The iceman. They weren't likely to call him a showboat. All business, no give to him. A stranger to his circumstances might have charged him with affectation, the arrogance of his grandfather Dwyer, whom Adam had watched as a boy condescend in an anti-trust case to the United States Supreme Court. Now Adam struggled for clarity of vision, and against jitters. In a hurry, he managed to counterfeit purpose, control, serenity. This was no small trick, because it had passed the notice of no interested party that the customary intervals between arrest, arraignment, pretrial hearing, and trial had been brutally truncated. Speedy justice? Hellbent: the narrative line—charge (that S. did willfully and with malice aforethought kill B., a "human being"), denial ("I did not!"), countercharge ("Frame!")—commonly developed with such profitable leisure on the front page and tube, had been condensed to a few weeks of synopsis: X was alleged by Y to have ended the life of Z. Hence the frenzy of curiosity.

All interests, rare occasion, now coincided. The Federally Protected Performing Bird happened to be in Providence, with no one else to accuse. Skippy Carbone languished unbailed from Old Max, bunked with a mate who never slept, who died laughing at matters unrisible, causing Skip to wonder if *he* might die unlaughing for matters simply reckoned. And Adam . . . say Adam hadn't a world of patience, or time. Thus, weeks after drinking mai tais with Lisa at Trader Vic's, Skippy found him-

self in a Providence courtroom, charged by an utter stranger
with having fired a nail gun into the face of his late best friend.

Imagine if Pavlov had had to untrain his dog. Imagine he was
given a few weeks to untrain him. Imagine you'd driven a car
quarter of a century, and they decided to reverse the placement
of the stop and go pedals. So think of Adam's task. It had required deceptions across the grain of every instinct to call in
markers from Jimmy not to bail Skippy the morning of the arraignment, and to importune Jimmy to call in markers to a similar end. No bail. It required concentration to violate learned
reflexes, to urge a swift course to trial when delays would have
been expedient for acquittal. (The Hairy Canary was fresh out of
news and losing credibility as well as the appeal of novelty;
every time he sang, time told against him; given time, nature or
contrivance would surely remove him from the world.)

When chance had first dumped this happy accident in Adam's
lap, he had thought to get the felon back on the street, chop-
chop, where it was said he would assuredly die, slap-bang. But
then the attorney learned from his police friend the clown that
all the street hit to be done on Skippy Carbone in the proximate
future had been done, a mere public piss on the Goblin. This
seemed to Adam not enough. It seemed to Adam unjust that the
young home invader continued to breathe out and breathe in
simply because The Boss, guilty of an obscure and antique
promise to a child on a Big Wheel, excessively zealous for peace
in his Golden Years, had failed in his duty. It was said, at Fountain Street and elsewhere, that a mischance might be dealt the
asthmatic terrorist in the joint, and Adam's mission was clear:
sell the boy out; sabotage this case; slam for Skip, till the cursed
dago died, and pray then was soon.

To win a guilty verdict. Tricky. Not in the sense of devious,
mind. The way through justice was never straight. Not that
Adam was crooked, of course, but these days an outlaw with the
right change in his pocket might think to give Dwyer a jingle.
For let's say ten thousand minimum (negotiable? sure) he'd
spring any piece of bent steel, coiled to do harm. The fee came

up front, because otherwise it wouldn't come, because if he won
the case, the badman was innocent, so of course "they" won. If
he lost, what fee? Up front, and where did it come from, the fee?
Who asked? What other profession had such liability, that the
healer was confused with the disease? Who asked a doctor if his
patient deserved to live? How did Adam feel about putting vicious punks back on the street? He felt fine, he said, just fine. He
said. He would defend *anyone* who had that fee, but no post-
dated checks, okay?

For instance, he had run all over town to keep the mayor,
Fuzzy (couldn't a human being in Providence be known by a
simple name: "Robert" or "Peter" or "Kenneth"?), out of the
jug. This had required some serious running around, until the
mayor chose to *nolo* his heavy assault charges and got five years,
suspended. Whether the storklike mayor, every imperial inch
the likeness of a man of authority and deliberation, whether the
elegant, bushy-haired Fuzzy ate or did not eat institutional food,
ate stone soup even, mattered not a fiddler's fuck to Adam.
What mattered was the game, shirts vs. skins, and the fee. Nice
fee. Nice fee too from a middle-management mobster picked up
a couple years back on suspicion of murder. State troopers had
swabbed this gentleman's arms, hands, and torso with benzidine,
which turns blue in the presence of blood. The suspect did not
turn blue, but benzidine did cause bladder cancer, sometimes.
And emotional distress, oh my Lord! Adam satisfied a jury just the
other day that those state troopers had behaved as though they
didn't care that the suspect's bladder might pull some weird
tricks on him after growing things on itself. In fact, the suspect
almost didn't testify, because he was embarrassed to talk in public
about his bladder. Half a million dollars. (By the way, had he
killed the dead man? Oh-oh, good question: Adam forgot to ask.)

Now Adam dove headlong into the putative justice of that
case. His life itself seemed to turn on the protection of his client's civil rights. Could you believe it? He didn't care if you
could believe it, but Adam cared. He gave the best advice he
knew how to give, which was pretty good advice. If it was true
that he didn't knit his brow in such cases over fine points of real-

ity, contingency, metaphysics, exegetics—what do we mean by
guilt, what by *innocence*—it was also true he sold quality hours
to his clients, and always had. Gentle Adam was a meat-eater.
He liked to whip unmerciful ass, to win cases.

Until now. Until the Goblin. Still, to go in the tank, take a
dive, this was tricky. As in difficult.

It was a burden breaking to Skippy the sad news about the loss
of the young man's single remaining asset, a square-cut emerald
engagement ring of remarkable clarity, luster and value. Adam,
whispering through the hubbub of visiting hour at Old Max, explained that he couldn't really explain how it had happened. He
had simply misplaced the gem. Was it insured? Should he report
the loss to the authorities?

"Don't *dare* try to rip me off, man," said the young man on
the other side of a wire-mesh barricade. "I'm not some helpless
chump you can jerk off," said the helpless chump.

"Oh my," said attorney Dwyer. "I knew you'd be cross."

"Talk plain," commanded the cageling.

"I'm more sorry about the ring, and my carelessness, than you
can know. To put things right, I'll shoulder the burden of your
defense. What do you say? Despite the injury done to the ring
itself—was it vandalized?—the stone was a pip. I can only imagine what it must have meant to you. My assistance will cost you
nothing, believe me."

"Why the fuck should I trust you now?"

Adam lowered his voice, obliging Skippy to lean into the dis-
eased man's sick breath. Adam Latinized his client, *"mala in se"*
this, and *"mala fides"* that. He jargoned him to remind the wise
guy who was dumb.

"Please talk plain," Skippy asked.

"I can't speak for you, make you trust me," said Adam.
"Would you prefer a PD?"

"You get what you pay for," said Skippy, recollecting something he once heard.

"Just so," said Adam.

Adam assured Skippy, "We only want what's best." If the

presumptive indirect objective pronoun reference was misap-
prehended by the criminal, it was clear to his counsel.

Jury selection was the first hurdle. Now all the local DAs and
defense counsel knew Adam to be an ace at picking and stroking
a jury. He had won cases in Mississippi, after all, black defendant and white jurors. He was courteous, didn't patronize, explained in English what he'd just said in Latin. From strength to
strength during selection, and better at no part of it than at *voir
dire*. Knew when to back off personal questions, sympathized
with the citizens' bleak prospects, maybe weeks of grinding
dullness, $12 a day. Understood too that even though the show
was a bore, jurors wanted a seat. Was niggardly with peremptory challenges. But when he saw a potential advantage, look
out, here he came.

Take that case of the benzidined man: Adam had spotted a
fine broth of a girl among the jury pool, and not a day over seventy she was.

"And would it prejudice you," he asked during *voir dire*, "to
know that my client's dear granddad and grandma came to these
shores from County Cork?"

"Why not at all," said she.

"And would it turn you against me," asked the DA, "to know
that I am descended from Orangemen?"

"Why not at all," she said, her eyes narrowed to slits.

So from that day, green tie for Adam, green felt-tip pen.

But that was before he got Skippy Carbone for a client. Jurors
hated faceless fugitive criminals, but treated defendants—
named, modestly dressed, almost normal, palpably *there*—as
underdogs; for compassionate men and women it could be a
blast to forgive. So Adam now selected pinch-mouths, people
who believed they hadn't got one fair shake all their lives, and
weren't about to offer a free lunch to his felonious client; Adam
exercised his six peremptory challenges against Italian men (explaining to Skip they'd hang him to prove Italians respected the
law); Adam hectored ("Do you drink? To excess? Have you
committed the sin of adultery? Are you prejudiced against

heavy-drinking adulterers?"); Adam spoke too low to be heard, and shouted when they begged him to speak up. Adam bored them to sleep (nappers were bad news; tedium irritated them, for which Skippy would pay the tab). He attempted to dismiss for cause (knowing he'd fail) any victim of any crime (better than two-thirds of them). He spoke with agonizing patience to black jurors, pronouncing every word syllabically. He delayed, demanded bench conferences, broke the flow of the testimony, disrupted the cohesion of the story. Trump, he insisted Skippy's jury be sequestered. If Adam wasn't a world-class fuckup, it wasn't for want of trying.

Trouble was, the charge was a crock, mere circumstance, jury-rigged, shoddy welds and obvious seams. What if Adam's hand-picked hanging judges, those twelve meanies, elected to set the Goblin free? Well, Adam wouldn't hear of it. If only the DA wasn't a third-stringer. He looked good enough, in gray-vested suiting, with hair too short at the neck (the military look) and long in front, some untamed locks falling boyishly across his blue eyes. But saw him in half, you'd find mostly vodka, house brand. His intro was unpropitious:

"Let the chips fall where it may . . . Crime scene search activity revealed . . . I concede the State's star witness is not somebody who you had a choice would be your son-in-law. In fact, I have a daughter of marrying age . . ."

This case was not attractive to the man's superiors. When the pool television camera rolled for its thirty-second spot, Adam thought the DA might wave at it, and yell *yoo-hoo*. When he lost himself in his notes, trying to remember who was accused of what and by whom, the DA wrapped himself in the flag and made fond allusions to the Celts, Bruins, Pats and Sox. When he found his place in his notes, he squinted like the small print artist he had once been, and tried to nickel and dime the befuddled jurors. Or he reached for conundrum, slyly: "A thing is most likely to be what it is most likely to be." Say again?

It was either "when the Great Scorer writes the score up there on the scoreboard it's not the winner but who tried," or it was "permit me to draw your attention to the events following Mr. Searle's dinner at Logan Airport. Just a minute, they're here somewhere."

This was not to have been a farce. Adam had to give off vibes, oh so subtle, nothing visible to an appellate court, that he conceded a bad man was on trial, that what this buffoon of a DA believed, that belief was so. But the DA couldn't keep Italian names straight: Carbone, Capone, Capolina, Carbini. . . . And who could have failed to notice the dandruff? The DA yelled and begged ("The victim, whatever crimes he may have committed, yes, even MURDER! The victim, Baby," said softly, as though about a baby, "was your BROTHER! You OWE him!"). The DA complained about his feet. He saved his best stuff for Judge Barlow, after the jury had been dismissed. It was difficult to treat the man with civility, yet it was Adam's purpose to encourage the jury to pity rather than despise the DA, to feel they owed him a guilty verdict for the work he had invested in this farrago of hearsay and perjury. Adam obliged himself to chat up the DA, to whack him on the shoulder, compliment his suntan.

"Where did you get those brogans?" Adam made himself ask.

What an overmatched gangbuster. The DA was punchdrunk, or maybe just vodka drunk. He banged the table to emphasize . . . what? He couldn't recollect. He walked the body through the courtroom twice; convention held that once was enough, the mental picture of a nail-gunned Baby had a way of lodging in the memory bank. Listening to him, Adam pictured the Steinberg drawing, two men arguing, the bubble coming from this one's mouth in the shape of a sheep, his opponent's the shape of a wolf.

So Adam's introductory remarks had to outshine the DA's for offensive stupidity, lapsed attention, arrogance, indifference, patriotic zeal, manifestly false religious conviction, compassion for the criminal "element."

The ballistics expert was first to testify. Plus the nails there had been bullets. It seemed to please Skippy to learn this, and Adam neglected to advise his client to perhaps suppress the evidence of that pleasure. Skippy often glanced at the jurors, meantime scribbling on a yellow legal pad. The jurors must have figured these were drawings of dead men and women, hanging from limbs, machine-gunned, stabbed in the back, doodles, you know, like kids do. In fact, Skippy drew pictures of flowers, or a single brand of flower, your daisy, the one he knew how to draw.

No legal niceties here, no landmark paradoxes, no invocations of the Exclusionary Rule. No high-tech voiceprints or handwriting experts (Jesus, could any of the principals read or write? Adam wondered. Yes, Skippy could read, write, draw a daisy, want to draw a daisy, and change a woman's life). But just now it was ballistics: lands and grooves, blow-ups of striations on the bullets removed from Baby's head, the head removed, recall, from his torso. Some photographs caused the spectators to nod off, and some, *that one*, for sure, caused them to sit straight on those oak benches. Adam had offered no objection to having entered in evidence a few pieces of Baby, his fingers, for instance, and his tongue; these were preserved in a jar of alcohol, and were meant to display to dramatic effect the brutality of little Skip Carbone. Judge Barlow was grossed out. Not in his courtroom. When Adam did not object, Judge Barlow shot his fellow Hope Clubman a look, not quite a warning, call it a question.

Then it was the Medical Examiner's turn. On his way to the stand, the forensic expert had remarked to Adam: "You don't look so good. Better ease off that diet, get some rest, back off the jogging."

So, in case somebody might have forgotten, an autopsy was "surgery on the dead." Adam itched to sink his teeth into the pathologist's throat. Experts were pushovers; they spoke from notes as though their story were history rather than a patchwork of hunch, questions asked after their answers had been selected by the state. Adam was a fair hand at questioning the integrity of a chain of evidence, when he wanted to. He knew how to make a jury wonder whether those pristine laboratory results might not have been contaminated by carelessness, or partiality, if that were what he wished to make a jury wonder. Today, he was tame as a pup.

The Medical Examiner explained, with perhaps needless patience, that it was difficult to estimate the nature of an entrance wound caused by a weapon held four feet from the body, or forty, or four hundred. But less than three feet: bingo, exact science. The Medical Examiner was cheerful now, a chummy lecturer:

"The weapon was held tight against the victim's skull, and neck. We know this from powder burns, a stippled smudge, what we call a 'tattoo effect.' Tight contact causes what we call an 'abrasion imprint,' as though the victim had been shot with pepper. The tissue, where tissue was traumatized, was, in effect, vaporized. If you will, melted. It is our best judgment that trauma caused by tenpenny nails preceded these terminal events. So too were the eyelids sewn shut before death."

Did Adam have questions? Were you kidding?

Later in the week Lieutenant Cocoran swore to tell the truth, the whole truth, et cetera. Defendants "lie." Police officers use a "ruse." This policeman lied. Tom had suborned perjury from a shopworn professional he had caught at new wickedness. This testimony would be the ex-killer's last hurrah, and Tom explained to himself that he had set up Skippy not from jealousy, or for revenge. Jesus, how he'd hate himself if that were all. No, he wanted to protect Lisa from Skippy's evil influence, to give her a shot at making a better human being of herself. Also, think of Skippy as bait; maybe she'd come home for the trial. He just wanted to talk to her one more time. To explain. Apologize, if she insisted. Jump her bones.

The police officer's story was brief, passionate, absurd. Did Adam have questions?

"Later, Your Honor. I reserve the privilege of cross-examination for a time later in this trial."

Tom winked. The wink angered Adam so powerfully he thought he might eat the cop whole, right now, lunchmeat. That conspiratorial wink punctuated how far Adam had strayed from the course he thought he had set himself, not just at the beginning of life, which he dated as that moment when he first held

himself accountable for his choices, but at the beginning of his
death, when he had chosen to stay put, be what he was. That
was a shyster wink, between accomplices in some cumshaw
scheme. Adam avoided "we" in the expression of his beliefs; he
had in fact a perfect loathing of "we," except in such a community of purpose and blood as he shared with Clara and their son.
What, Adam asked, had he done to himself? He looked at the
police officer, and for a moment Adam felt as though he had already left this world, or *his* world, as though he had been sapped
behind the ear with a sock full of beebees by some invisible
mugger. Then Adam looked at his client, and saw who had
mugged him. Mugged them. *Eye on the ball*, he told himself.
Adam had heard street buzz: this lieutenant was heading for a
Humpty-Dumpty fall. Pity, Adam had liked him.

The courtroom was like a metaphor mimicking order, much as
criminal life with its supply/demand and command/submit im-
peratives might be thought to parody industry. It required imagination to decode the process by which a punishment might
follow a crime, and Skippy, sixth day of his trial, began to suspect he was not imaginative, or anything else, except in a world
of shit. He understood some of the words, but none of the language. He recognized some of the players, but hadn't the fog-
giest which were on his team, which on the other.

His Honor, what to make of him? Sometimes sweet as pie,
especially to the jurors. When the jurors coughed, maybe after
one of those bench conferences that bored everyone to death,
whisper-whisper, about what? Oh, his Honor preached, some
studies showed that coughing was "born of" the frustration
jurors felt because they couldn't ask questions. (*Questions!* Boy,
Skippy had some questions he'd like to ask.) To suck Lifesavers,
the judge said, was to "ameliorate" the discomfort that caused
coughing. Gum too was "efficacious," but it was the judge's experience that jurors too often disposed of chewing gum beneath
the seats of those benches. No gum. Looney tunes. By the way,
the judge said, he regretted the inconvenience experienced by
"sequestered" jurors. How difficult it was to be prevented from

talking in person or by telephone with their "loved ones." Hard on jurors! How about Skip? The fucking judge didn't seem to realize Skippy was there. Fuck that, this was Skippy's future! Skippy's ass was on the line, and how about innocent? (Okay, he wasn't perfect, he'd maybe shoot out a person's windows, but not his eyes, wasn't there a difference?)

It was true, the judge didn't do much to conceal his dislike of the DA. The DA showed up late sometimes, and Skippy thought the man might have been shitfaced a time or two. The booze didn't seem to trouble His Honor, but tardy burned His Honor's ass.

Another thing, the judge seemed to be tight with Dwyer. Skippy liked that, at first. Now he wasn't sure. Who was *his* friend? No friend of Skippy Carbone came to his trial. His dad, dead, couldn't. Mike wouldn't. Grapevine said Lisa was already in Florida; she'd been handed up, handed down, handed over. Baby would have come. Skippy missed his mom. He wanted to see his mom in court. He told Adam.

The questions Adam would have asked Jumbo, had he wanted to ask him questions, were asked by the DA. How come Jumbo, an enemy of the Outfit the past year and more, in fear for his life, was privileged to witness a mob hit on Baby?

"I was in long-term parking at Logan, saw the defendant stuff the deceased into the trunk of a car, a Volvo, I think. I guess it was a coincidence."

"Were you familiar with the kinds of actions you observed?"

"Sure. Sometimes I used a chainsaw. Then put the guy in a trunk, or maybe a dumpster. Sent the leftovers to the landfill. People don't poke around landfills. Dirty shoes, you understand? I've used the trunk of a car, just like him."

"How many human beings, Mr. Searle, approximately, have you shot?"

"Shot, or killed?"

"Both."

"Twenty, I don't know, forty."

Adam said he'd have questions later, maybe.

Now Skippy began to wonder out loud. Adam explained, his only hope was to take the stand, let the jury see he wasn't the kind of fellow who could kill. Forget kill: he wasn't a man to hurt someone. Rob maybe (they'd have to concede it), threaten, okay. Sure, he'd lied. Led, okay, a bad, lawless, sometimes violent life. Wasn't Skippy personality plus? True, he'd done some home invasions, maybe once an upper invasion. Maybe some of this *would* leak during cross. In fact, there was his alibi for that night. If it came to it, and it might come to it, Skippy could tell about the night he broke in a house, and went upstairs in that house. But whoa, it probably wouldn't come to it.

Adam successfully counseled Skippy to eschew suit and tie for his customary Leisure Look.

"Have you got a Hawaiian shirt? Sale-table rayon? Something floral, perhaps, luxuriant with palm trees and bananas, bedizined with sailboats, figured with florid native girls showing their big tits?"

"Huh?" asked Skippy. "Are you jerking my chain, man?"

"Just some banter, to lighten your load. Take it easy, Mr. Carbone. You're innocent. You need not conjure what those of us in the field call an 'acquittal look.' Dress *your* way. As you'd say, *fuck 'em*. Don't explain. Don't apologize. Neither remorse nor shame, okay? I had hoped to beat them with the fine print. That hasn't quite panned out, so we'll put you on the stand."

"I don't know. I like to dress natty. I got pride."

"But of course you have pride. Show it. Leather jacket. Designer jeans. The silk shirt. The buckles. Let's see some gold, too. What you wore to your arraignment. Why hold back?"

"That's glove leather. Matched calf."

"I guessed as much."

"When do I go on the stand?"

"Tomorrow. We'll surprise them. Wait till you see their faces. It's all over, Mr. Carbone. Skippy. You'll see."

"I want my mom there. I want my mom to hear me say I never killed a person. Never since she gave birth to me."

"Count on me," Adam said.

Defense counsel found it a piquant touch. To put the youngest Carbone on the stand, ask a few desultory questions, retail his squalid history, and leave his bones to be picked clean by the DA, not such an oaf he couldn't smell carrion when it was put under his nose. It would be fitting to have Mother Carbone witness the carnage.

The bakery was within handgun range of Atwells Avenue. He smelled the cupcakes before he was abreast of the entrance. Adam's mother, preparing to embark on a bender, would begin to rev her motor a few days before. The manic phase, Adam was told. She'd be at her best, warm and witty, singing along with the radio, asking Amos to take her dancing, which he would not. Then, still sober, she would bake: pies, cupcakes. She must have gone at it all day, because when Adam would walk home from Moses Brown, turn off Brown on Benevolent, he could sniff them a block away. To smell that sweet fecundity, that warm, iced excess, this was to know his mother was soon to go away drunk, and that he'd next see Marguerita Dwyer days or weeks later, stinking of puke, hunched on their front stoop, or in Rhode Island Hospital, with things stuck in her arms, nose, mouth, hoping wanly that in her absence Adam and Asa had eaten abundantly.

Adam felt sick. Oh, how sick he felt, standing at the bakery window, watching a chubby woman talk to a woman just like her, behind the counter. They were laughing. The woman behind the counter—that must have been her—didn't notice Adam. Adam felt sick from the smell, from the side effects of what he took to keep himself more or less alive, from everything. He was sick with shame, and sick with fear. He was sick with rage. But mostly shame. He didn't trouble Mrs. Carbone's peace. There was a limit.

For Clara, there was no end. Her husband died and died, and so it seemed did she. What she thought of as her crazy time was behind her. She made no more ugly scenes, and no longer spoke of setting razor wire around their house. She had left off reading newspapers and watching television; enough ugly stories. When she wept, she first looked right and left, to see that she was alone. Clara had bled from her voice what was abrupt or loud. She studied the cadence of her speech like an actress, knowing that pitchlessness would cause Adam to be sad, wishing not to make him sad. She cooked for them again, and believed he did not notice that she did not eat. She dreaded his calls from the courthouse inviting her out to dinner, because out there among strangers she didn't know what to order or say, or how to behave. She'd be all right, she promised. Just tonight, she was finding it difficult to open the passenger car door. They were parked in front of her favorite Providence restaurant, The Blue Point. She had liked their grilled shrimp. Now she thought of the stink of the grilled shrimp lingering on her fingers, as though she could never get rid of it. Adam sat beside her, and she wanted to be brave, and she couldn't figure out how to open the car door.

"You used to love this place," Adam said.

"I'm just not hungry."

"I mean Providence."

"It's not mine."

"It's ours."

"Yours."

"You used to laugh at it. Great laughing. Like a kid in a burlesque house. At least the people here, all the trouble they get themselves in, they're not high-hat. You used to like that, the tolerance."

"Feelings change. People do."

"Do you really think so?" Adam held his wife's hand in the dark car. It had begun to rain, and Mr. and Mrs. Dwyer watched a young couple come through the swinging doors of the restaurant laughing, and watched them get hit by the rain, and watched them turn their faces to the sky and laugh, and let the rain beat warmly, harmlessly, lovingly down on their faces. Adam squeezed Clara's hand. "Remember the White Horse?"

Clara nodded, directed her fingers to respond to her husband's touch; they would not. She felt him slide it down her finger, and then she heard him say, "You're safe now."

Now she could open that car door. Now she could walk into that restaurant. Eat. Ask, like a woman coming awake, what time it was. What day? Was there news? Had the world been . . . busy?

And Adam told her the news. That he would put the thing on the stand in the morning, and there would be an end to that story, and that was his gift to her.

"I want to watch."

Adam said no. He didn't want tomorrow to be the end of *his* story, in her memory. He had been a good lawyer. Well, maybe a good man. It wasn't right that the last thing he did with the law was subvert it, but that would be the last thing he did with the law, and it wasn't right that she see it, and he didn't want the Goblin to know what had been done to him, because the Goblin's ignorance was a goal of this game. He didn't want her in that courtroom. He promised he would make it right, win.

"You mean lose."

"Yes, lose."

"Did you promise him you'd win?"

"Yes."

"I want to watch."

"Oh, Clara, no."

The groundlings shoved aggressively in their ragged ranks. Clara sailed past them, what a friend of the court she was this morning. She wore her square-cut emerald, and entered on Adam Dwyer, Esquire's, arm.

The courtroom, for all its seedy transactions and grubby theatricals, was a majestic place. Adam noticed after a long time without noticing its fluted walnut columns, the brass-capped jury-box railings, the sun falling weakly through that skylight. The effect here was of permanence, upkeep, polish, gravitas.

At ten to ten, Ann Hutchinson was seated in the press box, scribbling notes. When jurors saw her write in her little notebook, they listened more carefully. It was difficult to find terra firma in a place like a courtroom.

"How are we doing?" Adam asked the journalist.

The first person plural, a convention of such rites, gave no offense. Neither did Ms. Hutchinson dissemble: "I think you're a goner."

The prisoner, spiffy as a pimp, entering the courtroom at just that moment, hearing the reporter's judgment coincide with his own inexpert opinion, confounded perhaps by the exact person to whom the second pronoun (*I think* you're *a goner*) should have been addressed, seeing in the first row of spectators a woman he assuredly recognized, spying on her finger a large, green gem, spying on her face a frank smile, leaping now to an inference of common interest between that woman and his counsel, said to Adam Dwyer:

"I been boned. You ratted me out."

Enter the Clerk: "Rise please, the Honorable Superior Court of Providence Plantations, Judge Howard Barlow presiding."

Enter Judge Barlow, about half as learned as he believed, to Adam's delight a veritable doomsman. Also corrosive, prickly, a churl, an overburdened referee of volcanic petulance. The time? Ten-fifteen. The jurors were seated. The defendant's incomprehensible outburst, cries of "conflict of interest," and "I demand another mouthpiece," and "I been jobbed," and "I ain't taking the stand, no way, fuck you" did his cause no good. The defendant was silenced, restrained, and removed. Clara, disappointed to see him leave, managed anyway a bright, final smile.

It was ten-thirty. All parties present save the DA (more precisely, assistant DA, soon to be, as he knew, ex-assistant DA, canned in fact last week), who had been tardy every morning since the trial began. Who responded to the judge's reproofs with shruggy self-pardons, references to traffic, alarm clocks, a tetchy carburetor. At ten-forty, with the State of Rhode Island unrepresented at the bar, Judge Hugh Barlow dismissed the charge of murder in the first degree against Skippy Carbone.

"I have admonished counsel for the State not once, twice, even thrice. Four times. I will not tolerate in my court indifference to orderly procedures. A respectable argument could be mounted against my decision, but I would not expect to hear any learned or respectable argument, on any point of law, offered, judging from the quality of their performances, by either brother now at this bar. I hope by my action to teach counsel for the State a lifelong lesson, and rescue respect for my robes, if not my person."

For sure, Judge Barlow had a lifetime appointment, and counsel for the State did not. The soon-to-be-ex-assistant DA, at ten-thirty, was being fitted for corrective arches; his dogs were killing him; the podiatrist had sprung an opening in a busy schedule. The assistant DA was sore as hell at the judge, and he figured he'd have to answer to someone for this sorry outcome, but frankly, seen from his point of view, it was worth it.

17

▲ ▲ ▲ ▲ ▲

AFTER ALL

THE third morning of his freedom dawned on Skippy Carbone well-positioned in a ragged queue at the Providence Civic Center; he hoped to cop ducats for a Grateful Dead concert that night. To see those aged hipsters was not this young criminal's ultimate ambition. His plan was to buy at list price, scalp at triple list. Take his profits to Lupo's Heartbreak Hotel, hear A Roomful of Blues, Little Rhody's own wicked band, Skippy's kind of sound. He was standing among dead-head freaks, and then he was sitting among them. A tie-dyed concessionaire, stoned as he was, noticed the shift in Skippy's posture, from erect to sort of prone; he had to laugh: "Man, that boy has smoked some devil weed. What you using, bro? Tragic magic?"

Not at all. He'd met with an evil valedictory, was all. He'd been found by a sharp-dressed man in a blazer, who had been three days and nights seeking him, and had found what he sought. Who said the last words Skippy heard:

"So long," Tom went, "you're gone."

Skippy sat dead on the sidewalk with an ice pick buried in his ear. The stoned freak thought it was like a costume, a Steve Martin kind of thing, the way Steve liked to wear that arrow growing out of his head? Closer examination by ticket-aspirants shuffling toward the ticket window revealed this wasn't like that after all.

"Wow," remarked more than one of the music lovers.

The Biltmore-Plaza was an easy walk from the Civic Center. Tom checked in carrying a suitcase, wanted to pay up front. The manager said there was no need, but Tom wouldn't have it any other way. The manager reminded Tom what a good customer he'd been all summer, but Tom insisted.

The bellhop showed him up. Manager insisted. Top floor, right below L'Apogee, clear view of the State House behind the railroad station. Tom could make out the Independent Man. While the bellhop switched on the television, Tom fingered his room key. The cast bronze fob weighting that brassy little key seemed cheap. It was an awful ornament; he'd always thought so.

Deirdre had filed for divorce. Maisie wouldn't talk to him. Just like Tom had imagined if he ran off with Lisa to Mexico. Except he'd never gone anywhere.

He'd gotten a card from her yesterday, at Fountain Street. They gave it to him while he was cleaning out his desk. Boy oh boy, after Judge Barlow pulled the plug on that trial, Ann Hutchinson sure cut Tom a new one. She wrote a good story, give her credit. She got most of it right. Not *why* he stole the cocaine, of course; what did she care? Steal it to sell; steal it to use; steal it to give to a friend. Unrighteous. Still, that reporter cashed Tom in; what had he done to her? She was too pretty to be such a hard customer.

Oh, the card: no return address. Sunny climes, though. America. It would have hurt Tom to get a card like that from Mexico. Lisa had heard the talk.

I'm going to change my luck. You're just a guy, with a weakness, like they said on the street, just like anybody. You're good people. Be nice to yourself. It was a hoot. Gotta blaze. I'm a memory. XOXOX

One of his clown pals at the 19th Hole had told Tom, when Tom was getting too good at grief, "You've got a soft heart is all. No one should have to apologize for loving another person."

Tom thought that was bullshit. Knew it was. He'd let love turn him into a bum. Maybe love was a word it didn't deserve. Maybe it was just touch and tickle, smell and feel, push, pull, come. Go. He had been scared of cocaine, stealing and using.

Instead he got addicted to her. Her was worse. Before he bot-
tomed out, or shallowed out, Tom put in many hours in his car,
hunting her. She had said she wouldn't run off, and he had believed that. Jesus. Finally, he quit looking for her convertible
Bug in his rearview mirror; then he forgot her license number,
and how exactly she looked laboring on top of him, sweating
down into his eyes, her sweat as salt as tears. Bottom came later,
when he wished she would die so he could rid himself of her
memory. Or that Deirdre would, would die, so he could run off
with the other one. Or that he would die, so he could be free of
wishes.

The bellhop was still fiddling with knobs and faucets. What
did he want? The first night Tom slept with Lisa, she told him a
story. Something about the Newport Bridge, some poor fool had
jumped, she'd seen him about to go. She was so wasted on weed
she forgot what she saw before she got to the other side of the
bridge. Where were Tom's alarm bells, his red lights? It was an
ugly story. Tom had talked people out of the jump; he got
medals. He remembered the woman on the Mount Hope Bridge,
out of Tom's jurisdiction, but he was celebrated for the gift of
saving. Portsmouth had *begged* for Tom. The wife and mother
was out there on the wind-whipped brink, holding a .22 target
pistol.

"There's a round in the chamber, so don't act up."

Tom had said he couldn't talk to a woman holding a loaded
weapon, but right away he went back on his word, and kept
talking. He said he was going to come close, now, she could say
where to stop. Tom was scared. The woman's mascara ran down
her cheeks. She said her husband had run off and left her.

"Another woman?" Tom had asked.

"You guys. You don't know shit. His pride's hurt. He's an
electrician. He went color-blind, so they laid him off. He can't
tell apart the color-coded wires. So he ran off. What am I supposed to tell him, if he comes back? Huh? Tell me. 'It's okay,
sweetie. We'll do welfare?' Forget it. He won't come back. I'm
going now, no one will even notice."

Tom had thought that was probably true.

"I don't know. I'll notice. You're a good-looking woman," he had lied.

"What is this? You coming on to me? I'm a married woman. He took off on me."

"What did you do today?" Tom had asked the woman.

"I'm going to jump so I don't have to hear your boring questions no more."

Then the woman had laughed. Tom had laughed.

"Tell you what," he said, "give me that pistol, how about it?"

"Everybody wants something," she had said. "That don't mean they get it."

What did the bellhop *want?* Tom remembered. He gave the fellow a tip. The door shut, and Tom climbed into his clown suit. Went through that shut window headfirst, dearly beloved. The bellhop, fingering his tip, had touched the elevator button before he heard the glass go. He wished he never heard it. He rode down the outside elevator, the principal marvel of Providence Plantations, thinking to report a suspicious noise, but he could see from the glass-sided elevator that the mystery of that noise would be solved ere he was at street level. He hoped he didn't have to hang around answering questions he couldn't answer, even though the cop was a handsome tipper. Chummed with Whosis, that waitress with good lungs? The bellhop was holding tickets to a concert, Grateful Dead, believe it or not, just about the dearest ticket there was. As generous as the officer had been, he didn't want to see him now, or think about him again. But just for drill: did a guy ever go through a shut window, down from the apogee, because he wanted to?

That day, with Ike in his third month at Exeter, with Adam at sea, Clara sat on the bottom step of the stairs, ten feet from her front door, waiting. The November afternoons blinked off early now, and she had sat there, adjusting her eyes to the gloom, several hours. Last night, too, through the night, and dawn to dark today, waiting for the Goblin or whoever to test her unlocked door. She held a flare gun in both hands, steady. He'd come, she knew. Somebody with a knife, like last time. When that door-

knob turned, when that door opened, she'd do it; she was ten
feet from that door; she'd light him up with white phosphorus,
willy-peter him, lay the flare center of his chest, burn a hole in
that chest, hear the wound suck.

Here came the newsboy, maybe with larceny in his heart. His
hand was on the knob.

Now Clara stood on the sidewalk, lofting distress flares into
the night sky. Clara needed counsel.

He couldn't help anymore. She wouldn't let him. He thought he
understood. It was beyond their reach; it just got away from
them. The cells first, and then the rest.

Adam had raised sails at his Jamestown mooring. He left behind his first boat, a gift now to Ike, an eight-foot Penn Yan sailing dinghy with white-canvas topsides and varnished mahogany
strakes. It had given Adam satisfaction to watch Ike, when Ike
was younger, row that dinghy as Adam had, as though in flight
from danger, helter-skelter, till he stopped abruptly, backwa-
tered, spun in circles, the demented ballet of a child alone in his
first boat, free of land. Then, watching his son rest on his oars,
Adam knew his son's thoughts, because they had also been his
thoughts.

November was late for *Warlock*. Adam and Clara and Ike
liked to shut down the season end of October, when they'd sail
north up the bay through protected water. If they were lucky,
and once upon a time they were often lucky, the sun would
shine as they beat toward Potter Cove. They'd wear sweaters,
and the sun silver against water washing the lee rail was like em-
eralds spilled on velvet. When the wind went northwest they
could see beyond the edge, so far it was possible to believe the
earth curved. At such times, watching Ike braced against the til-
ler, wanting to teach his boy what he had been taught, to move
with care on deck, piss to leeward, steer a delicate, steady
course, it seemed to Adam he had all the time in the world. He
wished now he had been a better teacher, a perfect father, but
he hadn't been, but who had?

If they were lucky those final October days, if that black anvil of a thunderhead kept its distance, they'd ghost on the dying wind into Potter's Cove, sneak up on the geese, provoke their noisy takeoff, watch the sun set behind the marshy saw-grass. They'd go below, light a wood fire in the Tiny Tot, cook spaghetti, spark up the brass cabin lamp. *Warlock* was Bristol-built, a concoction of teak, cherry, and fir. Adam and Ike and Clara would play poker or word games; Clara couldn't lose. Adam would take Ike topside for a final look around, and to let out more scope on the anchor rode. Adam was known for prudence; the other two laughed at him. He hated to be stupid at sea, took pains. It felt good to do things just so, to navigate without incident from here to there and home, without losing nerve, knowing you could depend on them; they on you. To look for a shackle, to find it where it was meant to be; this felt good. It was possible to know everything about a sailboat of *Warlock's* dimensions. Adam knew her mysteries, improved her circumstances. If he sometimes lay awake fretting about dry rot, the wood hull's malign mystery, Adam's imagination did not run to metaphor, and if an ugly surprise befell her, he thought he would know how to heal it.

Now Adam sailed seaward, out the bay, east southeast, running toward Noman's Land. This was not his favorite point of sail; he liked a bravura reach, all noise and strain, green water awash in the rails. Or to beat, pinch close to the wind, sail the hard way. Adam wasn't a single-hander by choice. He cleared Brenton Reef. He had practiced this with the deliberation he once brought to man-overboard drills. Seven hours out, off soundings, night fell. The November sea-night was cold, and Adam left his running lights unlit. The boat was insured. He was insured against accidents. South of Devil's Bridge off Gay Head, dead reckoning from Lone Rock to the Old Man Ledge, Adam would go forward, secure that spare forty-pound plow to this spare anchor chain, clasp the shackle to his belt, and drop himself into the water. No morphine. No priests like crows hovering over his bed. He couldn't kill for her—Tom's final, awful wink in Courtroom 9 the morning of miscarriage let him know Skippy was settled. He promised Clara she was safe. She had no faith, thought she wanted him to kill for her. Adam could try now to believe he was dying for her, but he knew better, and so would she. They were clever, the adjusters. There would be questions. But without answers, they'd have to do the right thing.

He made out the loom of Noman's light. No, that was the moon, just when it was meant to rise, 8:56. The astronomical tables did not lie; the enactment of those scheduled motions, the appearance of that moon in its regular way, had once been a consolation to Adam, a companionable response to a friend's expectation.

Adam didn't see the red umbrella flare hang in the night above Providence, where some kid was knocking over his first liquor store, and another chose not to swipe a pack of gum. Between Noman's Land and Lone Rock the fog appeared. Some say of fog that it "rolls in," others that it "descends," like a curtain. Another thinks of fog as a wall, of bumping into it. Adam believed otherwise, that fog occurred; it wasn't, and then it was. Such a fog! Seasmoke, really, not a summer's dense stillness, but a wind-driven confusion, primitive, the blindness of newborn creatures. The wind blew a fright, and Adam, answering reflex, reefed down. This fog froze him; it awed and terrified him. And then it interested him. Now he was a sailor and not a lawyer who sailed a boat. The seasmoke was *Warlock*'s enemy, but with care, and attention, with patience, a seaman might sail through such a menace into a clear day. Now there were hazards to navigate. The wind blew obscurity into Adam's face, and he braced against its menace.

And then he heard above the talk of *Warlock*'s timbers and the complaint of her rigging sea-noises he had long imagined: the rusty-hinged creak, a great sound of breathing, the squawky click of whales. They were talking to one another, and by the way to him. Their talk was healthy, not the desperate squeals of pilot whales so enigmatically morose that they beached themselves to die in their dozens, their navigational systems out of calibration, or misled by disease, or by some subterranean magnetic shift along an unfathomable fault. He heard them breathe, the chuff of horses uneasy in a corral, but these things were at

ease, and knew their place, exactly. Adam smelled the brine
stink of huge mammals guiding one another through oceans
blinder than any night he had known, helping one another.
Adam was gaunt, blear-eyed from looking too close at strangers
and himself. *Warlock* had a compass. Adam looked at it, and
came about.

Born in Los Angeles in 1937, Geoffrey Wolff has written a biography of Harry Crosby (*Black Sun*) and *The Duke of Deception: Memories of My Father*. Author of four other novels—*Bad Debts* (1969), *The Sightseer* (1974), *Inklings* (1978), and *The Final Club* (1990)—and the forthcoming book of personal recollections *A Day at the Beach*, Mr. Wolff lives in Jamestown, Rhode Island.

VINTAGE
CONTEMPORARIES

___ **I Pass Like Night** by Jonathan Ames	$8.95	0-679-72857-0
___ **The Mezzanine** by Nicholson Baker	$7.95	0-679-72576-8
___ **Room Temperature** by Nicholson Baker	$9.00	0-679-73440-6
___ **Chilly Scenes of Winter** by Ann Beattie	$9.95	0-679-73234-9
___ **Distortions** by Ann Beattie	$9.95	0-679-73235-7
___ **Falling in Place** by Ann Beattie	$10.00	0-679-73192-X
___ **Love Always** by Ann Beattie	$8.95	0-394-74418-7
___ **Picturing Will** by Ann Beattie	$9.95	0-679-73194-6
___ **Secrets and Surprises** by Ann Beattie	$10.00	0-679-73193-8
___ **A Farm Under a Lake** by Martha Bergland	$9.95	0-679-73011-7
___ **The History of Luminous Motion** by Scott Bradfield	$8.95	0-679-72943-7
___ **First Love and Other Sorrows** by Harold Brodkey	$7.95	0-679-72075-8
___ **The Debut** by Anita Brookner	$8.95	0-679-72712-4
___ **Latecomers** by Anita Brookner	$8.95	0-679-72668-3
___ **Lewis Percy** by Anita Brookner	$10.00	0-679-72944-5
___ **Big Bad Love** by Larry Brown	$10.00	0-679-73491-0
___ **Dirty Work** by Larry Brown	$9.95	0-679-73049-4
___ **Harry and Catherine** by Frederick Busch	$10.00	0-679-73076-1
___ **Sleeping in Flame** by Jonathan Carroll	$8.95	0-679-72777-9
___ **Cathedral** by Raymond Carver	$8.95	0-679-72369-2
___ **Fires** by Raymond Carver	$8.95	0-679-72239-4
___ **What We Talk About When We Talk About Love** by Raymond Carver	$8.95	0-679-72305-6
___ **Where I'm Calling From** by Raymond Carver	$10.95	0-679-72231-9
___ **The House on Mango Street** by Sandra Cisneros	$9.00	0-679-73477-5
___ **I Look Divine** by Christopher Coe	$5.95	0-394-75995-8
___ **Dancing Bear** by James Crumley	$8.95	0-394-72576-X
___ **The Last Good Kiss** by James Crumley	$9.95	0-394-75989-3
___ **One to Count Cadence** by James Crumley	$9.95	0-394-73559-5
___ **The Wrong Case** by James Crumley	$7.95	0-394-73558-7
___ **The Wars of Heaven** by Richard Currey	$9.00	0-679-73465-1
___ **The Colorist** by Susan Daitch	$8.95	0-679-72492-3
___ **The Last Election** by Pete Davies	$6.95	0-394-74702-X
___ **Great Jones Street** by Don DeLillo	$7.95	0-679-72303-X
___ **The Names** by Don DeLillo	$11.00	0-679-72295-5

VINTAGE
CONTEMPORARIES

VINTAGE
CONTEMPORARIES

___ **Angels** by Denis Johnson	$7.95	0-394-75987-7
___ **Fiskadoro** by Denis Johnson	$6.95	0-394-74367-9
___ **The Stars at Noon** by Denis Johnson	$5.95	0-394-75427-1
___ **Mischief Makers** by Nettie Jones	$9.00	0-679-72785-X
___ **Obscene Gestures for Women** by Janet Kauffman	$8.95	0-679-73055-9
___ **Asa, as I Knew Him** by Susanna Kaysen	$4.95	0-394-74985-5
___ **Far Afield** by Susanna Kaysen	$9.95	0-394-75822-6
___ **Lulu Incognito** by Raymond Kennedy	$7.95	0-394-75641-X
___ **Steps** by Jerzy Kosinski	$9.00	0-394-75716-5
___ **The Garden State** by Gary Krist	$7.95	0-679-72515-6
___ **House of Heroes and Other Stories** by Mary La Chapelle	$8.95	0-679-72457-5
___ **White Girls** by Lynn Lauber	$9.00	0-679-73411-2
___ **The Chosen Place, the Timeless People** by Paule Marshall	$12.95	0-394-72633-2
___ **The Beginning of Sorrows** by David Martin	$7.95	0-679-72459-1
___ **A Recent Martyr** by Valerie Martin	$7.95	0-679-72158-4
___ **The Consolation of Nature and Other Stories** by Valerie Martin	$6.95	0-679-72159-2
___ **Suttree** by Cormac McCarthy	$6.95	0-394-74145-5
___ **California Bloodstock** by Terry McDonell	$8.95	0-679-72168-1
___ **The Bushwhacked Piano** by Thomas McGuane	$8.95	0-394-72642-1
___ **Keep the Change** by Thomas McGuane	$9.95	0-679-73033-8
___ **Nobody's Angel** by Thomas McGuane	$9.95	0-394-74738-0
___ **Something to Be Desired** by Thomas McGuane	$6.95	0-394-73156-5
___ **To Skin a Cat** by Thomas McGuane	$8.95	0-394-75521-9
___ **Spider** by Patrick McGrath	$10.00	0-679-73630-1
___ **Bright Lights, Big City** by Jay McInerney	$5.95	0-394-72641-3
___ **Ransom** by Jay McInerney	$8.95	0-394-74118-8
___ **Story of My Life** by Jay McInerney	$6.95	0-679-72257-2
___ **Homeboy** by Seth Morgan	$11.00	0-679-73395-7
___ **The Beggar Maid** by Alice Munro	$10.00	0-679-73271-3
___ **Friend of My Youth** by Alice Munro	$10.00	0-679-72957-7
___ **The Moons of Jupiter** by Alice Munro	$10.00	0-679-73270-5
___ **Mama Day** by Gloria Naylor	$10.00	0-679-72181-9
___ **The All-Girl Football Team** by Lewis Nordan	$5.95	0-394-75701-7

VINTAGE CONTEMPORARIES

___ **Welcome to the Arrow-Catcher Fair** by Lewis Nordan	$6.95	0-679-72164-9
___ **River Dogs** by Robert Olmstead	$6.95	0-394-74684-8
___ **Soft Water** by Robert Olmstead	$6.95	0-394-75752-1
___ **Family Resemblances** by Lowry Pei	$6.95	0-394-75528-6
___ **Sirens** by Steve Pett	$9.95	0-394-75712-2
___ **Clea and Zeus Divorce** by Emily Prager	$10.00	0-394-75591-X
___ **A Visit From the Footbinder** by Emily Prager	$6.95	0-394-75592-8
___ **A Good Baby** by Leon Rooke	$10.00	0-679-72939-9
___ **Mohawk** by Richard Russo	$8.95	0-679-72577-6
___ **The Risk Pool** by Richard Russo	$8.95	0-679-72334-X
___ **Mile Zero** by Thomas Sanchez	$10.95	0-679-73260-8
___ **Rabbit Boss** by Thomas Sanchez	$8.95	0-679-72621-7
___ **Zoot-Suit Murders** by Thomas Sanchez	$10.00	0-679-73396-5
___ **Anywhere But Here** by Mona Simpson	$9.95	0-394-75559-6
___ **The Joy Luck Club** by Amy Tan	$10.00	0-679-72768-X
___ **The Player** by Michael Tolkin	$7.95	0-679-72254-8
___ **Myra Breckinridge and Myron** by Gore Vidal	$8.95	0-394-75444-1
___ **All It Takes** by Patricia Volk	$8.95	0-679-73044-3
___ **Philadelphia Fire** by John Edgar Wideman	$10.00	0-679-73650-6
___ **Breaking and Entering** by Joy Williams	$6.95	0-394-75773-4
___ **Escapes** by Joy Williams	$9.00	0-679-73331-0
___ **Taking Care** by Joy Williams	$5.95	0-394-72912-9
___ **The Final Club** by Geoffrey Wolff	$11.00	0-679-73592-5
___ **Providence** by Geoffrey Wolff	$10.00	0-679-73277-2
___ **The Easter Parade** by Richard Yates	$8.95	0-679-72230-0
___ **Eleven Kinds of Loneliness** by Richard Yates	$8.95	0-679-72221-1
___ **Revolutionary Road** by Richard Yates	$8.95	0-679-72191-6

Available at your bookstore or call toll-free to order: 1-800-733-3000.
Credit cards only. Prices subject to change.